Thoroughbred Legacy

The stakes are high.

Scandal has hit the Preston family and their award-winning Quest Stables. Find out what it will take to return this horse-racing dynasty to the winner's circle!

Available September 2008

#5 *Millions to Spare* by Barbara Dunlop
Identifying with your captor is one thing. Marrying him is quite another! But when reporter Julia Nash is caught snooping, she's faced with saying goodbye to her freedom…or saying *I do* to Lord Harrison Rochester!

#6 *Courting Disaster* by Kathleen O'Reilly
Race-car driver Demetri Lucas lives hard and fast—and he likes his women to match. Until he meets the one woman who can tempt him to slow down and enjoy the ride.

#7 *Who's Cheatin' Who?* by Maggie Price
Champion jockey Melanie Preston has a firm no-men-with-secrets policy. Especially when it comes to her family's horse trainer, who has more secrets than anyone that sexy should….

#8 *A Lady's Luck* by Ken Casper
After one glance, widower Brent Preston finds himself feeling emotions he thought long since buried. But pursuing his gracefully elusive English lady may mean heading straight into the arms of danger!

Dear Reader,

Y'all should know that I was born and raised in Texas, but have spent the last six years living in New York, writing books about New York City, with nary a "y'all" or "fixing to" in sight. When the editors in New York talked to me about this book, and it dawned on me that I could write a character who actually talks the way I do, I was happier than a pig in molasses.

I adored writing the character of Elizabeth, and she's a conglomeration of several of my best friends who I grew up with, all smashed together into one (although none of them sing country and western, bless their little hearts, and all have been known to drive fast on occasion). I didn't want to stop writing Elizabeth, and I hope to high heaven that I get to write another Southern character someday.

I love hearing from readers, so please write to me at Kathleen O'Reilly, P.O. Box 312, Nyack, NY 10960, or e-mail me at kathleenoreilly@earthlink.net.

Best,

Kathleen

Thoroughbred Legacy

COURTING DISASTER

Kathleen O'Reilly

Published by Silhouette Books

America's Publisher of Contemporary Romance

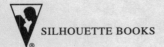

SILHOUETTE BOOKS

ISBN-13: 978-0-373-19923-5
ISBN-10:   0-373-19923-6

COURTING DISASTER

Special thanks and acknowledgment are given to Kathleen O'Reilly
for her contribution to the Thoroughbred Legacy series.

Visit Silhouette Special Edition and Thoroughbred Legacy
at www.eHarlequin.com.

Printed in U.S.A.

KATHLEEN O'REILLY

has done nothing extraordinary in comparison to other authors whose bios she has read. She is not a former CIA agent, nor has she ever been president of the United States (nor slept with him, either). She graduated from Texas A&M in 1987, which her parents do consider extraordinary, and she has been married for sixteen years, but not to Mick Jagger or Justin Timberlake. No, she merely lives with her husband and two kids in New York, and not even Manhattan, just your typical suburb. Due to the mundaneness in her life, she has chosen to write fiction, which seems best, all things considered.

With great appreciation to Julie and Dee,
who continually amaze me with their writing genius.

Special thanks to Stacy for the spot-on editorial
advice, and to Marsha for giving me the shot.

Chapter One

The long driveway leading up to Quest Stables was nearly a mile and a quarter straightaway, a first-class temptation for a man who did his most memorable work in the fast lane. On some other day, Demetri Lucas would have shifted into sixth, pealed out and torn up the road with the eighteen-inch sport tires. All in the name of testing the drag coefficient his engineers swore was nearly zero, of course.

Today, however, wasn't the time for testing drag coefficients. For one thing, his host's guests were beginning to arrive for this weekend's wedding—not for an exhibition in speed and mechanical prowess. Although Hugh Preston might have done the same when he was younger, the years had mellowed him, and he probably wouldn't appreciate Demetri offering them a glimpse of such unique entertainment…at least not in the Preston backyard.

More than that, as difficult as it was for Demetri to believe, there were actually things on his mind that weighed heavier than drag coefficients, Formula Gold racing or even his upcoming race in Louisville. Things like Hugh's financial straits. Not to mention Demetri's own "Married Princess Incident"—otherwise known as the three weeks in Monte Carlo that the Sterling PR team had labeled "boneheaded and reckless."

Reckless was a label that seemed to follow him around like a black cloud. When he was seventeen, it had been fun and daring. Now that he was thirty-five, it seemed…sad.

Invariably, Demetri could feel his collar tighten, feel the high-velocity impulses kick up a notch, and in response, his foot floored the gas, gravel flying. The six-hundred-horsepower engine was street-legal—on the autobahn, not the horse country of Kentucky—and the answering roar was sweeter than music, better than sex.

Almost.

Within seconds the main house tore into view, a sprawling redbrick that was home to the Preston family and Demetri's current destination. As his foot moved over the clutch, he smoothly downshifted, the engine quieting to a more respectable purr. Someday he'd learn how to live a little slower, how to live a little safer, but today wasn't it.

Parked cars lined the drive, including one sturdy tan Volvo that was trying to park—and doing a piss-poor job of it. Demetri didn't have a lot of respect for cautious drivers as a matter of principle. They tended toward cars that were heavy tanks, built to withstand a nuclear blast, and all those safety features added weight. Pounds were a liability to a race-car driver who valued things like acceleration and whip-quick handling.

Demetri downshifted again, suspicious that this was the Fates' way of making him pay for speeding down the drive. Maybe the Fates were expecting him to be grateful to the sensible tan Volvo standing between him and sixth gear. Maybe the Fates were wrong.

He watched—it was actually more of a penetrating glare—

as the sedan slowly reversed, inching to the right, braking, inching, braking, inching, ad infinitum. With the Volvo steering system and the driver's conservative refusal to cut the wheel properly, they were going to be here for a long, long time.

It took six more tries, inching, braking, inching, braking, but at long last the Volvo eased into the space. *Finally.* There was the small matter of the tires ending four feet from where the lawn lined the drive. However, in the big scheme of things, four feet wasn't awful. The rear end wasn't out too far. In fact, it was almost…

Hell. Demetri took the shot.

Easily he slid his car in behind the other, wheels perfectly aligned along the edge of the lawn. Now *that* was how to park a car….

He was still smiling smugly to himself when the back-up lights of the Volvo flashed. Surely the Volvo would notice the car behind it. Surely the Volvo would stop. Surely…

Nope.

The sound of slowly crunching metal was never a happy sound for a race-car driver. The specially designed aluminum chassis collapsed onto the honeycomb frame, pushing up into the middle of the car in slow motion. The aerospace-quality chassis made of autoclave carbon fiber might have had a drag coefficient of zero, but when rear-ended by rock-solid Volvo, the car was toast.

Demetri swore again, ripely, violently.

Of course, the Volvo escaped without a scratch.

Perfect. It seemed fitting, poetic justice even, and he rubbed his eyes. Fine. Round one goes to the Fates. *Lesson. Learned.*

He flung open the door, not happy, yet prepared to apologize, prepared to own up to his own impatience. It was the right thing to do. It was the responsible thing to do, but then he noticed the driver and stopped.

He couldn't see her face, because she was leaning against the car, her hands at her temples, rubbing in circular motions. Instantly the anger disappeared. Was she about to pass out? He didn't see any blood, and with a suspension system that could withstand an earthquake, no way the Volvo would give her whiplash....

"Are you all right?" he asked, rushing to her side, then stopping when she held out one hand. He stood there, staring at the palm hanging in midair in front of his face. His gaze dipped lower, watching her breasts rise and fall as she took deep breaths.

Probably watching more than he should, all things considered, but at least he knew she wasn't about to pass out anymore. From what he could see, her breathing was great.

Then the hand dropped, and she turned to look at him, her face flushed, eyes shooting fire.

"When the heck did you zoom in behind me?" she demanded.

"Obviously while you weren't looking in the mirror," he said, happy to see that she wasn't going to faint on him. Anger was much better. Especially since anger looked so...*hot* on this woman. A cute, trim blonde with nice curves...standing in front of his crumpled car, because he had been reckless.

Oh, the Fates were killing him today. He made himself stop noticing her curves.

"Couldn't you see I was parking? What did you do? Descend from the sky? And *why?* Why on earth would you do a stupid thing like that?" She waggled a finger at him. "You should have waited. It's that sort of reckless maneuvering that will get you in trouble."

He laughed, mildly amused. Demetri crashed on an almost monthly basis, and he'd never had anyone lecture him before. It was refreshing. *Arousing.* He was noticing the curves again, because in the tight, faded blue jeans, it was impossible not to. The denim jacket was old, as well, with some froufrou fringe around the chest that drew attention back to her...

Not looking.

"Are you listening to me?"

"Absolutely," he said, eyes firmly on her face.

She drew in a breath, her mouth twisting as if she were going to argue. Then she took a step away from her car, looking back toward the front of his. The mouth twisted more. "Oh, heck," she whispered, the denim-clad shoulders sagging. "Are you all right?" she asked.

Her voice was a rich Kentucky drawl that slid down his throat much smoother than bourbon ever had. He had always had a thing for blondes, but lately they'd been tending toward the icy cold of professionally done platinum rather than the warm taste of golden amber. Still, professionally done platinum had bought him a world of trouble, so maybe it was time for golden amber....

No.

Bad actions. Bad consequences. Lesson learned.

"I'm fine," he told her. "How are you?" he asked, looking her over, ostensibly checking for injuries. The narrow glance she shot him told him better than words that she didn't buy the act for a minute. "You looked like you were going to faint."

"Mister, the only thing dented on me is my pride," she said, meeting his gaze before shaking her head sadly and turning her attention back to his car—what was left of his car. "Good God almighty, I can't believe this. Look at that thing. Folded like a cheap lawn chair. I've never even had an accident, and my first one has to be some European whoop-de-do that would crunch up if you hit it with a cotton ball."

"European wh—"

"That could have been *you*. That is exactly what I'm talking about. Why do something so *stupid* in a flimsy little car like that? Do *you* want to end up all smashed like your car?"

Demetri swallowed, then took an involuntary step backward. "I'm fine. In fact, I'm more than capable of handling that machine," he began. "You're the one—"

"Who doesn't have a crunched-up car," she said, pointing to the bumper of her Volvo, which had escaped completely unscathed. "Barely a scratch." Then she looked at his vehicle. "I don't know why carmakers make cars like tin cans. You'd think they'd make them sturdy."

"That makes them slow," Demetri explained, feeling strangely compelled to defend his car, possibly due to the way the fender was dragging the ground like a broken leg, and the hood was folded up into the windshield. The pain was like his own. An Italian work of art was not designed to withstand the impact of a Volvo. It seemed…ignoble, somehow.

Her head lifted, the bright eyes capturing his imagination in ways she probably wouldn't appreciate. "You got a problem with slow?" she challenged.

"Some people like to drive fast," he pointed out, not really wanting to argue with her, but he did like the way she talked, even if he didn't completely like the things she said. And he couldn't kiss her, and an argument kept her talking…and so he was human. So what?

Her hands settled on her hips, cute, curvy hips that he had told himself not to notice. Not noticing, not noticing at all.

"Some people like to die. I prefer neither." Her face paled, and fire lit her voice. "That really was a mighty fool thing to do."

"Yeah," he said. "It was."

She blinked. "Excuse me?"

"I should have waited. I didn't. I'm sorry." He'd been prepared to own up to his impatience from the moment he'd stepped out of the car. This was the first solid opening she'd given him, and seeing the look of surprise on her face made him supremely glad he'd waited. "I get a little impatient sometimes."

"Mmm." She pondered him for a moment, and Demetri enjoyed the way her gaze softened and cut over him, like a physical caress if a man were inclined to think that way—which Demetri was. As quick as it came, the moment was gone, and she focused on the car again. "You know, I'll be able to feed an entire undeveloped nation for what it's going to cost to repair that little ding in your fender."

He took in the damage to his car, one of only five experimental versions in the world. Rockefeller couldn't afford to fix his car. No way was he going to make her pay for it. It had been his fault. He'd be the bigger person. "If you need to settle this under the table, that'd be fine, but I'm not sure you could afford it. Don't worry about it." He looked at her, waiting for her to appreciate his generous offer.

She laughed at him. *Laughed* at him. It was humbling, demeaning and slightly irritating.

"When you get an estimate, send it to my assistant, and I'll take care of it." She scribbled a phone number on a piece of paper. No name, just a number. If it hadn't been for the way her mouth bowed up like a flower, or the way her blue eyes reflected turquoise in the afternoon sun, he probably would have left it at that.

Nah.

"You're a friend of the Prestons?" he asked curiously.

"Family," she snapped, looking mildly insulted.

"I've never seen you before."

"I've never seen you, either, but that doesn't amount to a hill of beans, does it? Next time you should be more careful with that driving. You could get yourself killed that way."

"I could give you lessons," he offered.

"In how to drive like a crazy person? Thanks, but no." It was a dismissal, and in case he didn't get the point, she presented him with a perfect heart-shaped rear, tightly encased in denim. As she walked toward the house, her hips swung back and forth like a pendulum. A connoisseur's smile flared on his lips. A man could get lost in that rhythm, or at least distracted.

Maybe better men than him had tried, but probably no one more stubborn. If he were smart, he would ignore his urges, leave her alone, get his car fixed and pocket the bill.

But Demetri was reckless, and he spent most of his life laughing at the Fates. Habits were hard to break, and some were impossible.

Once out of sight of the stranger, Elizabeth Innis caught her breath, and resumed fanning her face, because Lord knows, she was overheating, and it had nothing to do with being twenty-eight years old and in her first car accident ever. Not that the accident wasn't traumatizing, but the hot flashes running in her blood weren't anxiety. That was one hundred percent pure, all-natural lust.

As a rule, she stayed away from men like that: dark and handsome in those ways of soap-opera villains who were always hiding deep, traumatic secrets. No, Elizabeth had sky-high standards.

In her world purview, she clung to the idea of true love, but knew that for every prince, there was a whole oceanful of frogs that were green and slimy and caught flies for a living. No, thank you. She was holding out for the one, the only—true love, with a capital *T* and a capital *L*. Not that that meant she wouldn't be picky about finding Mr. Right. None of that high-living, high-loving, hotdogging for Elizabeth, no sir, which meant staying away from exotic-looking men in exotic-looking cars when just the thought set her off fanning again.

This was going to have to stop, she reminded herself, giving herself one last wave for good measure, and then tucking her hands away. After all, she had a reputation to preserve. The magazines said she wore a chastity belt under her tight-fittin' jeans and was so clean that she squeaked when she walked. Elizabeth didn't mind the talk one bit. Her music fans ate it up, and in Elizabeth's mind, that chastity belt was worth its weight in gold—gold records that is. Still, her reputation had one drawback—men saw it as a challenge.

Like the exotic-looking driver of the car she'd crumpled.

Hopefully he'd contact her assistant and let Elizabeth pay for the damage and then she could put the whole matter behind her. After all, she wasn't here to puddle at the feet of some dark stranger. She had a wedding to sing for, a woebegone cousin to cheer up and two weeks' worth of R & R.

Her chastity belt was staying right where it was, because there wasn't a place in her life for hot-looking strangers who took darn-foolish chances…

Even if he could overheat her with a glance.

Her hand started fanning all over again.

Shoot.

The Preston study was an impressive testament to the legacy of Quest Stables, the stables that Hugh Preston had built from scratch, one winner at a time. Dark wooden bookshelves lined the walls, filled with a mix of business books and racing books, the two skills that had made Quest Stables one of the largest racing operations in Kentucky. Hugh had handed over the reins to his son Thomas a long time ago, but was still active in the process, picking out horses with the same eye for a winner.

As Demetri waited for the old man to arrive, his gaze wandered over the room and all the racing memorabilia that it contained. A trophy case was filled with the old-style, two-handled cups that had been awarded so long ago, and pictures of the horses that had raced under the Quest name. The green walls were covered with framed news clippings of the stable's winners. And now, all that history, the Preston legacy, was in doubt.

Not if Demetri could help it.

As a rule, Demetri didn't play Sir Galahad well. Racing was a solitary occupation, and kept him moving from place to place. When the cars hit the track, friends turned to competitors, never a good idea. And as for his family, all that was left was his father, and he didn't speak to Demetri unless he was forced to. It made for a solitary life.

Yet Hugh Preston had always been there for Demetri—a lot of the times with a sharp rebuke, or a shake of the grizzled head. A poor substitute for family, but Demetri would take what he could get. And for his friend, Demetri would wear the Sir Galahad mantel, no matter how badly it fit.

"There's a tow truck dragging a cracked-up car from my drive, and I'm certain it belongs to you. You, a prizewinning Formula Gold driver, with a slew of records behind you. Which leaves me scratching my head, wondering how it came to be in such poor shape?"

Demetri turned and greeted the old man with a one-armed slap against the shoulder. At eighty-six, Hugh Preston still moved with the hurried pace of a much younger man, and spoke in a voice that was almost musical, with long-ago traces of an Irish brogue, the hard swagger of Brooklyn and the meandering drawl of Kentucky, all blended together in one.

"The accident wasn't my fault," defended Demetri, although technically, if someone wanted to split hairs or argue over "fact," then yeah, he probably shared some of the burden of responsibility, or most of it.

Hugh settled his frame in a leather chair and poured out two glasses of bourbon. "That's what the guilty ones always say," he said, taking a long sip of bourbon, and ending with a contented sigh.

"It'll take a few weeks for my engineering team to repair, but Louisville in the fall has a certain appeal." A blond appeal, with wide blue eyes and a smart mouth. A smart, extremely kissable mouth...

Nope. Not going there.

"Hopefully your driving skills will improve before the race next week. Are you coming to the barbecue dinner tomorrow?"

"I don't know," answered Demetri, because Preston social events were different from the social events of the racing circuit. On the circuit, Demetri was on display, a showman for the cause. The Prestons would expect merely the man, and Demetri wasn't comfortable when the mere man was on display. Some things were best left in the dark.

"So who's the blonde that backed into me?" he asked nonchalantly, deciding to go there after all. In the end, the sun rose on a daily basis, an old dog couldn't learn to play fetch and Demetri was born to pull the wheel against the skid. "I think I scared her. Drives a tank of a Volvo."

"That'd be Elizabeth."

"Elizabeth who?" he asked, rolling the name over in his mind. *Elizabeth.*

Hugh frowned. "That'd be 'just Elizabeth' to you, Demetri. She's like family to me."

The slight hurt, but Hugh would never realize that. Demetri's smile was too polished, too practiced. "I would guess she doesn't need your protection, Hugh. She seems capable of making up her own mind."

Hugh's harsh bark of laughter was answer enough. "Now what was that I was reading in the tabloids about you? A married princess? Whatever got you thinking that was a good idea?"

Demetri shrugged, the picture of casual indifference. "She was lonely. I thought I could help. I didn't know her great-aunt owned forty-seven percent of Valencia Products and would pull her sponsorship of the team."

"Elizabeth isn't lonely. She doesn't need your help."

"All right. Lesson learned. Message received. Hands off. But she should have checked her mirrors," he felt the need to add, because she should have looked behind her. However, Demetri wasn't here to play, and he'd made polite small talk long enough. "Tell me what's going on, Hugh. The stalls are empty. I heard there won't be any Quest horses at the Keeneland sales. Thomas said that he's losing McMurray's horses and the Thornhills', too. How much longer until this racing ban goes away?"

"Not long," answered Hugh, which wasn't much of an answer.

Thoughtfully Demetri swirled the ice in his glass before looking up. "Let me give you the cash to cover the expenses until then."

"No," said the old man, not even waiting to reply.

"Talk to Thomas. He'll agree."

Hugh scoffed at that. "You don't know my son very well."

It was true, Demetri had never bonded with Thomas the way he had with Hugh. Thomas had a hard, uncompromising edge that reminded Demetri of his own father, whereas Hugh had been impulsive, reckless, a risk taker, but a man who had grown wiser as he had gotten older. "He can't be prouder than you," Demetri pointed out.

"Prouder, and in some ways, more stubborn."

Demetri sighed, taking another long sip of his drink. This was going to be harder than he'd thought, and he had known coming in that it wouldn't be easy. That was all right, though. For Hugh, he'd work a little harder. Demetri polished off the last of the bourbon and then put the glass on the table next to him. "Ten years ago, somebody spotted me a loan to move my father's start-up to the big leagues. I repaid the money, but that man wouldn't take a decent interest rate on the loan."

Hugh smiled and waved the reminder off with a careless hand. "I liked you, Demetri."

"It was a boneheaded move," Demetri reminded him.

"You were a friend."

"So are you. Take the money. It'll be an infusion of cash to tide Quest over until the ban has lifted."

Hugh shook his head, not even hesitating. "Put your wallet away. First Elizabeth, now you."

There was that name again, rolling in his head. He could feel the itch in his fingers, the ache in his body, the challenge. Always the challenge. "Elizabeth?"

"The money's not needed here," answered Hugh, slamming down his glass. "Thomas won't take any loan, and I don't want to discuss it any longer. For over sixty years I've been picking out the best legs, the biggest hearts and the horses that kept going when they had nothing left to give. After I retired, Thomas ran these stables with honor and integrity. They're not going to take that away from us now."

"Talk to Thomas. Please."

Hugh sighed, downed the remainder of his bourbon and shook his head. "No."

Okay, so the honest, aboveboard ways weren't going to work. Not a surprise. "My teammate wants to stable some horses here. Would you mind if I show him around?"

"Stabling horses here? While people suspect us of cheating to win, and we can no longer race our own horses? Is this another cockamamy way of throwing money in my direction?"

Demetri had been stabling horses at Quest for nearly ten years. Last spring the Prestons' own champion Leopold's Legacy was on his way to winning the Triple Crown when a DNA test was required because of a discrepancy in the Jockey Association's computer records. The results revealed that the stallion's sire was not Apollo's Ice, as listed, and a racing ban was imposed on all majority-owned Quest horses. The integrity of the stables had come into question and owners began to remove their horses. But Demetri could help add more horses to Quest Stables. Boarding fees didn't bring in nearly as much as stud fees or racing purses, but whatever worked.

"No," he lied. "Definitely not. He's new to horses." Actually, Oliver didn't know that he was stabling horses at Quest. But he would soon. Demetri would buy them, Oliver would "own" them and Quest would stable them. Everybody was a winner.

Oliver was in his debut season as the number two driver for Team Sterling, with the promise of a great career ahead of him, assuming he didn't muck it up. Young at twenty-two, he was powerful and aggressive, and what he didn't have in brains, he made up for in *grande cojones* and gamesmanship.

Some of the other drivers didn't care for Oliver. They said he was too aggressive, too manipulative, always chasing the top step of the podium, rather than driving for the team, but that was the exact reason that he and Demetri worked well together. It wasn't about the team, it was only about the win. And James Sterling, former CEO of Sterling Motor Cars, and the principle executive for Team Sterling, was building up his reputation by picking drivers who drove to the edge.

Drivers like Demetri.

For a moment Hugh studied him, looking right through him, but Demetri didn't flinch. Finally Hugh nodded. "Bring him to the barbecue with you tomorrow. Maybe he can keep you out of trouble."

"Sounds like a plan," answered Demetri, rising from the chair and heading for the door. "I'll see you tomorrow."

"Are you forgetting something?" asked Hugh.

Demetri looked around blankly. "No."

"Are you planning on walking all the way back to town?" The faded blue eyes danced with mischief.

"Call me a cab?"

"You're a cab, and if you give me your promise to keep your hands off my great-niece, then I'll let you borrow one of the trucks."

"You don't need my promise," answered Demetri, because he knew it was a promise he couldn't keep.

Elizabeth.

Hugh moved to the desk, rummaging for a moment before throwing a set of keys in Demetri's direction. "I know I'm going to regret this. And try not to smash up this one, Demetri."

Demetri grinned. "I always try."

"That's what I'm afraid of."

Chapter Two

Elizabeth found her cousin Melanie riding in the paddock, sitting on top of a big gray with flashing white stockings who looked speedier than Elizabeth ever wanted to travel. However, Melanie was of a different mind. She wanted to ride faster than some nuclear-powered rocket, and Elizabeth wished her all the luck in the world with that.

Everybody had a gift. Elizabeth could sing, and Melanie could talk to horses. Maybe not in words, but when you saw Melanie with a horse, you knew that two-way communicating was going on. Melanie would murmur sweet nothings to the Thoroughbreds, and when they were out on the track, those sweet nothings could make them move like nobody's business. Baby talk, was how Elizabeth used to tease her cousin. After Melanie started winning her races, Elizabeth stopped her teasing.

For a few seconds she watched her cousin ride, noticing the way the horse and the rider moved together, and noticing the telltale droop in Melanie's smile. At that disturbing sight, Elizabeth squared her shoulders and pushed all the bad things out of her mind, including the inopportune car-crush—along with the correspondingly inopportune, hot-looking car-crusher. Out of her mind, and hopefully out of her loins. Briskly, she waved, looking just as bright and perky as a woman who had not just wrecked a car that cost more than God, or lusted after a man that she had no business feeling the heat for. "Hey, cuz. Ready to race?"

Melanie's mouth curved up at the corners, and she dismounted, hopping down to the dirt. "Bet you twenty I can beat you out to the ridge."

Elizabeth snickered. "I don't bet with jockeys. I'm absolutely certain there's something against that in the Bible. Don't know where to find it, or specifically what it says, but I'm comfortable in my decision."

"Spoilsport," answered Melanie, pulling a face. She hollered at one of the stable hands, asking for another mount for Elizabeth—hopefully something not quite so zippy. Elizabeth found herself more than satisfied when the man led out a pretty little broodmare, soft brown with a coal-black mane. Courtin' Cristy was what they called her. A pretty name for a pretty horse.

Gingerly, Elizabeth climbed into the saddle, taking a deep breath and adjusting to the discrepancy in heights.

The stable hand opened the gate and the two cousins took off "racing," which was Elizabeth's word for a nice, steady trot, curving among the sturdy branches of the black walnut trees. Riding with her cousin through the hills and valleys with the wind at her back, Elizabeth felt like a kid once again.

The afternoon was crisp and cool, the last of the bright yellow leaves valiantly fighting against the November wind, carpeting the grass in a patchwork quilt of red and gold. In the distance, the smoky smell of burning leaves drifted in the air as the rituals of the first true cold snap of autumn commenced.

The ridge overlooking the winding valley had always been

their place to go, a place to forget all the troubles of the world. They pulled up in a plush field of bluegrass, perfect for sitting and watching the clouds skate by. Melanie sighed, her face not nearly as happy as Elizabeth wished it were.

Quest Stables was in serious financial trouble, and to Elizabeth's way of thinking, it was time for the Prestons to face facts. Their prize Thoroughbred, Leopold's Legacy, had been pulled from the racing circuit because his pedigree was in doubt, and until the Prestons could get the mystery of his parentage resolved, things weren't so rosy.

"Melanie, you should be happier. Your brother's getting hitched day after tomorrow, but you don't look happy, and Robbie's going to see right through those fakey smiles. I keep wanting to help, y'all keep turning me down, and it's getting real old, real fast. However, because I am determined, I'm not giving up, and by the way, how are y'all paying for this wedding? At least let me help with that."

"Grandpa's being stubborn. He put some money down on a race in Saratoga, won big, enough to cover the wedding, but I thought Dad was going to blow a gasket."

Elizabeth clucked her tongue. "And now Uncle Hugh's been driven to gambling…"

Melanie snorted inelegantly, a sound echoed by the mare behind her. "Grandpa isn't driven to anything he doesn't want to do. Elizabeth, do you remember when you were in bad financial straits and needed help? I tried to help, and what did you tell me?"

"I didn't say anything," lied Elizabeth.

Melanie glared, and Elizabeth felt a twinge of remorse. So Elizabeth repeated her words in a quiet whisper. "I said I didn't want charity, not from my family, not from anybody. But this is different."

Melanie nodded, in a completely annoying fashion. "And you made it all on your own, didn't you?"

"Yes," answered Elizabeth, wishing Melanie didn't have to be so…right.

"So, why do you think the Prestons are any different?"

The Prestons. Elizabeth sighed, because there was that dividing line again, like the Mason-Dixon line, the Great Wall of China or the Berlin Wall, before they tore it down. The Prestons were her family, God bless 'em. Melanie's momma and Elizabeth's momma were sisters, but Elizabeth and Diane weren't part of the inner circle. It wasn't something that was rude or snooty or mean-spirited at all, but geographical instead. The Prestons lived right outside Lexington, and Elizabeth had grown up in Tennessee. Between the mad dash from one singing gig to another, guitar and singing lessons, and the odd jobs to pay the bills, it was only during the holidays that Elizabeth spent time with her cousins, and sometimes, on a rare golden occasion, a whole summer week.

Those hot summer days were the best, riding horses until she could barely walk, eating watermelon on the porch, Brent and Andrew trying to outwrestle each other, and giggling with Melanie over Robbie's goofy little-brother antics. On those days, Elizabeth had watched her cousins with greedy eyes. She wanted that warm closeness of the Prestons. That after-dinner moment when two thousand conversations were all going on at once, and it didn't really matter that nobody could hear a word. The Preston family kept together through thick and thin and that was all that counted.

Staying with the Prestons had once again reminded Elizabeth of what she had missed growing up. The grass was always greener, especially in Kentucky. She blew out a wistful breath.

A few feet away, the two horses were grazing under the scraggly canopies of the bur oaks that dotted the countryside. Melanie's mount, Something to Talk About—now that was a true character. The gray was showing off and prancing around, as if he just knew people were watching.

Horses were the Prestons' lifeblood, and now that blood was slowly being squeezed off. If the Prestons truly thought Elizabeth was just going to pack up her marbles and go home, they had another think coming.

"I have the means, you know it, and y'all are family."

Furiously Melanie shook her head, short blond waves flying from the force. "No. I think it's nice of you to offer, Elizabeth, but we're not angling for handouts. We're not that desperate yet. I don't want to hear another word."

"I want to help," Elizabeth insisted.

"Elizabeth, you sing. You don't know anything about horses or stables or financial matters. You help out by being here. Let somebody else take care of the rest."

Elizabeth sighed, throwing a piece of grass at her cousin, wishing it had magical powers that could make her family see sense, instead of having Melanie look at her as though she were some space alien come down from Planet Helpless.

"I'm capable of doing a whole lot more," she said, but her cousin went right on talking, as if Elizabeth hadn't said a word.

"Yeah, like getting into car wrecks. I heard about your accident in front of the house. At first, I didn't believe it was you. I mean, it's not like you drive fast enough to do any damage to anybody, but then they said Demetri ran into *you*." Melanie started to laugh, and Elizabeth could see no humor in this situation and thought it was downright…*tacky* to laugh at someone who had suffered such a tragic misfortune.

"It's no cause for laughing, Melanie," she answered, wounded, *wounded* to the quick.

"You don't know," answered her cousin, gasping between giggles.

"What don't I know?"

"Demetri Lucas. He's a race-car driver."

Demetri Lucas. Race-car driver.

Oh, she didn't want to know his name. She preferred to

keep him as the hot-looking driver with the heavy hands and the lead foot.

A race-car driver, and didn't that beat all? Elizabeth didn't like car-racing. Cars were tools, a means to get from one place to another, not some durn-fool bleacher sport that took away good Sunday-afternoon television programming. "Driving cars. Now isn't that the most useless pastime ever? I mean, why in heaven's name does anyone want to zoom around that track, flying round and round, wheeling around the corners, and oh, Lord, I'm making myself queasy just thinking about it."

Melanie stopped her giggles and her eyes got that sly little gleam that indicated she wanted to pry. "So what'd you think?"

"I didn't think anything," Elizabeth answered, lying through her teeth. "What's there to think?"

"Elizabeth, you're not blind."

"And I'm not dumb, neither."

Melanie nodded once, in that smug, supercilious way of people who know they've discovered the truth when someone doesn't want them to discover the truth, because sometimes the truth is better left undiscovered. "He's hot."

"If you like that sort of look," answered Elizabeth, idly strumming her fingers through the grass, because she didn't usually go for the dark-and-dangerous look in men. Her normal type was clean-cut and upstanding. Men who took "no" for an answer and didn't quibble.

"Every woman likes that sort of look."

Elizabeth looked up and arched a brow, smug and supercilious, too. "Even you?"

"Oh, no."

"Still nursing a hurt?" she asked, because Melanie had fallen for the wrong sort once. It seemed like every woman was destined to be a fool once.

Melanie shook her head. "Older and wiser, just like you, I bet. Are *you* still nursing a hurt?"

There was forgiveness, and then there was spotted-dog stupid. Elizabeth blew out a breath. She had been snookered once—and by the man who sired her—but now she was older and wiser, too.

Sadly she checked her watch and sighed. Playtime was over. She walked over to her mount, leaves snapping under her feet. Gently she rubbed the velvety nose, letting the mare know that even though she wasn't as fast as the colt, she was still special to Elizabeth—especially since she was taking her back over the ridge to the stables.

"Courtin' Cristy, you're a nice lady, aren't you?" she crooned, the horse neighing softly.

Melanie nodded. "She is, too. Not a mean bone in her body."

"She should have a nicer name. Flower or Buttercup, with those flirty eyelashes of hers."

Melanie shot Elizabeth a telling look. "I don't name them. I just ride them. And speaking of which, I do have a job to do."

Elizabeth took a last look at the long, sweeping valley. "Don't remind me. I've got a meeting in the city tonight. Album covers. You would not believe all the hoop-di-do that goes into deciding what goes on a cover. I could tell you stories that would curl your hair."

"You're going to leave? I thought you were staying at the house until after the wedding?"

"I'll be back late tonight, Melanie. You think you can sneak out a bottle of apple wine and we can sit on the veranda and gossip?"

Melanie raised shocked eyebrows. "I don't drink apple wine anymore, Elizabeth, only Chardonnay. Do you?"

Elizabeth was shamed. "No," she lied. Three lies in one day. It was a world record, but Elizabeth knew exactly where the blame belonged.

The hot-looking driver with the heavy hands and the lead foot.

"So did Robbie invite him to the wedding?" she asked, the words flying out of her mouth before she could stop them.

Melanie leaped into the saddle, as graceful as a ballet dancer, and waggled a warning finger at Elizabeth. "Be careful, Elizabeth. That snowy-white reputation that you're so proud of can disappear like that." Melanie snapped her fingers, as if Elizabeth couldn't comprehend the graphic on her own.

"Like I'd do something stupid with that man? You know me, cuz. Cautious is my middle name, my first name and my last name, too," she answered, dismissing the idea, all while new ideas were seeping into her mind, ideas that were distinctly uncautious.

She shook her head, flicking all those ideas out of there.

Hopefully this time, it'd work for good.

Whenever there was a wedding in the works, the wind blew a little softer, the nightingales sounded a little prettier, and even Seamus, Hugh's Irish wolfhound, walked around with a bounce in his step and a song in his bark. The Preston household might have been dreary lately, the pall of the scandal touching everything in ways that Elizabeth had never imagined, but in the hectic days leading up to Robbie and Amanda's wedding, things were perkier and livelier. Betsy, the capable manager who ran the house, had the staff take out the best china, guest rooms were dusted, the silver was polished, and everything was set out for Jenna Preston's white-glove inspection.

That evening, when Elizabeth got home from the meeting in town, she opted to do a little inspecting of her own. Said subject of inspection? One Demetri Lucas, whose car she had recently demolished, and whose image kept cropping up into her mind, and other places that she didn't want any man cropping up into. Hopefully a hard dose of reality would help matters. After climbing atop the fluffy yellow guest room bed, she studied her laptop screen, and stumbled across the first of many, many, *many* damning sins. The most recent being that he had just lost a key endorsement from Valencia Products because he'd been boffing royalty. Elizabeth sniffed contemptuously.

Married?

Royalty?

Not only was he irresponsible, but he was also plain stupid. Thinking he wouldn't get caught? Durn. The man might as well be blond.

To be fair, he did have some business sense, but it was that hard-nosed, hard-hearted shark behavior that Elizabeth didn't like. Besides his race-car driving, Demetri Lucas bought and sold companies the way other men played the slots. He didn't care, didn't participate, only signed on the bottom line, made a bucketload of cash and then moved on to either the next venture, or the next princess, whichever caught his roving eye first.

And apparently his roving eye had been caught many, many times.

She was cursing the man six ways to Sunday when her cell phone rang.

"Liz?" Her manager was the only person who called her Liz. Thank God for small favors, because Liz was a shortcut name; it didn't have nearly the regal grandeur of Elizabeth. And at five foot four, Elizabeth wanted all the regal grandeur she could get.

"Tobey?" she said, kicking back on the bed. "What are you calling for? If you're calling me about the album cover, I'm not going to listen. I told you tonight that I didn't like that last mock-up of the cover, and I meant it. I sing country, not heavy metal. Use something prettier than black. What's wrong with yellow? Or pink? Or maybe one of those soft teals? I think—"

"Liz."

Elizabeth stopped. "What?"

"I'm not calling about the cover. They're going to change the background color."

Elizabeth blew out a breath. "Well thank heavens for that. So why are we chatting when I'm supposed to be on vacation?"

"I got another call from the shampoo company Softsilk. They're determined to get you. The woman said they have a new line coming out next year. Soft, sexy, womanly. Those were their words. They want you to do the spots."

"Why did you call me with this? I sing. That's it. I don't want to do commercials or product placements, or be some shill for some shampoo that will probably make my hair fall out. I told you no the last five times you asked me. No, no, no. What I use on my head, what I put on my face, what jeans I wear, what car I drive is nobody's business but mine, and I'll be damned if Elizabeth Innis is going to help sell somebody else's products. I'm not telling you something that you don't already know, Tobey. Why are you calling, and this time, please tell me the truth."

"Frank called. He heard you were in Kentucky and thought it'd be good for you to do a local concert the week after next. It's for the University of Louisville, the Wednesday night before their homecoming game. Skew your demographics younger."

Frank was the manger of Five Star Records, Elizabeth's label, and when Frank told Tobey to jump, Tobey asked how high. Elizabeth didn't mind, that was Tobey's job, but Elizabeth wasn't a business person. She was an artist. And everybody knew that artists were temperamental. Even though Elizabeth wasn't temperamental, that didn't mean she couldn't pretend when it worked to her advantage.

"Tobey. I'm on vacation. My cousin is getting married day after tomorrow and I'm singing in the wedding. I need this break. I've been on tour for the last twelve months. Now, I love my band, but do you know how many hotels that is? Do you know how many frequent flier miles that is? More than I can count, Tobey, but I bet it's not more than you can count. I bet you can tell me exactly how many frequent flier miles I've logged, can't you? Let me make this clear so you can understand. I'm not doing any concerts here. I'm tired. Can't you hear the tension in my voice? I don't know why you can't, 'cause this phone connection sounds pretty good to me."

"Frank's got something lined up, Liz."

Elizabeth glared at the phone, which did absolutely no good, but it made it her feel better. "Let me repeat what I said, because I'm thinking this phone connection must not be as crisp as I thought. I'm not doing any concerts here. Not one. I'm tired. This is my family time, and nothing gets between me and my family time."

"Frank already lined it up," he answered, just as if he hadn't heard a single word that she'd said.

Elizabeth snorted. "Well, tell him to unline it up. I'm on vacation. It's three weeks, Tobey, not three years. Nothing trumps family for me. You know that."

"The money's good, Elizabeth."

Elizabeth humphed into the phone. "Do you think that matters? If it's going to start mattering to me, then I need to fire you, because I'm not making as much money as you're telling me I am. Do I need to fire you, Tobey? Don't tell me yes, because you're about as L.A. as I can handle. Everybody told me to get a Nashville agent, but I liked you, even if you were L.A, but maybe they were right, Tobey. Maybe I should get a Nashville agent."

"Don't make me go back to Frank and tell him no," he begged.

"Go back to Frank and tell him no."

"Oh, Elizabeth…" Which he only called her when he was really, really, really up a creek.

"Oh, Tobey…" she said, and she knew she was starting to get all soft, and she didn't want to get all soft. She needed to be tough and hard-edged with a spine that wouldn't break, no matter how much battering it took. Elizabeth drew in a deep, strength-injecting breath, happy to feel the steel return. "Now you listen—"

Suddenly she stopped, a lightbulb flashing in her head.

"How much money are we talking about?" Elizabeth asked carefully.

Tobey named a figure that raised her brows, and her brows—

which were perfectly arched—didn't usually rise that far. That was all it took for her to change her mind. "Sign me up, Tobey. I'll do it. Get the band down on the next plane out of Nashville. Actually, not the next plane, but maybe Monday after next. At least let's give them the weekend off, then we can have two days' worth of rehearsal."

"Why did you change your mind so fast?" he asked suspiciously. Rightly so. A wise one, that Tobey. That was why she liked him.

"Might want to buy something," she hedged, even though the plan was already formulating in her head.

"Couldn't you give me a hint?" he asked.

"Whoa. Gotta go, Tobey. This phone is breaking up. Darn cells. Hate the things." Elizabeth made crackling noises into the phone and then snapped it closed. A concert would be the perfect solution and hopefully the Prestons would think so, too.

"It looks rather deserted, don't you think?" asked Oliver Wentworth, squinting in the direction of the empty pasture, and Demetri tried to see the stables through Oliver's eyes.

Oh, yeah, the grounds of the Preston homestead were impressive. A thousand acres, perfect for the Thoroughbred horses that were being trained there. At one time, there had been over five hundred horses stabled on the premises. Today the numbers were dwindling. The practice track stood silent, only a few horses wandering in the pasture, grazing quietly.

Demetri took it all in, and shook his head sadly. He didn't want to see Quest through Oliver's eyes.

Next to him, Oliver leaned against the wooden fence and looked around, completely unimpressed. "So this is what a horse farm looks like?" he asked.

"Normally Quest is a little busier," Demetri answered, feeling the need to defend the proud stables because of course, soon "Oliver" would be stabling horses here, as well, but they had a long way to go, and Demetri was going to have to work this slowly. Oliver was from England, and his idea of horses ran toward polo ponies and fox hunts, not Kentucky Thoroughbreds.

At first, Oliver hadn't wanted to come to the barbecue, but Demetri had casually mentioned that there might be women there—single, attractive and lonely women—which immensely perked up Oliver, who was tall and golden haired, with a playboy's eye.

When Oliver had made the team last year, the press had kidded that Demetri was like an older brother to him—a lousy older brother. People expected a lot from the elder sibling. They expected responsibility, maturity, vigilance and watchfulness. Demetri had none of those qualities. He never had, and he wished that people would stop expecting it from him. No matter how wild his antics, or how reckless his driving, they still expected more. *Idiots.* At one time, he'd had a younger brother, Seth. Demetri had come up short for Seth, and he hoped that Oliver wasn't watching too closely, because he worried that someday he would come up short for Oliver, as well.

Demetri had yet to tell Oliver his grand plan to have Oliver stable some Thoroughbreds at Quest, because Oliver's first priority was always Oliver, and Demetri had yet to figure out an angle, or possibly a debt obligation, which he could hold over Oliver's head. But he would. Eventually.

Oliver grinned. "Fascinating, now can we go have dinner?"

"You're hungry?" Demetri felt vaguely disappointed that Oliver hadn't gone all cowboy at the sight of horses. It seemed…un-American, which, considering Oliver was British, wasn't a total surprise. Still, Demetri had hoped.

"I'm not hungry for food, old man. I'm only here for the women."

Demetri slapped him on the back, not hungry, either—except for her.

Elizabeth.

A smile crossed his face, and he could feel the burn inside him. "Watch and learn, Oliver. Watch and learn."

It took a foolish woman's heart to skip a beat when she saw six-foot-something worth of trouble walk out onto the manicured lawn. The barbecue dinner for Amanda and Robbie had gone along smooth as molasses, but then he walked outside, and Elizabeth found herself looking, which turned into ogling, which turned into lusting, and it was all downhill from there.

Dressed in dark jeans, exactly like ninety-nine percent of the other men, he still stood out. He was handsome, but there were other nice-looking men here, too. No, there was something distinctly different about Demetri Lucas. Some dangerous song that called to every woman in the place, some unspoken melody that played havoc with the female senses. Greece is where the gossip sites had said he was born, and now Elizabeth understood the appeal of exotic, foreign men.

His face was proud and arrogant, as if he didn't care what anyone thought, and Elizabeth mused to herself that well, if you looked like that, you didn't have to care, because the women were already lapping it up in spades. She could tell. They'd walk by him, a flirty gleam in their eyes, hoping to earn a smile or even better a touch, but Mr. Demetri Lucas was too busy—

—too busy looking at Elizabeth.

There was a dark gleam in those appraising eyes, as though she were some prime piece of horseflesh, rather than the bubble-brained woman who smashed up his car.

What was even worse than that was the shiver in her arms, the compulsive need to lick her lips and the general twitch under her skin that made her nervous as a twelve-year-old.

Frankly, that wasn't quite the truth. That wicked gleam made her feel every single bit of her twenty-eight years, reminding Elizabeth that she was long past puberty, knew the real story about the birds and the bees and had woman parts that were designed to fit a man's parts—perfectly. Although she'd recorded a few songs that delved into the shadowy mystery of passion, they'd been written by someone else, because Elizabeth had never felt the burn herself. She had never known that long lick of desire between her shoulder blades. Never truly felt that heavy throb between her thighs.

Until now.

Restlessly she stalked around the yard like a stray dog looking for a place to land. She moved from one place to another, always trying to escape the magnetic draw of his eyes, but never quite succeeding. Elizabeth pulled up a lawn chair and talked with Melanie, with Uncle Thomas, and Aunt Jenna, chattering like a blue jay, all nonsense, because if she didn't talk, she'd find herself looking in his direction, checking to see if he was still watching.

Which he was.

Elizabeth shivered again.

Oliver was already in his element at the party. The junior driver for Sterling Motor Cars was standing next to Demetri, and in less than an hour, he'd met one long-legged blonde, one brunette with sultry eyes and one redhead with pouty red lips. Still he wasn't satisfied. Oliver loved them all with passion rarely seen in Britain, his stunts nearly, but not quite, eclipsing Demetri.

From across the way, Hugh met his eyes, and Demetri nodded once, lifting his beer. If Hugh had noticed the way Demetri's attention kept slipping toward Elizabeth, he showed no sign of it. In the large crowd, it was unlikely, and Demetri's attention slipped toward her once again.

Oliver saw where Demetri was looking, and nudged him in the ribs. "Do you know who that one is?"

Demetri frowned. "She's one of the Prestons," he said, sounding as if he knew exactly who she was.

"It's Elizabeth Innis. Country-and-western singer. Her last

eight records went platinum. Pity she's not your type," commented Oliver, his wandering eyes firmly fixed in Elizabeth's direction.

"I didn't know I had a type," said Demetri, stepping in between Oliver's wandering eyes and the country-and-western singer that Hugh—who was his friend—had warned him off.

Oliver sidestepped Demetri neatly. "That white dress isn't just for show. Pure as the lamb, but eyes that promise so much more. Sexy, but innocent enough to drive a man wild with anticipation. The advertisers have been after her in droves since she first went platinum, but she consistently tells them no. I think even Valencia was trying to get her to sell some toothpaste or shampoo or something. She told them no, too."

"Definitely not my type," said Demetri with a regretful sigh, but wishing he could change types—for a little while.

Oliver grinned as if he could read his mind. "What a shame. Why, if you were to hook up with someone like her, we'd have sponsors plying us with money left and right. Advertisers love that happily-ever-after fairy-tale world that she sings about."

"Why don't you go into advertising?" asked Demetri, because Oliver lived to manipulate the press, always thinking of new and better ways to play games. At twenty-two, Oliver was too young to know that the man who lived by the media, died by the media. Demetri knew it, only he usually didn't care.

"I hate the pesky buggers, but a man has to survive, and until I get your notoriety, then I'll content myself with my little machinations."

"That's fame, not notoriety," corrected Demetri.

"You say tomato, I say, how do they say it in Kentucky? Horse pucky. Now, if you took up with a woman like that, it would benefit the team immensely," said Oliver, nodding back in Elizabeth's direction.

Demetri shook his head regretfully, his eyes never leaving Elizabeth. "When I look at her, I'm not thinking about a PR opportunity."

Oliver quirked a golden brow. "Even better."

Demetri knew Oliver's bent for trouble, and he felt the need to intervene. Prudent. Sensible. Responsible. "No, Oliver."

Demetri's teammate watched Elizabeth, a wicked gleam in his eyes, and he heaved an exaggerated sigh. "If you won't, then maybe I should," he said, with just enough lust in his voice to make Demetri look twice.

"Stay away from that one," warned Demetri.

Oliver only smiled.

Chapter Three

The late-afternoon sun provided a fitting setting for the couple, poking gilded holes through the clouds sending yellow sunbeams playing on the lawn, until it finally settled down low over the horizon. After that, the air turned a little cooler, and people filtered inside the house, where there was plenty of room. The wedding rehearsal was all through, nothing left to be done but have a good time.

A lively band played in the corner, and bubbles frothed from a silver champagne fountain in the center of the room. However, Elizabeth was too nervy to dance or drink. She had thought she had managed to escape the spider's web, but exactly when she felt most safe, she bumped into a long, hard thigh, and the temperature notched up three hundred degrees. She didn't even have to turn around. She knew. She hadn't planned on giving Mr. Demetri Lucas the satisfaction, but then he laughed at her, deep, with a huskiness that was best described as criminally sexy.

Curious as a cat bent on suicide, she turned, not quite managing to stop the moonstruck sigh.

Dang.

"Imagine that," he said. "Crashing into me again? It's becoming a habit. Or fate?"

Elizabeth cocked her head, staring up at him, locking her knees so she wouldn't embarrass herself and swoon. This was silly. He was a man. A mere man. She frowned, at the moment not caring what her stylist said about premature wrinkles. If ever there was a time for forbidding frowns, this was it.

When he grinned at her like that, a momentary flash of teeth, she felt something stop inside her, and she hoped it wasn't her heart. That would be bad.

For the devil, he sure had a nice mouth. A nice, firm mouth. A kissing mouth, she thought, and then quickly tamped the image back down. *None of that, Elizabeth.*

If only he wouldn't look at her, the dark eyes trapping her, hot waves of want spiraling inside her. She'd had men look at her with desire before, but this felt personal. Way too personal. She could feel that look in places that he had no business affecting.

Elizabeth summoned up the forbidding frown once again. "If you'll excuse me, I believe I see someone I need to talk to," she muttered, completely lacking in manners. She didn't think he'd mind.

"But not me?" he asked, obviously minding.

She stopped and gave in to temptation, looking her fill, as she'd been wanting to do all night. Not surprisingly, that only made things worse.

Truth be told, this was the most dangerous-looking man she'd ever met in her entire life. The boldness in his dark gaze, the wicked twinkle that said, "what the hell," better than words ever could. That same devilish twinkle fired her blood, and the phrase "what the hell" tumbled from her own mind, too.

There was danger in him, and she knew it. He was fairly

humming with it, like a live wire destined to burn the living day-lights out of anyone that dared to touch. But oh, she wanted to touch. Her body ached with that want. Words that she'd never even known were suddenly haunting her lips. Pictures she'd never dreamed of before flashed behind her eyes, tempting her with sins that she'd never ached to commit. It would be easier if she couldn't see those same pictures of those very same sins reflected in the warm russet depths of his eyes.

Sweet mercy, those were fascinating eyes.

It took her a second to breathe again. "No. Definitely not you," she answered, trying to put as much certainty as possible in her voice, but it didn't sound certain enough.

"What a shame," he said, still watching her with that bold gaze, and something inside her started to melt. Slowly, treacher-ously…and stupidly.

"Isn't it, just?" she answered, and without another word— which was a true testament to her fears—she ran.

After that, Demetri had actually planned on leaving her alone. He sat through endless toasts, and didn't even glance in her direction. It wasn't easy because one heated look from her had shot straight to his groin, and made him ache ever since. However, trying to be on his best behavior, he had counted and recounted the hundred and one reasons he should stay away. First and foremost, Hugh was his friend. A man he owed a tre-mendous debt. A man he was here to help—not hurt by tangling with a lamb. He normally didn't mix with "lambs"; they were too complicated, and Demetri didn't have time for complicated. His life was too fast, the racing circuit too demanding a mistress.

And then there was that dreamy light in those bright blue eyes that scared the hell out of him.

Everything was going along well, until after dinner, and he saw her dancing with Oliver—the junior driver formerly known as his friend.

Demetri couldn't help himself.

She'd changed from the virginal white dress she'd worn earlier, and this new one killed off brain cells left and right. It was green, a short jade green silk that was cut low in the front and back, flowing around her hips like water. It was a dress meant to be pulled off inch by luscious inch, and his fingers flexed, greedy and more than up to the task.

As they danced around the floor, Demetri could see she was light on her feet, the green fabric catching the candlelight and reflecting its glow. He tried to tell himself that of course she could dance well, every move was probably profession- ally choreographed. Somehow it didn't help. All he wanted to do was touch her, and see if she was real, or some vision that had stepped out of his boyhood fantasies. And that was the biggest part of the problem. She wasn't some X-rated goddess that a man tumbled into bed with one night and then forgot the next.

Elizabeth Innis was Hugh Preston's niece.

But even with all the alarms flashing inside him, he couldn't help it. She was irresistible.

Once more, damning the fates, Demetri tapped on Oliver's shoulder. "You don't mind if I cut in," asked Demetri, more of an order than a request. Seniority had its privileges after all.

His teammate released Elizabeth—reluctantly. *Suck it up, Oliver.* "Not at all," Oliver answered.

"Excuse me. Did anybody here think that I might mind?"

Demetri took Elizabeth in his arms, and swept her up in the lilting strains of the "Tennessee Waltz." "No," he said, getting used to the way her eyes lit up when she was mad. "One dance for running into my car. It's the least you can do."

"I absolve myself of all responsibility, because your sort of driving— Well, it's a train wreck waiting to happen."

When she talked, it was like warm honey, and he could all too easily imagine what that voice would sound like, whispering in bed. His arms tightened around her, his fingers sliding over the smooth skin of her shoulder, just once, just to know.

"I told myself I was going to stay away," he admitted, willing himself to remember how to dance. "Hugh told me to stay away."

"Are you waiting for me to tell you to stay away, too?" she asked, never missing a step.

"Would you?"

She paused. One second. One momentary hesitation, before answering, "Of course." However, she didn't pull away, and they danced together, Demetri expertly leading her around the other dancers. One hand memorized the curve of her hip, the warm clasp of her fingers in his other hand fitting as if it were custom-made. Something was making him dizzy, the tempo of the music, the snap of her eyes, the full pout to her lips, he wasn't sure what. In the blur of that moment, the hundred and one reasons to stay away from her—reasons that he had carefully recited to himself all evening—faded into nothing. There was no way in hell he was walking away. Not tonight.

When the song came to a close, the crowds drifted one way, and Demetri lifted two glasses of champagne from a passing waiter. Then he guided her through the tall glass doors that led out to the sanctity of the veranda, his hand pressed firmly against the soft skin of her back, shamefully taking advantage of another chance to touch her.

Outside, the moonlight flickered through the trees, bathing the veranda in a soft glow. Demetri handed her a glass, then clinked it once, toasting to absolutely nothing.

"What are you afraid of?" he said, as if he didn't know.

The dreamy eyes narrowed to sapphire slits of death. He didn't even mind.

"You don't have one single move that hasn't been tried before. Don't think I can't take care of myself."

But he could do such a better job, Demetri thought to

himself, studying the full upper lip, and the tiny depression there that was made to be savored. "You're Hugh's niece?"

"Great-niece, but not by blood. My aunt Jenna married into the Preston family, but he doesn't mind when I call him uncle, and I protect him just like he was my own," she answered, eyeing him over the rim of the glass. There was suspicion and disdain, but there was a flicker of other things in those eyes, too. Things that gave a man hope.

"I've been trying to help them," he told her, hoping to erase some of the suspicion. "Just like you."

"But they turned you down. Smart of them," she answered, suspicion still the emotion du jour.

"Do you always make up your mind so fast?" he asked, as if he didn't live and die by snap judgments as a race-car driver.

"Not normally, no, but your track record isn't so stellar, Mr. Lucas."

"You know?"

"Maybe," she said, shrugging carelessly.

"Why didn't Thomas and Hugh accept your offer?" he asked, needing to talk about her, not his past indiscretions. His past wasn't interesting. She, on the other hand, was fascinating.

"They don't want my help," she answered quietly, the perpetually smiling mouth pulled into a frown. Demetri wanted the smile back in place.

"Ah…"

"And you don't need to be ahhing here, like you understand everything, because you don't."

"Why don't you tell me?" he invited, because he wanted to understand everything about her.

She studied him for a minute, and he must have passed some test, because she shook her head, resigned. "Do you really want to know why I'm mad?"

"I'm dying to know."

Then she started to pace around the space, high heels

clicking on the stones, green skirts twirling, exposing a long length of leg. His attention was torn between watching the sway of her hips and the restless way she circled the champagne flute in the air. "I have tried every which way to get my family to take money, ever since I heard about the problems with Leopold's Legacy, but nobody will listen. A few years back I had…some financial issues, and the Prestons wanted to help. I told them all no, that I didn't need it. I could take care of myself. I wasn't some poor cousin looking for charity handouts. And now, well, who knew that they'd listen to my own words so well. I have money, but oh, no, I'm not in the horsey business, I'm in the 'music' business. Elizabeth, she's just a simple little thing." She downed her glass in one gulp, and he handed her his.

"They turned me down, too. That should make you feel better."

She polished off his glass, too. "And that's the only reason I'm still dancing with you, Mr. Lucas."

"Technically, we're not still dancing."

"Don't get all particular on me. I get enough of that when I'm working, thank you very much." She lifted herself up on the edge of one of the wooden railings, crossing one delectable leg over the other, exposing more thigh than he thought she realized. Wisely he didn't say a word.

"Sorry," he answered, trying to keep his gaze firmly fixed on her face.

"Apology accepted," she said, her mind still firmly fixed on helping her family.

"Do you know your way around Louisville?" he asked, his mind firmly fixed on other things.

"Some."

"Enough to show me around?"

She shook her head once. "I bet there're a lot of women that would be interested in showing you around, Mr. Lucas. Fast women who aren't a thing like me. I'm not your type."

He crossed his arms across his chest, sensing a depressing change in the infamous Lucas luck with women. "Why does everyone keep telling me I have a type?"

"If the shoe fits…." she answered, one heel bobbing up and down.

"I'm trying to reform," he said. It was not quite the truth, but if he thought it'd earn him a dinner, drinks and long hours in her bed, he'd be willing to try.

"Ha!" Her arms crossed her chest, plumping her breasts nicely.

"Don't be so skeptical," he answered, his eyes glued to her face as if his life depended on it. Currently he thought it might.

She watched him, noticed that his gaze kept dipping down. "Sorry. Skeptical is my nature."

Reluctantly, he looked up from her cleavage. "No, that's not even close to your nature. You don't have a skeptical bone in that luscious body—excuse me, that slipped out, but it's true. The nonskeptical part. Actually, the luscious part is, too." Demetri stopped. "Sorry."

She started to smile. "That's all right. I liked you better, then."

Humility seemed to work with her. He would remember that. "Why can't I take you to dinner?"

"I don't think that'd be wise."

"Why not?" he answered, although he knew there were one hundred and one reasons that it wouldn't be wise. That wouldn't stop him from trying.

"Trust me," she replied, and he knew people did. Contrary to trusting him, people would trust her with their life.

"You crash into my life, and one dance is all I'm going to get?" he asked, not hiding the disappointment in his voice.

She nodded.

From the distance, he could hear the sounds of music once again, but he didn't want to go back to the crowd. He could stay here forever. Alone with her, listening to the soft music of her voice, drowning in the teasing light of her eyes. *Forever* wasn't normally a word in Demetri's vocabulary. He drove fast cars for a reason. When the world went by in a blur, you never knew what you missed, and Demetri had a feeling that he missed a lot. Yet sitting here, doing nothing more than talking with this woman, made him want to slow down.

"I don't know if I'll survive with only one dance," he told her, the words harmless enough, but deep down, he wondered if it was the truth. He'd never felt this before. This obsessive need to do nothing more than sit in her presence and breathe.

"You certainly turn a lady's head."

"But not yours?"

The teasing light in her eyes dimmed. "Not enough," she said. There was some imaginary line in the room, some piece of rope between them, and she was determined not to cross it.

"What if I made you a deal?" he asked softly.

"I don't make deals with the devil," she said, obviously seeing temptation for what it was.

"There you go again with the name-calling."

"If the shoe fits…"

He glared, and she had the grace to look ashamed—a little. "Tell me what you're proposing, and it had better be aboveboard."

He wanted her across the line, and there was an easy way to get what he wanted, and he wasn't above using it. "You want to help your family?"

She angled her head, watching him carefully. "Yes."

"So do I. We should team up."

"I already have some ideas of my own," she said haughtily.

"What sort of ideas?" he asked, because his mind was brimming with ideas. Glorious, detailed, mostly porno-graphic ideas.

"Not those sorts of ideas," she answered, her eyes knowing.

Demetri willed his mind back to the issue at hand. "Pity. I want to hear more about your ideas. I'm staying in town for the race. You should come."

"I don't do car races, Mr. Lucas," she told him, as if they were the lowest form of entertainment on the planet.

"Could you please call me Demetri?"

"Since you begged so nicely," she teased, and she had no idea how much he'd be willing to beg for her.

"Demetri," he added.

"Demetri," she complied, and he planned on hearing his name on her lips again. And again.

He smiled to himself. "So you'll come?"

"I didn't say that," she answered, and his smile faded.

"You could sing. At the start of the race. Oliver says your voice is lovely. I'd love to hear you sing."

"I'll give you a CD. Truly, the quality is amazing. Can't tell the difference."

He took a chance, taking one step toward her. "You're going to make this difficult," he said, noticing that she didn't run. Progress.

"No, Mr. Lucas. You're making it difficult. I know what men like you are about, and I'm not going there, so you might as well give up."

"I don't give up, Elizabeth. Sorry."

"You're destined for bitter defeat."

"I'm a race-car driver. I live for defeat."

"Why don't I believe that?"

"Because you're a lot smarter than you let people think."

"Maybe."

He took her palm in his, twining their fingers together. She had long, elegant fingers with perfectly polished nails. He could picture those fingers trailing down his chest, the polished nails digging into his back…. Demetri shook his head. "You'll have dinner with me?" he said, his voice huskier than he intended.

"No," she answered, obviously sensing the more explicit train of his thoughts.

"You'll let me help you help your family?"

She looked down at their hands, staring for a moment. Eventually she looked back up at him. "Maybe."

"You'll sing at the race next weekend?"

"Don't you think you need to check with somebody before you ask?"

"I can pull some strings."

Regretfully she removed her hand from his, and for a second his fingers flexed, still feeling her warmth before it finally disappeared. "Yeah. And I bet she's female and you just flutter those thick lashes of yours at her, and she doesn't dare tell you no."

Demetri looked at her, surprised. "I don't think I've ever had anyone notice my lashes before."

"It's a weakness of mine. Don't read too much into it."

Immediately Demetri's imagination shifted to high gear. "Are there any other weaknesses I should know about it?"

"None," she answered promptly, hiding all sorts of delightful secrets.

"I guess I'll have to discover them on my own," he murmured, already dwelling on the infinite possibilities.

"Over my dead body."

"Body, yes. Dead, no."

"Is your mind always this immoral?" she asked, exposing a charming dimple in her left cheek.

"Not normally this immoral. Usually some other thoughts manage to crowd in there, but since the first moment I saw you, no, that's pretty much it."

Her lips curved up in an irrepressible smile. "You're going to be honest about it?"

Demetri shrugged without remorse. "If I lied, you'd see through it, so why try?"

That kept her silent—for a minute. "Assuming my agent says okay, I'll sing at the race," she said at last.

"Was it all those immoral thoughts?" he asked, teasing, but still dying to know.

"No, it was the eyelashes," she answered, dashing his more immoral expectations.

"There's the qualifying lap next Friday. You should come and watch."

"No, I don't think I should."

"We can talk afterward. I've got some ideas of my own."

"I bet you do," she answered.

"About the Prestons," he said, wounded that she would think so low of him. Yes, it was true, but he still was wounded that she thought it.

"I bet."

"Does that mean you'll let me kiss you?"

"Not tonight," she said primly, but he liked the sparkles in her bright eyes, sparkles that reflected the moonlight, the candlelight and the better part of a man's dreams. No wonder the advertisers loved her. *Driving a man wild with anticipation.*

"Hope is a marvelous thing, Elizabeth."

"Isn't it, though?" she told him. "I think it's time to return to the real world."

"I won't see you at the wedding tomorrow."

"You don't do weddings? Now there's a surprise."

"I have practice. Racing stuff."

She gave him a long look, and he knew he didn't measure up to her standards. He knew he never would, but Demetri had been chasing his tail for longer than most. She turned and left.

"Good night, Elizabeth," he whispered after her. When all was said and done, Hugh Preston was going to hate him. But Demetri had always walked into the fire, no matter the price.

It was who he was. It was who he always would be.

Chapter Four

Early Tuesday morning, Demetri escaped from his hotel in Louisville to Quest Stables to watch the training of Courting Disaster, Demetri's one-year-old filly, who was the offspring of Courtin' Cristy. Last night, Team Sterling had a meeting with Jim Sterling, the team's owner, who commended Demetri on his responsible behavior, chastised Oliver for playing too much and not taking practice seriously and updated everyone on the search for a new team sponsor, at which point, Demetri shifted uncomfortably in his seat.

A visit to see his horses and do some riding seemed the second most perfect way to take the edge off before the racing trials started. Sex was his traditional first most perfect way to take the edge off, but Demetri knew at this point, sex was not in the cards. He only wanted one woman, and unfortunately, with Elizabeth, he knew sex was a long way off. Over the weekend, he'd bought the entire Elizabeth Innis collection, and read up on her between practice laps, scanning the pages of the music magazines like a fan-girl. Thank God he hadn't been caught.

It was hard to believe that no man had climbed that mountain before and fought for the right to take off that virtual chastity belt she wore with pride, but seeing the pictures of the men she'd dated in the past? Heh. Nothing but boys. No wonder she expected every man to take no with a smile on his face.

Yet good things come to those who wait, even those who were impatient by nature. Like Demetri.

In the interim, he had Disaster. She was a flashy bay with a mean temper, and a way of tossing her mane when she didn't like what she was being told to do. From the moment he spotted her, Demetri knew that this horse had more in common with him than just a name. He leaned against the fence, watching as Marcus Vasquez, the head trainer at Quest, handled her like a champ, bringing her to heel until she turned and nipped in Marcus's direction. Demetri had been watching Marcus with the filly, and knew there was talent there, but Marcus was quiet, and didn't say much, and Demetri wasn't going to press.

"Looks like there's still work to do," Demetri commented.

"She'll come around," Marcus said, obviously more patient than Demetri.

For a few minutes he continued to watch them, Marcus talking quietly to the filly, leading her by the reins, using his magic to keep the head tossing to a minimum. Demetri's cell phone rang, interrupting the quiet. Marcus glared.

Demetri ignored him and answered, but he did walk away from the paddock, because it was his father, and some things were best handled in private.

"Demetri."

"Hello, Dad." If his father noted the sarcasm, he surprisingly ignored it. There usually wasn't much that Andre Lucas ignored.

"I need to see you."

"I'm really busy," answered Demetri. "You know how the racing circuit keeps me on the road most of the year."

"You're driving too fast. You're going to get yourself killed."

"Yeah, too bad. I bet you're all broken up about it." Demetri rubbed his eyes, not that it did any good. The glare of the morning sun was a little too bright, and a headache was already pounding at his temples. "What do you want?"

"I read you have a race in Vancouver near the end of the month. You'll be close to Seattle."

"Yes." Demetri could feel the walls looming around him. It didn't matter that he was in the great outdoors, because there were always walls, and his father was the world's biggest expert at making them compress.

"The Japanese are closing on the deal next week. I'll have the money I owe you from your loan."

Demetri sighed, not caring if his father heard or not. "I don't want it," he snapped. "I've told you that a thousand times." He knew it had been hard for his father to ask him for the money. Two years ago, Andre Lucas had flown out to see Demetri, which was testament enough to what it cost him. As a rule, Andre didn't fly anywhere to see Demetri. Sometimes two people weren't meant to be in the same state at the same time.

"Do you think your money can bring him back? Do you think your money will make me forget?"

Demetri heard the pain in that voice. Always the heart-aching pain over Seth. It always came down to his brother. "No, I don't think anything can bring him back. He's dead," he answered, careful to keep the pain out of his own voice. "I still don't want it. The money was a gift to you for your business. It had nothing to do with him." At one time, Demetri had thought that money could fix things. That fame could fix things. But no, nothing could fix things. Sometimes things just were.

"I won't owe you," his father answered, and then hung up without saying goodbye.

Demetri could take a corner at Nordschleife doing two-hundred and forty, ski down Verbier with black ice caked on his face, dive off the Punch Bowl cliffs in California without blinking once. But a conversation with his father made him sweat with terror.

Theirs had never been a good relationship. Andre Lucas was a disciplined man with an eye for order and stability, and a disdain for chaos, as compared to Demetri, who lived for chaos.

As he walked back toward the normalcy of the exercise ring, he noticed Marcus looking at him curiously. Demetri wiped his brow, waiting a few seconds, and like clockwork, he felt the familiar rage rise up inside him, bitterness tasting like bile in his mouth. Quickly he tamped it down.

The bay looked at Demetri, teeth bared, eyes filled with contempt.

"You mind if I take her for a ride?" asked Demetri, not really caring if Marcus agreed or not.

"She's your horse."

"Good answer," said Demetri. The spirited filly was exactly the rush he needed this morning. Efficiently he mounted the horse, and she reared up with a scream that would have scared a lesser man. For Demetri, it was perfect.

His face grim with determination, Demetri dug his heels in, shouted, and Courting Disaster took off as if the devil was giving chase. Faster and faster they went, hooves thundering against the soft ground. Demetri had bought this horse for her spirit and her strength, knowing that someday he was going to need it. Sadly, he'd thought it would be for a race, not to exorcise old demons. The bay didn't disappoint.

The paddock fence was approaching, and the filly took it, not once shying away. The powerful hindquarters gathered up beneath Demetri, and he leaned forward until they were sailing through the air, flying without wings.

Demetri's blood pumped, the rush of adrenaline drowning out everything else inside him. In the distance, he could hear

Marcus shout, but it would take more than a shout to stop Demetri at the moment, not when all things, including blessed absolution, seemed possible. The wind whipped against his face, nearly blinding him.

One thing he'd say for the bay, not only was she pretty, but she was fast. Over the pasture they went, farther and farther away from the exercise yard, the filly's legs pounding with powerful strength. Demetri's heart stretched tight in his chest, a ticking bomb waiting to explode. The rush of adrenaline did its job, and for a moment, he could stay lost. Unfortunately, the moment was always gone too soon.

Not surprisingly, the horse couldn't keep up the pace, her speed slowing, the clip easing into a gentle canter. Nothing ever lasted. Demetri abandoned the useless quest, and wheeled the horse back toward the ring.

"What the hell was that about?" Marcus asked as Demetri brought Courting Disaster back through the opened gate.

"My property," answered Demetri, slipping off the heaving flanks. The horse was winded and exhausted, but the contempt still flared in her eyes.

The anger in Marcus's face wasn't much better. "Find another trainer."

Feeling the well-deserved condemnation in the trainer's gaze, Demetri felt something else as well, which years ago he would have thought was a conscience. "I'm sorry. I didn't mean to take it out on the horse."

"Don't do it again, Demetri. She's not a car."

Demetri patted the bay, a stupid, futile gesture, and handed her off to Marcus, who took a towel and rubbed the sweat from her flanks.

Demetri watched, the headache back, worse than ever. "It won't happen again."

Marcus looked up from the horse, seeming to understand. "Thank you for that."

"I was..." started Demetri, then shrugged. "You know, never mind. I've been watching you work with the horses. You're good."

"I've been watching you race. You're nuts."

Demetri laughed. "So they say. You should come to the race on Sunday. I can get you tickets."

"I'll stick to the horses, but thank you."

"If you need anything..." offered Demetri, his hand outstretched.

Marcus shook it. "Thanks."

Demetri started back toward the driveway, but then stopped. No. He had other things to do here, as well, things more important than his family issues. He looked back at Marcus. "Is Hugh around?"

Marcus jerked his thumb toward the offices behind them. Demetri took off, leaving Marcus and Demetri's own stupidity behind him. A three-story brick building sat between the stables and the main house, overlooking the exercise yard. Demetri found Hugh at the viewing window, watching two horses on the practice track. The old man never used a stopwatch for his horses; he had an innate knowledge for how fast they ran. Hugh was never wrong.

"Is that the new colt?"

Hugh nodded once, his eyes never leaving the glass. "Yeah. Something to Talk About. He's fast. Faster than his daddy."

For a few minutes they watched in silence, and Hugh was right. The colt was fast, blazingly fast, leaving the bigger gelding several furlongs behind. When the jockey pulled him up, the colt wasn't even winded. It was a crime that as a Quest horse, he couldn't race because of the ban.

"How're you doing? Glad to have the wedding behind you?" Demetri added a note of buoyant high spirits to his voice. It wasn't perfect, but he wasn't feeling particularly chipper, anyway.

Hugh pushed back from the polished brass railing and looked at Demetri with a note of buoyant high spirits in his eyes. It looked fake, too. "The wedding was beautiful. Got another one in a month," he answered. "Shane and Audrey. This one won't be nearly as big. Must be something in the water."

"As long as they keep it away from me."

"I saw you dancing with Elizabeth at the party."

"I didn't go near her at the wedding."

"Because you weren't there…" Hugh said neatly.

"You asked me to stay away. I did."

"Thank you," replied Hugh, and Demetri wisely avoided telling him that Elizabeth would be singing at the race. Hugh would figure that one out soon enough.

"What's the latest on the investigation?" asked Demetri, quickly changing the subject.

Hugh locked his hands behind him. "Brent's working with the Jockey Association to track down a missing computer analyst from there. Hopefully he can tell us why Leopold's Legacy's sire was listed as 'unknown' in the backup data. But we don't even know if he's in the country or not."

"The analyst lives in Lexington?"

Outside, the jockey was leading the two horses off the track, and when they had disappeared from view, Hugh abandoned his horses again. He ambled over to the conference table and chairs that were situated in the middle of the room, and tiredly settled into one of them. Demetri joined him there, not knowing what else to do.

"He was supposed to be living in Lexington. Brent's been looking into his finances because his apartment has been cleared out. This fellow recently acquired himself a pretty house in Savannah. Eight thousand square feet with a five-car garage."

Demetri arched a brow in surprise. "On a computer tech's salary?"

Hugh frowned. "I'm not thinking he's from a wealthy family, Demetri. The whole thing smells."

"Does Brent have any more leads?" Surely there was something to follow up on.

"Not yet," answered Hugh, the eternal optimist. But there was a time for blind optimism, and there was a time to face reality.

Demetri was tired of sitting still. He jerked out of his chair, needing to move. Something. Anything. "The stables are running out of time."

"Do you think I don't know it? Thomas looked beat this morning. I want to help, but there's nothing."

"But you bet for the funds for the wedding?"

Old gray brows settled into a solid line over the man's eyes. "How'd you hear that?"

"I have my sources. Why don't you bet on my race?"

"Come on, Demetri. I bet on you, and it's even odds. That's not interesting."

"I'm not the favorite this time. Giovanni Marcusi is racing for McLaren. He's put in a new Mercedes engine, 770 bhp. It'll burn the paint off anything close. That alone should bring him in first on the pole. And he'll probably take the podium, too. I want a private bet. You and me."

Hugh looked at him, a wily glint back in the blue eyes. "For what?"

Demetri braced his hands on the table, feeling the momentary thrill course through him. He knew what drove Hugh. A lot of the same things that drove Demetri.

More. Everything was about more.

"If I win, you'll take my winnings. Give them to Thomas to put in the stables. An interest-free loan. Payable when the Quest horses are racing again."

"What if you lose?" asked Hugh.

"Bite your tongue. But if that happens, you sell me Leopold's Legacy." Demetri backed away from the conference table and watched the old man, waiting. Demetri knew his limits. He knew his capabilities. On Sunday's race, Giovanni was going to lose. No matter what it took.

"I think we're getting the better part of this deal. The horse can't race."

"Don't look a gift horse in the mouth, Hugh."

Hugh smiled. "You've been practicing that line, Demetri, haven't you?"

"It's a bet?" asked Demetri, holding his breath.

Hugh nodded once. "You're on."

On Wednesday afternoon, Elizabeth moved her things from the Prestons' into the Seelbach Hilton Hotel in Louisville and began rehearsing with her band at a little bar near the college. The place had not only great acoustics, but the ability to keep a secret, as well. There were times that Elizabeth went gunning for the fame—mainly when she needed something—but most of the time she yearned for a regular life without all the flash-bulbs blinding her, without all the reporters shoving a micro-phone in her face and without all the gossip columns making up wild-hair stories about her.

Ten years ago, when she was just starting to get noticed, she hadn't thought much about walking the straight and narrow path, and keeping her nose clean; she didn't have time for breathing, much less having fun. But then something happened. In a world where absolute fame corrupted absolutely, Elizabeth became the exception, and Tobey, being the smart man he was, had told her that she could milk her virginity all the way to the top, and so she had. As a cautious and prudent person, it hadn't been hard up to now. As a rule, Elizabeth didn't take chances. Not with her career, and not with men. She frowned—which she'd been doing a lot recently—because Demetri was making her think hard and long about her principles.

Yeah, her principles were a good bit of Pollyanna idealism,

and a lot of wanting to believe that there was only one man for her, but there was also the sexy allure of putting a roof over her head, and food on the table. For Elizabeth, home and security meant everything.

Someday, when the restlessness inside her stilled, she was going to buy a little place in Woodford County, Kentucky, and spend her days watching the sunsets, drinking lemonade and learning to quilt. But for now, every morning she jumped out of bed ready to tackle something new, like next week's concert, the continuing debate on the album cover with the art department at Five Star and the one thing that she tried to avoid thinking about. Singing at the race on Sunday.

The main reason she wanted to avoid thinking about it was that from Mr. Demetri Lucas, car driver extraordinaire, she had heard exactly zero words. Not that she was expecting to. Not that she was sitting by her hotel room phone waiting for his call, or even a bill for the car damages. No sir, Elizabeth wasn't going to wait for any man, no matter how much he stirred her blood, or no matter how much he affected her songwriting skills.

Pitifully, instead of robbing her of things to sing about, now she had tons of things to sing about. Songs with a brand-new tone. Something sultry, wicked and knee-wobblingly sexy. Of course that had absolutely nothing to do with Demetri, nothing at all.

If she kept telling herself that often enough, eventually she'd start to believe it.

The band, of course, noticed. Her "band" wasn't really a band in the proper sense of the word. There was Rebecca Townsend, who sang backup. Tobey had found her singing in an old bar in Nashville when she was only seventeen. Calder Jones was the bass guitarist, a big strapping man who was pushing sixty, although he told everyone he was just a more mature-looking twenty-nine. Peter Sanderson was the keyboard magician who had the fastest fingers that Elizabeth had ever seen. The four of them had been playing together for almost five years, and although it was a mostly professional relationship, that didn't mean that Elizabeth didn't want to hear about Rebecca's man troubles, Calder's grandkids and Peter's latest man troubles, too.

After rehearsal on Thursday, Rebecca trapped Elizabeth in the tiny ladies' room, her eyes sly with suspicion. "What's up with the new song?"

Elizabeth pretended ignorance, because she knew what Rebecca would say if she spilled any of the truth. "Frank gave it to me."

Rebecca's mouth curved into a knowing smile. "Tobey said you wrote it."

Elizabeth swallowed, but bravely climbed deeper into that hole she had now dug. "Are you calling me a liar?" she asked, hands on hips.

"Yes," answered Rebecca, not even a little ashamed to be casting such aspersions on Elizabeth's character.

So Elizabeth promptly changed the subject. "Tell me about this new fellow you've been seeing."

Now, Rebecca was born and bred in Virginia, so there wasn't much that sailed past her. "Only if you'll tell me about the inspiration for the new song," she answered, not budging an inch.

Elizabeth didn't want to talk about the inspiration for the new song. She didn't want to think about the inspiration for the new song. She didn't even like being inspired, which was saying a lot since she made most of her money as a songwriter.

There'd been almost a week of sleepless—or nearly sleepless—nights when she imagined she was still dancing with Demetri around the Prestons' dance floor. She had memorized that blood-thumping gleam in those warm eyes, and every time her brain fired up the memory—which was often—she felt those deviously persistent tendrils of desire that were curling all through her insides, whipping around and, for all intents and purposes, making mush of her brain.

It was a low moment for a woman who secretly prided herself on her good sense, and quietly laughed at all those people who thought she was a dim bulb who fell off the turnip truck at regular intervals. Not about to confess her deepest shortcomings, Elizabeth prudently kept silent.

Rebecca humphed. "Fine. You don't have to tell me. Me, the person you work with day in, day out. Me, who has toured the last twelve months with you, sharing after-concert French fries, when Calder and Peter refused because it was bad for their hearts. Me, your friend. You don't have to say a word, you keep those secrets all to yourself, but I'll be watching…."

"There's nothing to tell," answered Elizabeth, wishing the words from her new song weren't whirling in her head. *So easy to fall into the dark pull of desire, to sell my soul for what I see in your eyes…*

"'…innocence lost can never be found,'" sang Rebecca, in a breathy imitation of a woman on the verge. "That's a woman ready to leap off the bridge, Bethy."

"I'm not jumping off any bridge," she said, sounding just like a woman on the verge.

"It's a metaphorical bridge, Elizabeth."

"I'm not jumping, metaphorical or otherwise," snapped Elizabeth.

"I think it's high time you did," said Rebecca, "We've been playing together for five years, and I've watched you go from one useless boyfriend to another, without a backward glance. Three dates and they're out, just like in baseball. But you never wrote a song about a single one of them. Ever. Now you think you're going to escape a full-blown interrogation? Oh, no. Honey, when you do, you have to tell me all about it. I want to hear every single, sordid detail."

Sordid details ran through Elizabeth's mind like late-night cable television—scintillating, titillating, late-night cable. Desperate to escape, Elizabeth checked her watch. "Peter is going to shoot you for keeping us late tonight, Rebecca. He's got plans for this evening."

Rebecca snickered. "He won't be mad after I tell him what we were talking about."

"You can't!" hollered Elizabeth, a lot louder than she intended.

Rebecca wiggled her brows. "See, I knew there was something to tell. You're getting a break today, but just remember...I'll be watching."

Chapter Five

She hadn't planned on watching the racing trials on Friday. Elizabeth had hair to wash, fingernails to polish, but there she was, sitting in the tippy-top row of the stands, camouflaged in a blue cotton skirt, with a scarf on her head and Hollywood sunglasses over her eyes—so hopefully he wouldn't notice. And she didn't think that he did, because the stands were full and the track down below was busier than any beehive she'd ever had the pleasure to study up close.

It was a hair-raising experience watching the low-slung cars and the whole crew of mechanics that did everything but wipe the windshield and buff the tires. She kept telling herself that driving a racing car was not hazardous to anyone's health, but her eyes were trained on the red car with the hot-looking driver, and every time he went around the track, her nerves followed in those same fast-wheeling curves, dragging her stomach along behind. It wasn't pretty, and Elizabeth thought it wasn't healthy—not only for the low-slung cars, but for her, as well.

The whole circuit format was new to her. These weren't circles, but sharp, winding turns that didn't seem to scare anybody but Elizabeth. The engine buzzing was loud in her ears. Even from the top of the stands, it was louder than the speakers at one of her concerts, ringing in her head. The first time around, all twenty-one cars raced, but then a few minutes passed and officials came and eliminated some from the track. Both of Sterling's red cars stayed in. A few minutes later, the officials returned, kicked off more cars, and this time there were only ten cars left, including the two red ones.

Those last laps were more nerve-racking than the first, which she hadn't thought possible. The cars whipped around the track, and the drivers seemed a lot more stupid, taking a lot more chances, especially the two red ones. It was nearly the end of the last trial, when one yellow car made a move on the blue car, and the blue car wouldn't let him pass. But the yellow car was determined and bumped him, and then the yellow car went into a tire-screeching skid, taking two long circles, before ending up smashed into the wall. Elizabeth gasped, and nearly keeled over dead, wanting them to stop the race. But she didn't die, and they didn't stop the race. The car wheeled back around, and then it started off, as though nothing had happened.

In fact, everybody kept going, as if it happened every day. Her eyes found the red car, two lengths behind the cocky blue car, and she didn't think he could catch up. He tried, good Lord, that man got determined when he wanted to, but in the end, the blue car was faster, which surprised her. Demetri Lucas seemed like the sort of man who did everything fast, and she didn't mean that in a good way. When the other driver beat him, she didn't want to feel a tinge of sympathy, but she did.

She was such a sucker.

He glanced up once toward the stands, but Elizabeth was secure in her anonymity. Besides, she had her escape all planned. She would duck out the front entrance, mixing in with the rest of the crowd before anyone noticed. At the edge of the stands, a security guard stood, looking in her direction, talking into his walkie-talkie, but she didn't think anything of it, until she got down to the first level, and she saw him—Demetri, not the security guard, waiting for her.

He hadn't changed, hadn't showered. He was simply standing there in those white coveralls, arms crossed over his chest, sweat dripping from his lean face, his dark hair soaked even darker.

A man in coveralls wasn't supposed to be sexy. A man who looked as though he needed a hot shower wasn't supposed to be sexy, either. Obviously Mr. Demetri Lucas hadn't read the same rule book that she had, because this man had sexy popping from his pores. As he waited, people came by, congratulated him, and he signed a few autographs. Some women—little hussies—stopped to flirt and probably proposition him in some sexually lurid ways. He sent them on their way, his eyes tracking her progress as she moved closer, each step a little slower than the previous one. Elizabeth pretended she didn't know he was watching, but his voice called out as she passed.

"The security guard told me it was either you, or Marilyn Monroe had come back from the dead."

She halted, and for the first time in her life, Elizabeth was grateful for the dark anonymity of sunglasses. "Were you speaking to me?"

He looked around, arched a brow. "Nobody else has your legs."

She felt the blush all the way up to her roots. "I was just leaving."

He took her arm and wheeled her past a set of doors and into a long, concrete hallway that seemed curiously, conspicuously, absent of people. He took off her sunglasses, slipping them into one of his pockets. She thought about protesting, but decided she'd pick her battles, and Elizabeth knew that bigger battles were just waiting around those sharp corners he was good at taking.

"I thought you wanted to talk about the stables? If you'll let me shower and change, I'll buy you a drink."

"That's a really bad idea, Mr. Lucas." She needed the formality now, because she didn't like the way he looked, all tousled and hardworking. A woman could forget a man's playboy ways when he looked like that.

"I thought you were going to call me Demetri," he said, leaning against the concrete wall, one foot crossed over the other.

"Demetri," she said, hoping it didn't sound as much like a purr as she thought it did.

He smiled with satisfaction, which she suspected meant that it had ended up sounding like a purr after all. "Why is that a bad idea? It's only a drink."

She took the opposite wall and leaned against it, putting a good bit of distance between them. Unfortunately, it probably wasn't enough. "Your reputation is not as, um, wholesome, as I'd prefer, and I have to be careful about the company I'm seen keeping."

"You can reform me."

"You keep telling me that, but I don't think I believe you. I bet you got a bridge you want to sell me, too."

"Something like that, yes," he murmured. "I need to get cleaned up. Wait here."

"I can't," she said, and then started on that long, lonely walk back out of the stadium.

"I thought you wanted us to do something for Quest," he called after her.

Elizabeth sighed. Stopped. Turned.

"Us?" she asked, wishing he didn't keep using that one word. She didn't need him to keep linking them together. In her head, in her mind, in her dreams, the link was already there, noose-tight, and it kept pulling her closer.

She took four cautious steps toward him.

"You," he corrected.

"If all we do is talk, then I'm okay with this."

His face wasn't happy, but it was resigned. He nodded once. "That's all we do. I give you my word."

Sure enough, less than ten minutes later he was back by the gates, wearing dress slacks, a white shirt and a leather jacket, looking like some hotshot cover model, or a Hollywood actor, or just a man that made her skin turn hot then cold, and then hot once again. Elizabeth wasn't a normal practitioner of foolish denial, but when he looked at her, when he smiled sometimes—not the Hollywood smile, but the other one—she wanted to trust him, if only for a little while.

"Ready?" he asked, taking her arm and leading her back toward the corridor.

"Where are we going?"

"Out the back way. The press is out front. I'm assuming you'd want to dodge them."

"If you hadn't taken my sunglasses, they wouldn't recognize me."

"Maybe not your face, but you are the only woman in the world that walks like that."

"Like what?"

"Don't make me put it into words."

"You don't like the way I walk?"

"I love the way you walk," he told her, the heat in his voice implying all sorts of decadent things, and all because of the way she walked.

"Really?" she asked, nearly stumbling, but then recovering. "Where're we going?"

"There's a bakery around the corner. I think your reputation would be safe there, and the only people who might recognize me won't hang out in a bakery."

A bakery. Now that sounded harmless enough. She smiled at him, liking the idea.

The bakery was a good old-fashioned sweet shop with big glass cases of chocolate desserts, elaborately frosted cupcakes and colorful cookies with tiny silver candies on top. Jawbreakers and lollipops spilled out of the row of glass jars on top. Vinyl-covered tables were banked by soft, cushy, red-leather booths. After they walked inside, the girl behind the counter looked at her twice, as if she might recognize her, but then shook her head. Elizabeth still wore the scarf on her head, and her old blue-jean jacket was something found in every mall across America.

He led her to a booth near the back, they ordered two soft drinks and he sat across from her like teenagers on a first date. That close, she could smell the remains of his shower and the sharp tang of his cologne on his skin. The steady seduction in his dark gaze reminded her that, no, he wasn't a teenager. This was a dangerously handsome man who wouldn't hesitate to take what he wanted.

Quickly she launched into an innocent conversation, not wanting to get sidetracked by thoughts of showers with dangerous men.

"How's your car?" she asked him, to remind herself that not looking before leaping could lead to serious consequences.

"The engineers are working on it. It'll take a couple of weeks, but I have a loaner in the interim."

"Engineers? Couldn't you just take it to the shop?" she asked, a frown on her face, because engineers sounded—well, it made it sound like a national disaster rather than a fender bender—or a car bender, as the case may be—which it was. Guilt was not a usual emotion for Elizabeth, because being a hardworking, small-town girl, she considered herself a morally superior person, and as such, didn't do things that caused guilt. Sadly, she suspected that was about to change.

"The car designer would never forgive me if I subjected it to a 'shop,'" he said with an easy laugh, and Elizabeth resigned herself to more guilt. Once again, she changed the subject.

"So you've been thinking about the stables? I tried again

with Melanie yesterday, and then I talked to her daddy, but he wouldn't listen. He thinks that they can take care of this on their own, so it looks like I need to do something sneaky and underhanded, so they won't catch on until it's too late."

"You could drop a wad of bills on their front lawn."

"If you're going to make jokes…"

"Sorry." The waitress came with their drinks and he downed his in one long gulp before putting it aside. Elizabeth took a hard look at that empty glass, knowing that however intently she stared, however optimistically she wanted to think, that glass was going to stay empty. He would put her aside, just like that glass.

With a regretful sigh, she took her drink between both hands and sipped carefully, because that was her way.

"You're very determined," he said, looking at her, his eyes intent.

"Somebody has to be," she told him, wishing he didn't keep watching her like that, as if he was still thirsty, and this time, she was next. "What if the stables go under? What about all those horses? *What about the horses?*" she repeated. "Could I buy a racehorse and stable it there?" Maybe if she stepped full-steam-ahead into the biz, Melanie and Uncle Hugh would pay attention to what she said.

"You want to buy a racehorse?" he asked. With curious eyes, he balanced his chin on his palm, a picture-perfect frame for a mouth that made her own water. He had such a strong mouth, firm and hard, not one of those poetic, pretty-boy mouths. No, this was a mouth that knew what to do with a woman. Her heart stumbled, and she took a long drink of soda before she looked up again.

Elizabeth, shake it off, she told herself, and then pasted her all-business smile on her face.

"Maybe three or four. You own a whole stableful of horses, don't you? You must know something about this."

"I don't quite own a stableful, but I know a little."

"So you could help me. I could buy some horses, and stable them there until the troubles are gone."

"You'd need more than three or four. They're down about three hundred horses now."

Elizabeth swallowed. Three hundred was a big number. "That doesn't scare me."

"It's not that easy, Elizabeth. Buying a horse isn't like buying a new pair of shoes. It takes a commitment and time and research."

"You haven't bought women's shoes lately, have you?"

He smiled at her, that nice smile that tugged at her heart, and made her want in other places. "Now who's making jokes?"

"Oh, fine, but I think I could do this."

"Would you like help?" he asked, so nicely, way too nicely.

"I have a feeling there's strings with this offer," she answered back, hoping there wasn't blatant anticipation in her voice.

"No strings," he said…thankfully. "Besides, I'll be buying some horses of my own."

"What sort of help were you thinking?"

"Horses are usually sold at auctions. The big one is Keeneland. It starts next week and runs through the end of the month. I could take you. Explain a few things, and we could look at horses. You'd learn a lot that way."

Learn a lot that way. Yeah, she figured she could learn a lot from him. But when she looked at his face, she realized he was being dead serious, and she suspected that he was doing this on purpose. Not being all sexy and flirty, when she was expecting him to be all sexy and flirty. Reverse psychology. It was working. He was talking horse auctions and her mind was ready to be ravished in the gutter.

Elizabeth sniffed in disdain, more for herself than him. "This auction. Keeneland, Kentucky. Here?"

"Yeah."

Regretfully she shook her head. "Can't do that one." Her virtue would thank her in the morning.

"Why not?" he asked, completely confused, and then realization dawned. "My reputation. Yours. Got it. Sorry. I can see this is going to be a challenge. Wait. I know. On Thursday, there's an auction at Seneca Stables. In upstate New York. Little place. They have some nice stock. I can take you to New York."

Again he was looking serious and sincere, and she wanted to take him at face value, but there was something tangible hanging in the air. So heavy, so thick, she was surprised that no one else in the bakery noticed. Elizabeth noticed, and she suspected he did, too. He was just better at pretending otherwise. Her eyes took another hard look at the empty glass next to him. That set-aside glass that he was probably never going to touch again now that he was done with it.

So after all that, did she listen to her instincts, warning bells screaming like banshees? Nope. "Seneca?" she said, so perky and foolish. "That might be fun. I'll have to work it into my schedule, but I can manage a day off, considering I'm supposed to be on vacation anyway."

He nodded once, in that quick, decisive way of his, as if he'd never considered her answer would be anything else. "What are you going to do if Hugh won't stable your horses after you buy them?"

"I'll have to make sure he doesn't know that they're coming from me, because he won't take them otherwise. Can I do that? I can do that, can't I? Put together a shell corporation, or something?"

"I'm certain there's an easier way. Let me talk to some people. So have we covered all the business obligations now? Can we get personal?"

"It depends," she said cautiously.

He gave her an innocent look. "It's harmless, I promise. Have you always had a voice like that?"

She grinned, because talking about her voice was truly harmless. "You bought one of my CDs?" she said, and he nodded. "You like my voice, huh? Yeah, that's the same set of pipes I was born with, but I worked hard and had some good voice teachers along the way."

"You're very good," he said, and she felt herself smiling. Every now and then something sincere slipped out of his mouth, and made it easier to ignore the empty glass sitting uselessly next to him.

"Thank you."

"So where's home?"

Okay, this wasn't so bad. Elizabeth found herself relaxing, nearly having a good time. "I got a little place in Memphis and an apartment in Nashville."

"No big mansion with servants and pictures of Elvis on the wall?"

"Oh, no, honey. That's not me."

His dark eyes flashed for a moment, something that was making it hard to breathe. "Say that again," he said, his voice whiskey-rough, sending one-hundred-proof shivers tooling down her spine.

"That's not me," she repeated.

"No, the honey part."

She felt herself blush again, her cheeks heating. She really was way out of her depth with him, but like a fool, she kept on wading in the water. "I call everybody honey, even the IRS, so don't get too excited."

"That wasn't even close to excited. I just like to hear you talk."

"You're in luck, because I like to talk."

"I noticed."

"Sorry."

"I don't mind at all."

"How come you race cars?"

"Why not?" he asked, as if everybody wanted to zoom around at insane speeds and crash into walls. Some things were completely incomprehensible.

"Is that all?"

"Cars only do what they're told to do."

"Unlike people, huh?"

"Some people." And it was back again. She felt it, that thick cloud of fascination surrounding her, that breathless anticipation kicking her pulse up a notch. When she noticed her hands twisting in her lap, she let out a worrying sigh.

"I should go," she told him, already picking up her bag.

"We could have dinner," he suggested.

Dinner. Three hours of conversation, before heading into a knock-down, drag-out battle between her moral self and the other self, this new Elizabeth, who was salivating at the thought of rolling in the sheets with him. "No," she answered, because she might be foolish, but she wasn't that foolish.

"You'll be at the party after the race? Melanie and Hugh will be there."

Oh, he was good. Throwing in the family element, and what would Melanie say if Elizabeth ducked out? Elizabeth should have wrestled with the decision more, but he was the devil, leading her right smack into temptation. "Maybe."

With a sigh she polished off the last of her soda. Somehow it never lasted as long as she wanted. "I need to get back to the hotel."

He pulled her sunglasses from his pocket. "You'll need these."

She donned the glasses, grateful for the dark cover again. "Of course," she answered tightly, and then walked out of the restaurant. The whole time she walked, she was supremely conscious of the dark gaze following her, watching her, wanting her.

She really shouldn't be so foolish, she kept telling herself, but it didn't seem to matter at all.

On Saturday, Elizabeth picked up her momma from the airport and took her to lunch at Lilly's, a chic restaurant on Bardstown Road in Louisville that served high-calorie food that would cost her an additional two sweat-drenching hours jogging on the treadmill, but Elizabeth thought it'd be worth it. Her mother had just come back from a cruise, and Elizabeth wanted to see her perky and happy and full of life, but her mother looked—just the same.

Since the time Elizabeth had earned her first platinum record, she had provided her mother with a nice home, a comfortable allowance and travel to most any place that her mother wanted to go. But there were things that money couldn't buy. Peace of mind, confidence and the ability to look back on your life with zero regrets. It was that last part that kept Diane Innis from smiling much. Even splitting a chocolate ganache drenched in warm caramel sauce didn't put the kick into her mother's coffee. She toyed with the sauce, staring into space with those manhandled blue eyes.

"You missed a pretty wedding, but Aunt Jenna is dying to look at your pictures from the trip. In return, I think she'll make you sit through four hours with Robbie's wedding album."

Her mother looked at her, her smile a little sad. "I should have gone, but I don't like weddings much anymore, unless it's yours, darling, and then I'll make an exception."

Elizabeth blew out an inelegant raspberry. "You know me. I'm too busy working. Always here and there, hardly time to breathe, much less time to get to know somebody properly."

"I hope you meet some nice man someday, Elizabeth. Somebody that's kind and sweet and gentle."

"You mean somebody not like Daddy," snapped Elizabeth, more harshly than she intended, and she saw her mom wince.

"Your father's not all bad." Her mother faked a smile, and took a bite from the dessert. "This is delicious. You have to eat some more. I can't finish it." Which translated to, I don't want to argue about your father anymore. Elizabeth sighed, because she didn't want to argue, either.

"You've barely started, Momma, and I can't have more than a bite or two. Tobey will have my hide, and then some, if I show up for the concert busting at the seams of those skinny jeans they pour me into."

"What concert?" asked her mother, blinking curiously.

Oops. Elizabeth hadn't spilled the beans yet to anyone, biding her time until the moment was ripe, which unfortunately hadn't happened. "Oh, some little charity gig they lined up for me at the university. I think the tickets went on sale today. You want to go?"

Diane looked at Elizabeth, and then shook her head. "I don't think so, honey. All those crowds do me in."

"You're still taking your vitamins, right?"

"Oh, yeah. Don't worry about me," her mother said, as if that would stop a dog from howling at the moon, or a daughter worrying about her one-and-only mother.

"What's wrong?" asked Elizabeth, keeping her voice gentle, but having bad suspicions nonetheless.

"Nothing," answered her mother, scooting the caramel sauce around her plate with her fork.

"Tell me."

Her mom shot Elizabeth a supposedly casual look, which made Elizabeth all the more nervous. "I got a call from Ray."

And speak of the devil. Well, that certainly explained the look. Elizabeth leaned in close and looked deep in her mother's eyes, because this was important.

"I hope you hung up. Although if he told you where he was, I could get the cops after him." Elizabeth had a soft heart, but her mother had the heart of a bar of chocolate melting in the summer sun. Sticky, gooey and just as difficult to clean up after.

"No. He didn't say."

"What did he want?"

Diane tucked a stray strand of hair behind her ears, and avoided Elizabeth's eyes. "Nothing."

"Momma," she said with a warning in her voice.

"Oh, the usual. He wanted to see me. Come out and talk about you."

"And what did you tell him?"

"I told him no," her mother answered, licking her lips and looking studiously at the wall.

"Momma…"

"Oh, what can it hurt, Elizabeth? If he asks for more money, I'll tell him no."

It was like something from *Oprah*: when good women turn spineless. Elizabeth speared a piece of chocolate cake on her fork more violently than she intended. Then she took a deep, cleansing breath. "You do what you have to do, but you're making a mistake."

"I still love him," answered her mother, as if the man hadn't deserted her for seventeen years, as if he hadn't stolen three million and change from his daughter's account, as if he had a heart capable of loving back.

"And what good is love when the man doesn't deserve it? You're not supposed to work this hard."

"You've just never been in love, Elizabeth. It's easier when you don't know."

Elizabeth stared blandly. Like her own ignorance with men made everything all right? Like hell. "Don't lecture me on love. I'm not going to make the mistakes you did." Elizabeth clung to her high ideals like a life preserver. They had gotten her to where she was, and when she fell, she was going to fall for a man who was honorable, and brave, and sensitive. A man who wouldn't steal three million dollars and walk away from his family. Elizabeth had standards, and no one, not her mother, not her father, not some hotshot race-car driver, would cause her to lower her standards. She'd seen the end result. Heck, she was staring at the end result.

"Everybody makes the mistakes I did," Diane answered quietly, in a world-weary voice that indicated that she'd do it again, even with all the hurt.

"Not me," retorted Elizabeth, because she wouldn't, and

she went back to mutilating her cake and not really caring about the treadmill. In the mood she was in, she could probably run fifty miles and still not get anywhere. They were almost finished with dessert when a woman approached, her cocktail napkin in her hand.

"Elizabeth Innis?"

Elizabeth smiled, because there were still good parts left in the world. With a Hollywood flourish, she signed the napkin and reminded the woman about the concert the next week. "It's for a really good cause," Elizabeth told her. "You be there."

After the woman left, Elizabeth's mother looked at her. "What charity?"

Elizabeth took a deep swallow of water before answering. "Some local family that's hitting some hard times. I'm trying to help out."

"Do I know them?"

"Oh, no. Frank lined it up for me, and you know I can't say no to Frank."

A few more autographs later, Elizabeth and her mother left the restaurant. Elizabeth gave her a long, squeezy hug. "I hope you don't see him, Momma. But if you do, don't tell me about it. I just don't want to know."

Diane nodded. She would see Ray Innis, they both knew it, but sometimes denial had its place in life—especially when it came to family.

Elizabeth had sung the "Star Spangled Banner" exactly one thousand, three hundred and thirty-seven times. She'd been nervous exactly once. Today. She changed her dress five times, eventually deciding on a demure little black number with a removable jacket that changed it from "meh" to not so "meh." The race coordinator had given her an invitation to the VIP party afterward, and Elizabeth really hadn't planned on going until she received a little white piece of paper with three words.

I can't wait.

It would be a poor, pathetic creature who would find herself moved by such an obvious ploy. Elizabeth smoothed out the card, and tucked it into her bag, like the poor, pathetic creature that she was, and even picked out a delicious chiffon yellow evening dress for the party afterward—because a girl always needed to look her best, even the poor, pathetic ones.

She told herself that when she walked out on the track, she wasn't going to look, she wasn't going to gape, she wasn't going to stare, she was going to keep her eyes firmly averted from the drivers that were lined up next to the cars, but her eyes were as stupid as the rest of her, and she peeked, catching her breath when the dark eyes locked on hers.

There, in front of the crowd of sixty-three thousand, Elizabeth's knees dipped for just a moment before she recovered like the consummate professional that she was. The accompanying music, courtesy of the Boyle County Community Orchestra, kicked into the opening notes, and she sang. Everything was good, she was wearing her serious smile as you do when you sing the national anthem, and all the notes were fitting into the right places until her poor, pathetic eyes wandered off to the right edge of the stadium, and he was still watching her with that thousand-degree gaze. The last high G fell flat for a second, and she saw his mouth quirk.

Quickly she recovered, and this time she didn't look again.

Elizabeth was seated next to her uncle Hugh and Melanie in the box near the top. She gave her cousin a quick hug, before settling into the plush, leather seats that rocked back and forth when you moved. The box had a bird's-eye view of the track, and for those with lesser eyesight, there were a whole row of monitors banked on all sides of the room. In the back was a buffet of food and drink for people whose stomachs were able to contemplate the idea of food or drink. Elizabeth was too nervous.

When she was sitting with Uncle Hugh and Melanie, she pretended that she'd never seen a Formula Gold race, never seen those trials yesterday and hadn't spent three hours last night poring over the safety requirements, the race rules and the mechanical intricacies of the Sterling team's engine. Besides, Uncle Hugh was doing a fine job of explaining it to her, and he looked to be having such a good time doing it.

However, even knowing everything she did, she couldn't conceal her first heart attack when he told her that cars would average over two hundred and forty miles per hour.

"That fast?" asked Elizabeth, and Uncle Hugh laughed.

"It's okay. They're actually very safe. The drivers use special fireproof suits and equipment."

"I read that people die in this sport," she stated, cutting to the heart of the matter.

"Not very often," answered Hugh, which wasn't much of an answer as far as Elizabeth was concerned.

"How often? Let's be specific."

"I don't know. There was a crash two years ago, and two drivers were killed."

That news got rid of any chance of an appetite, and Melanie patted her hand, obviously made of stronger stuff. "It's only a car race, Elizabeth."

"I know," she answered tightly. The flock of cars drove up to the little bitty grid area, the lights turned red and they were off.

Right off the bat, the cars started jockeying back and forth for position, blocking each other, and then shooting past each other so fast it made her head hurt, and the cars were basically a blur. A blue car started out ahead of Demetri. Uncle Hugh said that it was Giovanni Marcusi, who was running in a Mercedes engine, and was the favorite to win, not Demetri. She found Oliver's car, running two cars behind Demetri, and for a few laps, she watched as Demetri and Oliver moved up and down in their standings.

A green car bumped into another car, and ripped a front piece of it clean away. Just like that. A safety car drove out and for two laps everything was sane. But right when she remembered how to breathe again, the safety car was gone, and the insanity started over again. Demetri was taking some awful chances. She didn't know cars, didn't know racing, but she did notice that even Uncle Hugh looked a little nervous. This wasn't good.

Near the last lap, she got up and walked to the window overlooking the track, pressing her hand against the glass.

Melanie came over and rubbed her back. "You look a little green."

"I'm not like y'all, Melanie. I don't run horses, or drive fast cars or jump off cliffs for the fun of it. I sing. The most heartbreaking thing I experience is when I break a nail. I don't like stress. I don't like irregularities in my heart rhythms. All I want is to know, with absolute certainty, that tomorrow is going to be just as good as today."

Melanie shook her head and an awful whine sounded. Elizabeth turned back to the track in front of them. One hand gripped the other, but she'd moved far past hand-wringing. Right now, she had fingernails digging into the top of her hand, the pain easing some of the damnable panic inside her.

There were two laps left when Demetri made his move, just as she knew he would. That man would never be content with second place. The first time, the blue car blocked him from getting around, so Demetri pulled back, hanging and waiting, and when they took the next sharp curve, you could hear the red car's engine squealing, wheels nearly pulling off the ground, and Demetri shot into the lead.

Hugh hollered, all excited and happy, and Melanie was grinning, ear to ear.

In fact, out of the entire box, Elizabeth was the only one who frowned.

* * *

Demetri pulled into Victory Lane and climbed out of the car. It hadn't been classy, it hadn't been clean, but he'd won. In the end, that was all that mattered, although his shoulder stung like a mother. Oliver popped the cork on the champagne, and champagne spurted everywhere, into the crowd, up in the air. The team manger, Jim Sterling, walked up to the podium, looked at the gold cup in Demetri's hand and grinned. With the win, Sterling was four points off the race for the Constructor's Cup, and Demetri was seven points behind Marcusi. But that wouldn't last long.

Of course, that last race of the season did happen to fall in Vancouver, a street circuit with hairpin turns, elevation shifts that took the front wheels spinning in the air and a double right-hander that only the strongest driver was able to maneuver. Demetri never liked racing in Vancouver. It hit too close to home, but this time, no one would beat him. No one.

There was a short press conference, and then Demetri showered and changed into his monkey suit. As he was shrugging into his shirt, Oliver came into the Sterling dressing area, shaking his head in disbelief.

"I wasn't sure you were going to pull that one out. Didn't know you still had it in you."

Demetri grinned. "Neither did I."

Oliver drenched his head in cold water, before shaking it off like a dog. "You should have heard Marcusi's scream of agony into his headset when you took that last corner. Rossi told me he nearly deafened his pit crew. I'm sure Marcusi saw pieces of his masterpiece littered all over the track."

"It's a car."

"Don't let him hear you say that. Doc thought you hurt your shoulder. Did you?" Oliver started pulling off his suit, the picture of health for somebody so young.

At the same time, Demetri crafted his face into the perfect

imitation of a man looking his prime years in the eye and winning. In racing years, thirty-five was a dinosaur, and today he was feeling the dinosaur's pains shooting around his back and down through his arm. If it hadn't been for that last corner, he'd be fine, but if it hadn't been for that last corner, he wouldn't have won, either. "No problems here."

Oliver headed for the showers and Demetri took advantage of the quiet to pop two pain pills into his mouth. By the time the party started, no one would know. Tonight, he didn't want to think about his shoulder, he wanted to see Elizabeth again with something fast approaching hunger. As he pulled on the black cummerbund, he laughed at himself. At night, he went to sleep with her music playing in his ear. Sometimes, if he was lucky, she'd whisper to him in dreams that kept him from falling asleep, calling him honey in that lilting drawl that rushed through him in ways a lot more appealing than adrenaline ever did.

A few soft words, the long tilt of her eyes, the dip in her mouth. Simple things and his body responded like Pavlov's dog, expanding to an impolite bulge, and he hadn't even got to the naked parts yet. Not now, he reminded himself. He had to face the cameras first. So Demetri spent the next few minutes telling himself not to think about her. It didn't help. When Oliver returned from the showers, Demetri was almost grateful for the company. Almost.

"Will you ever retire?" Oliver asked, donning a tux as though he was born to it. When Oliver was like this, so young and eager, he reminded Demetri of his brother. Seth had been like that, young, eager and full of life.

Demetri shook his head, just as an older brother would, one brow arched to lofty heights. "And give you my spot? Hell, no, my friend, you're going to have to do this the hard way. You're going to have to beat me."

Oliver didn't look worried, which ticked off Demetri more than the original comment itself. "I will one day. Soon." He adjusted the bow tie on his tux, trying to look the part of an aristocrat, and not quite succeeding. "You didn't tell me who would be singing today."

Demetri shrugged, because Elizabeth was no one's business but his.

Oliver stared into the mirror, smoothed his hair. "She'll be at the party?"

"I'm not her keeper."

"Do you think if I danced with her tonight, if I looked sufficiently gobsmacked, we'd get Valencia back? It's Elizabeth Innis. The press would eat it up. I could be gobsmacked. I think I should."

"I think you shouldn't," he said, with a hard look in Oliver's direction.

"For the good of the team, Demetri. If we don't get Valencia back, or someone equally well funded, do you know who gets cut? One large hint, it's not you. One day, my engine is a wee bit smaller, my crew a wee bit leaner, and then one day, my car is gone. Poof."

"I'll take care of you. That won't happen." Demetri had the funds to ensure it wouldn't happen. There were some things that money could buy. Security, for instance. Absolution, not so much.

Oliver only looked mad. "I don't want you to take care of me, Demetri. I don't want you buying my place on the team. That's not the way racing works. It's not like you can buy a ticket in, not at our level."

It was a conversation that Demetri had heard before. The words were different, the tone was the same. The same wounded pride, the same independent spirit. He rubbed at his eyes, not wanting to think about Seth. Not now.

"You've earned your spot, Oliver. Jim knows that. You won't get cut because of lack of funds."

"Let me make this clearer. In a few years, I intend to be you, well, not exactly you, per se, because you're much more apathetic to the media than I would ever be, and I don't think that's very smart in this day and age, but that's beside the point. I will be number one, for Sterling, for the world. And I will do whatever it takes, whatever I can, to get Valencia back, because I want my spot. I deserve it. I want my chance. If Elizabeth Innis gets me closer—whatever it takes."

The Wentworth family was old and aristocratic, but like most old and aristocratic families, they didn't have the money to go along with it. Oliver needed this job. However, at twenty-two years old, he also believed that actions had no consequences. And why did he have such stupid delusions? Because Demetri was the bright shining example of "what the hell."

Demetri took a long hard look at himself in the mirror, before his eyes slid away. He *could* make this right, he had to. "I'm sorry, Oliver. It's my fault that we lost Valencia. It's my mess to clean up, not yours. I'll take care of it."

"She could get us the endorsement back. You know that, don't you?"

"Don't go there," warned Demetri. Elizabeth wasn't a business deal, meant to be bought and sold.

"You have this under control? You give me your word?"

Demetri nodded, knotting his own bow tie expertly. The race might be over, but now it was showtime.

Chapter Six

The press surrounded them like hyenas as soon as the drivers walked through the doors. The reception hall was decorated in black-and-white check, with the flags of the different teams hanging from the ceiling. The reception tables were decorated with not just food, but exact-scale replicas of the cars. Around the room, the last laps of the race were being replayed on television screens, in case anyone didn't know who won. A win in the States—it should have been a life-defining moment for Demetri, but instead his eyes were searching, looking for a smart-mouthed blonde with a powerful piston action in her walk that Mercedes couldn't engineer if they tried. Unfortunately, she was nowhere to be found. Demetri didn't want to analyze the pain that caused. He'd been sure after yesterday afternoon that she'd be here. He wanted to believe she trusted him, even though he wasn't sure he could live up to Elizabeth's trust. But for now, he was going to try.

Hugh Preston walked up and slapped him on the back, jarring

his left arm. Demetri groaned in pain, covering it with a forced cough. "You gave us some bad moments, there, Demetri."

Demetri picked up a glass of champagne, the bubbles sparkling in the lights, but not nearly as bright as Elizabeth's smile. "You think you were nervous? You should have been behind the wheel."

Hugh laughed. "Fifty years ago, I would have been."

It was good to see the old man with the fire back in his eyes. "I didn't know that Elizabeth would be here," he continued, and Demetri found the reason for the fire.

"I guess we were all surprised."

"Don't go there, Demetri. She's built her career on a clean-cut reputation, and you could destroy all that."

Demetri swallowed the hard rock in his throat. "I don't want to destroy that. I respect her."

"How much?"

"I'll be extra careful," he promised.

"See that you are. Congratulations on the win."

"I won the race for you," he said quietly.

Hugh gave him a respectful nod and lifted his glass of champagne. "I appreciate that. I'll be seeing you later, my boy, but right now I think there's a lot of folks that want a piece of you. Your manager, for one." Out of the corner of his eye, Demetri noticed Jim Sterling, the managing executive for Team Sterling, approach, waiting to pull Demetri away.

"We'll catch up later," he promised Hugh and then went off to meet Jim. Together, they made the rounds, greeting the sponsors, the political types that liked the photo op and the Formula Gold executives who paid the bills. Racing had been the perfect occupation for Demetri. In a normal business environment, reckless and rash were frowned on. In racing, it was a guaranteed crowd-pleaser.

Amidst all the congratulations and the hearty handshakes, Demetri kept watching for Elizabeth, telling himself that Hugh would be happier if she didn't show, trying to tell himself that it wouldn't matter if she didn't show, but that was a lie. He couldn't wait to see her again.

Demetri wasn't a man who did slowly or cautiously well, and yesterday wasn't nearly enough.

It was an endless twenty minutes later before he spotted her in the far corner of the room, nursing a longneck beer, and looking gorgeous in a bright yellow dress that hugged her body in ways a man could only dream of. Her hair was pulled up, a few tempting strands hanging free, soft and silky. Such beautiful hair, shining like gold sunbeams through the dark. Everything about her was sunshine bright, and Demetri wanted to stop and bask in her warmth. Across the room their eyes met, and she turned away.

Not a good sign for a man with his heart set on basking.

However, he knew one easy way to fix that. He grabbed a beer and walked over. If he'd just pulled out an upset win over Marcusi, how hard could it be to coax a smile from one female singer?

"I suppose you're waiting for me to tell you congratulations," she said, and her voice lacked its usual honey smoothness.

"Not if you don't mean it, but Giovanni would probably be surprised to know that you were pulling for him out there."

"Congratulations," she muttered, and lifted the bottle to her lips. Somehow her bright sunshine demeanor had chilled to subzero degrees.

Demetri sighed. "What's wrong?"

"How do you know something's wrong?" she asked, with a look best described as livid. Demetri felt a familiar tightening in his groin. She gave him attitude, he got turned on. She gave him honey-eyes, he got turned on. He suspected that whatever she did, it didn't really matter. His body seemed to have one gear around her. Overdrive.

If his smile looked pained, it was all her fault. "You're not talking. That's my first, and actually, only, clue."

She slammed the bottle down on the table. "You could have been killed."

Suddenly it started to make sense. The pale face, the tense jaw, the straitjacket posture. Demetri began to laugh. She had been worried about him.

Laughing probably wasn't the best idea because she started to walk away—until he stepped in front of her. "Elizabeth, wait."

Her chin lifted, her lips set in a mutinous line, and her eyes were cold shards of ice.

"I'm sorry," he said, not sure exactly what he was apologizing for, but he thought it wouldn't hurt.

Elizabeth ran a hand over her hair, shoving blond wisps away from her face, a few strands escaping in a haphazard fashion. This time when she looked up, her eyes were glistening with tears. *Tears*.

Now the transition was complete. He'd gone from world-class driver to world-class heel, and all in two minutes or less. Demetri took her hand and led her back around the corner, to a place where the press wasn't so omnipresent, where he could soothe her in private. Once he was sure they were safe from prying eyes, he gently smoothed her hair back in place, his hand lingering for a moment. Every time he saw her, the compulsion to touch her was still there, the powerful urge to touch her. Every time he saw her, the urge grew.

The thought unnerved him, but Demetri forced a smile. "The risk is part of what I do."

"Are the races always like that?"

"Not always," he lied.

Elizabeth met his eyes, slowly shaking her head from side to side. "Why don't I believe you?"

"Your choice," he answered, keeping his voice light. Demetri didn't want her to worry about him. God knows, he'd been taking chances since he was kid, and he'd always survived. She didn't understand that Demetri was indestructible. Other people around him got hurt, but Demetri would always walk away unscathed. Time after time, he risked death, thinking that this time, he would finally get what he deserved, and time after time, death laughed at his efforts. Before Seth had died, the risks were for bravado, a young man's quest for immortality. After Seth had died, it became a wiser man's quest for atonement.

Elizabeth searched his face, and eventually she must have found the answer she was looking for. "I'm not doing this," she stated, and then started to walk away again.

"Goddammit, Elizabeth," he said, and this time he grabbed her arm, sending shooting pains all the way to his wrist.

She glared at his offending hand. "You can let go now."

He wasn't letting go of anything until they'd sorted this out. "Don't walk away from me."

"You don't tell me what to do, mister," she said, her voice snapping with fury, and just as sharply, she shook his arm. Demetri couldn't hide his wince when pain shot through his arm once again. Man, this was getting old.

Her eyes gentled, anger cooling to concern. "What's wrong?"

Seeing the softness in her eyes cooled his anger, as well. He could understand a car's engine, understand the physics involved to maximize acceleration, but what he didn't understand was how this one woman could slip under his skin so easily. He usually didn't care enough to argue, he usually didn't care enough to put effort into a relationship. His life was spent two weeks in one place, before moving on. He didn't have time to make an effort, but this time he was trying hard. He didn't want to fight with her, he only wanted her to know he was making that effort. "There's nothing wrong."

With one fingertip she touched his arm, as if he were made of glass. "Why did that hurt?"

Demetri didn't want to talk about his arm. He wanted to talk about tonight. Today he'd been unable to concentrate, been unable to focus, been unable to do most of the things that were expected of a driver. Maybe for her it was no big deal, but for him it was career suicide. "It didn't hurt much. Why are you so mad?"

Her fingers fell and she took another sip of her beer. "You don't want to know."

"I do. I really do."

"You scared me half-crazy when you were out there. Taking that one curve, and then wheeling around, and then scooting up in between those two hot rods, and there wasn't enough room, and then…when you took that big turn and your tires were screeching out from under you, and that one guy lit up right beside you…I knew you were going to hit him. Sweet Lord, I wanted to look away so bad, but I couldn't. See this," she said, holding out her left hand, exposing three angry red gashes. "I did that. You scared the hell out of me."

He stared at those gashes, amazed, and couldn't help himself. He took her hand in his and tenderly lifted the wounded flesh to his lips. "I'm sorry," he said, and he was. Usually no one worried about Demetri unless there was a vested financial interest in the outcome. And no one had ever cared this much before. Until today. Deep inside his chest, his heart shifted uncomfortably.

"You should be," she told him, but he noticed that her fingers were curled tightly around his palm. He liked that, the way they fit together.

"I had a good reason," he said, fighting the urge to kiss her hand once again. Maybe kiss her mouth this time. She had a delicious mouth. Pink and ripe and yes, it was hot. All last night, he'd dreamed about her mouth. Dreamed about all the places she could put that mouth. It was a large part of the reason his focus had been so screwed today.

The ripe mouth pulled into a hard line. "I don't think so."

"I made a bet with Hugh. If I won, he had to take the winnings. If I lost, he'd sell me Leopold's Legacy." He finally told her. If he'd lost, she would never have known. But he had won, and he wanted to see it in her eyes. Demetri—the man, not the media creation—wanted to be the hero.

One emotion chased after another as she processed all that. He watched, suddenly anxious to see the final outcome. Eventually her eyes warmed, and she squeezed his hand. "So you won. Does Melanie know?"

Demetri shrugged. "Doubt it."

"You're supposed to be a snake in the grass," she told him, and he heard what sounded like disappointment in her voice.

"You're supposed to be a prude," he shot back.

"I am," she said, as though she expected him to believe it.

He shook his head, not believing it for one minute. A woman with a body like that, with a head-turning walk like hers, had warm, passionate blood running in her veins. "Nobody knows who you are."

She cocked her head to one side, all sass. "Well, yes, they do. I'm a simple country girl. And you, Mr. Big-City Boy, should have figured that out."

He stared for a minute, enjoying the simple pleasure of watching her, cornflower eyes lit up with danger, rosebud mouth poised for battle and the shadowy line of cleavage that was like a treasure map merely waiting to be explored. Helplessly he shook his head. "There's nothing simple about you."

"You're not going to get a chance to find out, if that's what you're thinking, and let me tell you, what you're thinking is mighty apparent." Sadly, it probably was. Lust was probably written all over his face. Yesterday he'd been able to pretend he was perfectly harmless, but today, after the demands of the race, the mind-drugging effects of painkillers and the lust that was snapping at his heels, he couldn't pretend. Demetri was tired of being someone else around her. He didn't have the energy or the will. At some point or another, she'd figure out that he wanted her more than he wanted to breathe.

"What you're thinking is mighty apparent, too." He'd meant

it as an accusation, but his voice was soft and gentle, and she'd be foolish to see it as anything less than what it was. The desperate pleadings of a desperate man. He'd been so confident, so sure when he first saw her tonight, but slowly she'd taken everything he had and tossed it right back at him.

She looked flustered, and pushed the hair out of her eyes, then back into her eyes once again. "I should go."

"Probably," he told her, because she was right. She should go. He should leave her alone, exactly as he promised Hugh. He should ignore all the fire that was raging up inside him, but he couldn't. It would be easier to stop his heart. There was something so compelling about her mouth, the way she spoke, the way her tongue flitted against her lips when she was nervous. For eleven days, he'd wanted to taste that mouth, and he'd plotted and planned, and told himself to go slow, but right now, those plans got shot to hell. He didn't have a choice anymore. Demetri was running on instincts he didn't even know he had.

Slowly, reverently, he took her lips in a kiss and was rewarded with an openmouthed gasp. For his own sanity, for what was left of the tiny scraps of his honor, he had tried to convince himself that kissing her would be like kissing a curvy block of ice. Not that he really believed it, but it would have been easier for both of them if she kissed like ice. He could kiss her once, walk away and never look back.

However, at that precise moment, when he tasted her rosepetal lips, Demetri knew he could kiss her forever. She was warm, and soft, and tasted like honey. Sweet, seductive honey.

His world blurred, dimmed, and he leaned in more, deepened the kiss, because he wanted to taste more. Elizabeth moved against him, a slow slide that made his blood quicken in response. This was no block of ice. Somehow little Miss All-American knew all about the birds and the bees, and the single quickest way to drive a man wild. One move and all gears went right back into overdrive.

Urgently, Demetri pulled her to him. Rough palms grasping against the bare flesh of her back, frantic strokes down the curve of her spine and lower still. He'd meant to seduce her, slow, gentle, easy. Somehow she'd shot that plan to hell, too. He took those perfectly shaped hips in his hands and pressed her into him, a graphic move that wasn't slow, gentle or easy at all. But Demetri needed her to know exactly what she did to him. Her answering shudder pleased him no end, and her soft, throaty moan would echo in his head for days, weeks, years....

Weakly she arched, pressing against him with sweet, seductive breasts that were made for one man's hands. His. Only his.

Slow, gentle, easy, he kept reminding himself over and over, but Demetri had never done anything slow in his life. His mouth went for her throat, tasting the salt of her skin, the frantic pulse of her blood until he felt her pull away—

—*away, from him.*

God, no. Not yet. Did she want to kill him with this? He raised his head, his breathing rough, blinking rapidly until his vision started to clear. They weren't done. They weren't even close to done. For a heart-stopping second Elizabeth stared, blue eyes steamed with desire, her mouth swollen and wet, and he was ready to pull her back into his arms. Then he heard his name over the loudspeaker.

The brisk, British voice belonged to the head of the racing association. They were looking for him.

Hell.

"That's your cue," she told him, her voice warm and dazed with passion, and he put the pad of his finger against her swollen lips, then traced down the dimple of her chin, along the velvety line of her throat, and then farther into the deep, warm curves of her breasts. She stood, motionless, her eyes locked with his, and Demetri knew that walking away was now pretty much impossible.

The announcer repeated his name and Demetri sighed.

"We're not done," he told her. "Not by a long shot."

* * *

Elizabeth's fingers kept stealing up to her mouth, touching her lips. Ten minutes later, and the sizzle remained. She'd been kissed before, technically she'd been kissed plenty, but never like that. Her heart was pumping frantically, and she was still standing frozen against the wall, grateful for the vertical support it provided her. God knows, she needed it now, because her knees didn't want to cooperate.

Good lord, whoever knew about that triple-X, promise-you-the-world mouth that would melt butter in an Arctic blizzard? In her G-rated world, she'd thought about running bases one to three with a slow, easy gait so she could gauge Demetri's intentions before determining if he was the one. But here with one kiss he had knocked the ball out of the park, and she was thinking how good, how very endlessly satisfying it would feel, when he slid right into home plate.

Sad. Very sad, Elizabeth. All because of one little kiss from a man who refueled his tanks on an hourly basis. The problem was, she didn't want to believe it. She didn't want to believe he was a playboy like some of the other drivers. Some part of her ached to believe he was different, and she was torn between the two. The sensible woman who listened to her cousins, and most of the international press, versus the foolish woman, daughter of Diane Innis, whose track record with men was pathetic, at best. Elizabeth was trying desperately hard not to follow in her momma's foolish shoes.

But, sweet mercy, she wanted to like Demetri. When he told her about the bet with Hugh, secretly she had been thrilled that he had such a streak of goodness in him, but then she worried that she only wanted to like him because he was sexy, and dear God, did any man have to look that pretty in a tux?

She took a long swig of beer, but even alcohol didn't help dampen the buzz inside her. That chastity belt that she'd been so proud of herself for wearing was getting tight. Extraordinarily tight. So tight that parts of her were starting to itch and hurt and throb, and in general, protest their sanctimonious conditions.

And it didn't help that she had seen that single wince of pain, seen the way his skin turned pale under the tan.

Nothing like a wounded man to make a woman turn all stupid. So, when all good sense told her to get the hell out of Dodge, Elizabeth sought out Melanie and decided to stay.

The two women watched from the sidelines as officials presented the trophy to Demetri, watched when some executive told him what a great driver he was, and did everything but throw palm branches at his feet. The man had nearly gotten himself killed, and did anybody but Elizabeth notice it? No, sir.

"It was a good race," said Melanie, an innocent remark that made Elizabeth even jumpier. Quickly she touched her mouth.

"Yeah. Real exciting stuff."

"I told you you'd like it," she said. "It's like being on the turf, that same pound in the blood, the same thump in your heart when you can feel the other horses coming up behind."

Elizabeth had never been in a horse race in her life, but she was fresh off the blood-pounding, heart-pumping experience, and she could empathize, so she nodded professionally. When she saw Uncle Hugh talking to Demetri again, thoughts of the upcoming concert broke though her lust-fogged brain, and she knew that this was the opportunity she'd been waiting for.

"We need to talk about something for a minute, Mel. Business."

Melanie's fair brows drew together in confusion. "What kind of business?"

Elizabeth led her by the arm where they wouldn't be disturbed, realizing she was going to have to slowly walk Melanie through the steps of Elizabeth's logic because as always, Elizabeth's logic was complicated. "Demetri gave Hugh and Thomas an interest-free loan. He bet with Hugh on the race."

"Grandpa told you this? No one told me."

"I don't know why he didn't tell you, but the fact is that he made a bet, he's taking money from Demetri, and I insist on the same sort of treatment. You know the concert they scheduled on Wednesday? I'm giving the proceeds to the stables, to do with what you want. When things get better, you can pay me back. Or not. Doesn't matter, I don't need it."

"Elizabeth, no. You're just getting over the financial mess because of your dad. You keep your own money." Melanie looked so dad-gummed elegant, coolly sophisticated in her black taffeta dress and designer heels, but there was no missing the stubbornness that was written all over her face.

Elizabeth bit back a cussword she wasn't supposed to know. "Don't make me get sneaky, cuz. You remember how you got busted when you snuck out to the party over at Troy Livingston's when his parents were out of town? This would be worse. Ten times worse. I'll go public that night onstage. There won't be a dry eye in the house by the time I finish telling the long, five-hanky saga of Quest Stables, Leopold's lost Legacy and how Something to Talk About is the new hope in a proud, *proud* tradition of racing greats that have come from right here in Woodford County. How the Preston family was brought to the brink of financial ruin because of some DNA mistake."

Now, here in Kentucky, dirty laundry was meant to be washed, and not aired, and Melanie's eyes narrowed dangerously. "Elizabeth…"

Elizabeth held out a firm hand, one finger wagging in Melanie's face. Rude, yet effective. Tonight Elizabeth had faced down the devil, and even though she hadn't won, it'd been a heck of a battle and powerful adrenaline was still pumping through her veins. "Don't you 'Elizabeth' me. Just take the damned money. Good Lord, you'd think it's toxic waste or something the way you people keep tossing it back and forth."

Melanie's lips pressed together, and Elizabeth knew it went against everything that Melanie believed in, but, as she was fast learning herself, beliefs weren't made of steel. "No press, Elizabeth. This is all going to stay under the tables. It has to."

"That means you'll take the cash?"

Melanie looked at her hard. "You're sure you can afford this?"

"Honey, yes. I'd be dripping with diamonds if I was the tasteless, tacky type, which we know I'm not."

Finally Melanie nodded. "I'll square it with my father, and Hugh."

Wow, it hadn't been nearly as bad as Elizabeth had thought, no bamboo shoots under the fingernails, no boiling in hot wax. "You're making me feel better already. Now why don't you find some nice young man and ask him to dance?"

Melanie's eyes drifted across the room. "Are you going to dance with Demetri?"

"That snake in the grass?" protested Elizabeth, who was a great actress when times demanded it—like now.

Unfortunately, Melanie didn't look to be buying what Elizabeth was selling. "He's a nice enough man, and he and Grandpa are great friends, but he's trouble."

"No trouble for me," answered Elizabeth breezily.

Melanie still didn't look convinced, but she lifted her hand and stifled a yawn. "I've been up since early this morning. I'm going to round up Grandpa and head for home."

"You're going to leave me here alone?" asked Elizabeth, more than a little panicked.

"My drive home is longer than yours. I can trust you to behave with that snake in the grass. Can't I?"

Elizabeth frowned, because she didn't want to be left alone with Demetri. Her fingers touched her mouth once again. "'Course you can," said Elizabeth, lying to her cousin once again. It was becoming a serious habit. Or maybe Demetri was becoming a serious habit.

While he made the circuit, she watched him with a woman's eyes, and noticed the way the left arm stayed pretty much by his side the whole time. The same left arm that she'd shaken off as though it had burned her.

As the night moved on, Elizabeth watched, heavens she watched, but Demetri stayed away. Sometimes their eyes met, accidentally. Sometimes not so accidentally. The press approached her, more polite enquiries than anything, but this wasn't her turf. Country music was about average people who went about ordinary lives, and her songs were full of that, but here, tonight… This was all diamonds and glitter, and she knew she didn't belong.

The other Sterling driver, the Brit, approached her, asked her to dance, but Elizabeth shook her head.

He wasn't one to be denied, though. "Do you mind if I stay here for a moment and drink? It's frightfully mad, don't you think?"

Frightfully mad. Elizabeth's mouth curved up at that. Oliver Wentworth was a pretty boy, too. He didn't yet have the lines of experience like Demetri, but she figured that would come in time.

"You sang beautifully, today, by the way."

"Thank you, sir. Congratulations on the win."

"It wasn't mine," he answered, and there was more than a little whine in his voice.

"It was your team's win," she reminded him.

"I don't count that," he said, looking bent out of shape that she would think he would.

"Well, better luck next time, then."

"Sometime soon I'll beat him," he answered, his eyes watching Demetri.

"Maybe."

"You like him?"

Bold statements like that made Elizabeth nervous. They could be construed, misconstrued, and, in general most times came back to bite you in the butt. "I'm a people person. I like everybody. Even you," she added for good measure.

He laughed. "I've been warned off."

Elizabeth swallowed, then looked helplessly away.

"They call me his protégé, you know," he told her, looking proud of that foolish fact.

Elizabeth had always been taught it was rude to stare, but she did anyway. Astounding, completely astounding. "You actually want to drive like that? Like *him?*" She sniffed at her drink, because there was something in the water that she didn't want to drink.

"He's the best."

"Best is no good if you're dead," snapped Elizabeth, not understanding why no one in the automobile industry seemed to appreciate the sanctity of life.

"Do you know how many accidents he's walked away from?" he asked, as if that was some badge of honor.

"At least one."

"Dozens," he answered, and she could see the abject hero-worship in his eyes.

"Why do you think I want to know this?" She didn't want to know this. She didn't want to know how fast Demetri drove, how many crashes he'd walked away from or how many women were in his past. Denial. That was becoming her new best friend.

Oliver ignored her new best friend. "Most women like his daredevil persona. I'm his teammate, and I'm only trying to help his cause."

"I am not 'most women.' I don't like being lumped with 'most women.' I've made my name by not being 'most women.' I'd like for you to remember that fact."

"But you like Demetri—"

"Like 'most women,'" finished Elizabeth drily. "I feel so much better now, Oliver. Thank you."

"He's a good man," he told her, finishing off the last of his champagne, his eyes no longer teasing. And she didn't want to hear that, either. "He enjoys taking risks, but I think you're the biggest risk he's ever taken," he added. "See you around. I hope."

She watched Oliver walk away, wishing they'd never had this conversation. Her eyes sought out Demetri, like the security blanket he was fast becoming. He looked up, his eyes meeting hers. Once again, all the oxygen got sucked right out of the room. She sipped on her water, restlessly biding time until the press obligations were done, and he came over, wearing his Hollywood smile, the one that didn't mean diddly.

"Can we leave?" he asked, and the thousand-watt smile dipped some.

"And go where exactly?"

"I don't care. A drive. Anywhere."

"Is everything all right?" she asked. He didn't look comfortable or happy, wearing a bit of that same restlessness that she felt herself.

He nodded in that curt way that some men do. "Sure."

She searched his face for a second, wanting to trust him, dying to trust him, and eventually, sucker that she was, she did. "Okay," she answered, and then followed him out the back corridors, where the press wouldn't notice. He started to take the stairs down, and then stopped, looking her over in a distracted manner. "Do you have a coat?"

"I'm staying at the same hotel as the party. It didn't seem necessary."

Gallantly he shrugged out of his jacket and wrapped it around her shoulders, still using his left arm gingerly.

"What's wrong with your arm?" she asked.

"Nothing that more heat and painkillers won't fix."

Aha. She had known he'd gotten hurt. "You should go see a doctor."

"It's a pulled muscle, nothing more."

They walked down four flights, into a darkened underground garage, his hand holding hers, and she wasn't sure that he even noticed, but she did. He led her over to a sleek, red car that sat lower to the ground than a snake. It was absolutely no surprise when he clicked the remote, and the lights flipped. This was his.

"This is your loaner?" she asked, thinking this man had more cars than she had shoes. Fast cars that should be outlawed if she had anything to say about it, which apparently, she didn't.

"Yeah," he said casually, not even bothering to explain.

"This thing has doors?" she asked, wondering how the heck she was supposed to fit in with a long dress on.

He came around and lifted the door up. "I see," she answered, lifting her skirts and climbing in.

"You want to drive?" he asked her.

"No, thank you. Right now, I'm just figuring out how to sit. I'll leave the driving to the professionals. Keep it under seventy, if you please."

He climbed in, flashed her a grin and unknotted the bow tie, the evening's stress disappearing like magic. Elizabeth began to understand. Upstairs wasn't his place, either. Some people belonged, some people didn't. For the first time all night she relaxed, which lasted two seconds, until he cranked up the engine and revved it a few times. Oh, my. That was no engine, it was like a jet airplane ready for takeoff, and sure enough, instantly they were zooming out of the parking garage, the floors passing by before she could count. Her hand grabbed the door for security and Elizabeth kept her eyes closed until the turning stopped.

"You all right?" he asked, as if her stomach hadn't been left somewhere back on the floor of the parking garage.

"Fine," she managed, and he laughed.

"Good." The red light turned green, and Demetri took off fast, leaving the hotel far behind.

"I bet the cops really like you," she answered, when she could manage to talk again.

"They usually can't catch me."

"Life has been too easy for you," she said with a shake of her head.

His grin faded a little. "Yeah."

Demetri handled the city streets with ease, even favoring his one arm. He shifted the way some people breathe, popping in and out of gears. His long fingers gripped the stick shift with a practiced ease, tight, firm, and she found herself watching his hands, watching him shift with a dry-mouth anticipation that had absolutely nothing to do with respect for his driving skills.

Slowly she began to relax, her stomach starting to regain its bearings. And slowly she got caught up in the moment. Driving had never seemed sexy before, but she'd never been in the car with someone who drove with so much…aggression. Now she understood. Demetri didn't seem to notice.

"You should drive her. Can you handle a stick?"

"Of course," she answered, shocked that he would think otherwise. Her momma had taught her to drive in a '73 Chevy Nova that didn't have air-conditioning. It wasn't close to this car, sometimes you'd have to push start it when the heat was really bad, but Elizabeth hadn't cared. At sixteen, a driver's license had given her a freedom that she'd never had before.

The car slid to the side of the gravel road, and she realized he'd found some back roads to the west of downtown. "I don't think I should drive," she answered. "This dress…"

"Just pull it up. You'll be fine."

"No, Demetri. I'll crash."

"Please," he said, and it was the *please* that did her in, and she fiddled with the handle of the door, because she didn't want to see him soft and vulnerable. It made her want things that she didn't want to want. Not with him.

"Tell me how to open the door," she said, and he reached

across her, his arm brushing against her breasts, sending twin bolts of pleasure straight from her chest to her thighs. Elizabeth gasped, and he jerked back. "Sorry. I forgot. Let me open it up from the outside," he said, nearly rushing to get out of the car.

He helped her out, his hand lingering on hers for longer than necessary, and she didn't mind. Something had changed in that one moment. The cold night air had turned thick and hot, and her mind was acting slightly tipsy, but it wasn't the single beer she'd had earlier. She skirted around him, darting back to the safety of the car. After she climbed into the driver's seat, she raised her skirts to a respectable level.

He grinned at her. "I don't know why you wear a long dress with legs like that."

Now this she could handle. This easy teasing that soothed her nerves. Not that moment earlier when the urgent need in her had scrambled her mind. "Is that the only reason you wanted me to drive?" she asked. "So you could ogle my legs?"

"Shoot me," he answered, completely unashamed.

"At least you're a man of good taste. I don't think I should drive this thing. You got insurance, right?"

"I'm covered," he said, and then explained the dash to her, followed by an in-depth explanation of tires, brakes and the engine cooling system. When he got to the transmission, she made him stop.

"You like your cars, don't you?"

"Yeah, but there are some things I like better."

Elizabeth knew when to keep her mouth shut. It was all there in the devil in his eyes. She pretended that she didn't understand. She turned the key, and the engine pulsed to life. "Peppy," she muttered.

"You need help with the shifter?" he asked.

"Do I look like I need help?" Elizabeth asked, popped the gear, and the car promptly died. "Maybe a little. Some of us don't do this for a living."

"You said you could drive a stick."

"I'm going to try. Just give me time to ease into it."

He sat back, watched her, that too-smooth smile playing on his mouth. If he didn't watch her so much, with those eyes that knew too much, she would have had an easier time of this. But eventually she got used to it, told her body to calm down, and pretty soon, she was tooling around the back roads, handling the sleek car like a pro, all at the top speed of thirty-seven miles per hour. "Take a left at the next turn. There's a straightaway. She'll go over two hundred."

The blood drained from Elizabeth's face. "I don't think so."

"Just once?" he asked, so warm and seductive that she wasn't sure that she could manage the car at all.

"I'll hit a tree."

"There are no trees for miles around."

"I'll get a ticket," she said, searching for an excuse, any excuse.

"There're no cops for miles."

"Is there anything around for miles?" she asked desperately, like the coward she was.

"Just me."

That's what she was afraid of. Elizabeth opted for the lesser of two evils, and took the turn, slowing down and taking a deep breath.

"You can do it," he said, as if he really believed it.

"I don't think I can," she said, needing to put that out there, in case something bad happened, and then it could be all his fault for ignoring her good sense.

"Yeah, you can. Just close your eyes."

She stuck the car in neutral and looked at him sideways. "I don't think that's smart."

"You're not going to hit anything," he said. His arm curved over her seat, and she felt his fingers at her neck. Brushing, playing, seducing. Suddenly this car was way too small; suddenly he was way too big.

"Except maybe you," she warned, but was completely hypocritical because she leaned back against those playing fingers like the wicked woman she was.

He laughed. "Just do it," he said, and Elizabeth took another deep breath. Heck, she'd sung in front of the President of the United States, surely this wasn't so hard.

She gunned the accelerator, shifted into gear, and the car shot forward. She shifted, gunned a little more, the car went a little faster. Wisely Demetri kept his driving comments to himself, letting her find her rhythm. Third gear, seventy miles per hour. Fourth gear, one-twenty, fifth gear, one-fifty, sixth gear—*sixth gear?*—they were going over two hundred, and the countryside was a blur. Quickly she slowed the car down, her heart pounding, her hands sweating all over his fine leather gearshift, but she'd done it.

She'd done it.

"Was that so hard?" he asked.

"No," she answered with a quiver in her voice. "I think you should drive now."

"Scared?"

"Exhausted."

He raised an eyebrow.

"I'm an amateur," she said, defending herself.

"All right," he answered, opened the door and got her out. This time his hand definitely lingered, trapping her between the car and him. "You did good."

"I did okay," she said, flat back against the side of the car, the tension in the air, the tension inside her starting to come to a boil.

"Elizabeth." His voice pitched low, a husky whisper that was cutting through everything she didn't want cut through.

Her hands lifted to his shirt, with the sole intention of slowing him down, but her hands felt the warm skin that was so alive through the thin white fabric. She'd known he was muscular, but she hadn't known exactly how much until her hand settled there, feeling the sculpted muscles in his chest. Sweet mercy, all she wanted to do was to touch, to feel.

So she did.

Chapter Seven

"I shouldn't be doing this," she told him, lifting her disobedient mouth to his. He did what he did best, and took it. Her back was flat against the chilled metal of the car, but she wasn't cold. Good Lord, she was burning up. His arms held her like bands of steel, almost painfully tight, but she didn't care. That seemed to be her mantra lately. Foolish? Stupid? She didn't care.

Yet how could she care about anything but this? Now, there was no one around for miles, and she knew it. His kiss was all about sin, and her body seemed to like that plan fine. Judging by the hard length of his arousal, which was fitting perfectly between her thighs, she knew exactly what his body was thinking, too.

It was a perfect night for a kiss under the stars, everything so quiet, so beautifully quiet that a woman could hear two hearts beating if she listened. The sounds of staggered breathing, and greedy fingers that needed to touch. Elizabeth sighed into that perfect mouth, and her arms curled around him, pulling that hard body closer, even tighter.

She told herself that she didn't want to feel responsible and sensible, that she was ready to jump off that bridge, but some last little whisper of sanity was telling her that she couldn't.

"Demetri," she said against his mouth, desperately needing to stop him before it was too late.

His mouth lifted from hers, fed on her neck, and she could feel the rasp of his late-night stubble against her skin. Elizabeth moaned, openmouthed and not shy at all. It was like someone else was living in her mind, some hot-fired woman who couldn't wait for her lover's bold touch. Sure fingers slid his jacket from her shoulders, but she barely noticed. The air was thick and liquid, and hot. So terribly hot. Brazenly, his lips moved lower, deeper into the V of her dress, blazing a trail of fire in the wake of his mouth, his teeth, his tongue.

"I've been waiting seven long days to taste you, to see you," he said, and she could hear the throb in his voice, need barely held in check, and it didn't help her peace of mind at all. Somebody needed to be in control here, and she wasn't sure if it would be her. She felt his warm fingers slip aside the strap of her dress, the cold breeze puckering her nipple, and when his lips closed tightly over one breast, all her control was gone. Her knees buckled, her chest arching him closer, pleasure coming sure and fast.

It shouldn't feel so good, so perfect, but everything felt right to her. He felt right. Her eyes drifted open and she watched his dark hair against her white skin, lightning shooting through her with each tug of his mouth. Her fingers tangled in the soft strands, she nearly sighed in relief. Good heavens, she wanted this, she needed this…. He slipped the other strap down, and she was bared to the waist in the middle of nowhere, and she didn't care.

But she really, really, really needed to care. "I can't do this," she told him, her voice quivering with something that was a far cry from righteous indignation.

"We're not going to," he told her, pulling her close, his hot, hungry mouth closing over hers to kiss her again. "I just need to touch you. That's all. Only a little."

She couldn't think when he kissed her like that, and she kissed him right back, wanting to be even closer. Her hands slid up that brick wall of a chest, and she delved beneath the studs on his shirt, aching to touch all that hard skin. He felt so good against her, so safe.

Men had tried this before with her. Tried, and she always shooed them away with a flirty pat of her hands and her trademarked good-girl smile, but tonight she didn't want to smile, she wanted to explore under the velvety cover of darkness. Demetri's hands were under her skirt, the air cool on places that felt like fire. She didn't protest one bit when his cunning hands slipped between her thighs, stroking lightly until her legs slid apart. Then his fingers moved the damp silk of her panties and slipped inside, and Elizabeth heard her own gasp.

"Perfect," he whispered against her mouth, and then he brought his mouth back to hers, his tongue playing the same song inside her mouth, and she could feel the world slipping away. She only wanted to be here with him, his sure hands, his hungry mouth, his big body so tight with coiled tension.

There was no witness but the moon as she fell into the dark pool of desire. No one to hear her pleas—except for him. Sweet heaven, she had never imagined. Her whole body was coming apart into pieces.

"Just do it, Elizabeth," he told her, and the ache in his voice sent her over the edge, the release coming on wave after gilded wave. Her fingers twisted into his shirt, pulling at him, until finally the world stopped spinning and she stilled.

Slowly her heart began to thump again.

Against her lips, she felt him smile. Smile, as if everything was the same. How could he smile when the world had just crashed around her?

Elizabeth dragged her mouth away, needing to breathe, needing to regain something because she was absolutely sure she had just sold her soul, and it wasn't coming back anytime soon. With shaking fingers, she pulled up the straps on her gown, and pasted a confident smile on her face.

"Now," she said, trying to be mature and sophisticated, and acting as though he hadn't just swung a two-pronged pickax right into the heart of her unsullied reputation, but the look in his eyes did something far worse. There was a look there so warm, so tender, so perfect that she forgot all about her breathing. It wasn't the knowing look of a no-good, playboy driver with a wild reputation. This was the sort of look that she sang about. Simple and ordinary, a man and a woman alone.

Where her hands had been, his crisp, white shirt was pulled to one side, exposing a long strip of gloriously brown skin. The remains of his elegant dinner jacket were crumpled on the ground, and even seeing all that damage that she'd done, she still had to fist her hands to keep from touching him again.

He looked like one well-used man.

Restlessly, he ran a hand through his hair, silvery moonbeams caressing his face as the clouds drifted through the night. This is what the moon does, she thought to herself. This is why there is moonlight, and moonflowers, and people howl under a lovers' moon. This madness that fell from the sky like summer rain. It was the only explanation that she would believe.

Tomorrow, in the cold light of day, perhaps she'd think more clearly, but now she was entranced by the spell of the night. It had to be.

Demetri picked up his jacket from the ground, and she noticed that he was careful not to touch her. He stayed a long two feet away from her. A safe distance, but the magic was still there, the air nearly singing with it.

"Cold?" he asked, holding out his jacket, and silently she shook her head. She wasn't cold. She didn't think she'd ever be cold again. Demetri looked at the jacket, looked at the tie, and then glanced back to her. "Sorry. I'm not used to this," he told her.

It was so patently untrue that she rolled her eyes. "I don't think so."

His lips quirked in a smile. "That's not what I meant. That, I'm used to. This, I'm not."

"What is this?" she asked, curious to know if he was thinking moonbeams and madness, too.

Again he pulled his hand through his hair. "Being with someone like you. A woman who's still…intact. Hell, I haven't been with a virgin since I was fourteen."

Nope. Not moonbeams and madness at all. "Isn't that special?" she asked, because he was deflating this perfect moment bit by bit.

"You are still a virgin, aren't you?" he asked as if they were discussing whether she flossed after meals, or brushed two times daily instead of her most personal secrets.

"Not necessarily," she answered tightly, feeling the heat in her cheeks. It was as if she'd grown some new, never-before-discovered membrane, instead of the one that every woman in the world had been born with.

"All that press is for show?"

"No," she muttered, looking down at the ground, because she had the sneaking suspicion she was being laughed at.

She didn't hear him approach, but then he was there, invading her personal space. He tilted up her chin, and the tender look was back in his eyes. "I'm glad. I've never gone slow in my life, but I don't want to scare you off, either. I know you're different. Can I see you tomorrow?"

"Rehearsal. Sorry."

Sadly, his hand fell away.

"After rehearsal?"

He acted as though things were so normal, as though they were two normal adults sparking under the moon. But he wasn't normal. She wasn't normal, and the reason he didn't like to take things slow was because he didn't have the time for it. Ten days in one place, then on to someplace new. Someplace new without her. "When are you leaving Kentucky?"

"I'm supposed to be in Rome next week for a driving exhibition, but I can cancel. That'll give us seventeen days until the next race."

Her heart sank. Seventeen days was a flash in the pan, nothing more. Elizabeth told herself to get a grip. This was a man who went through women like glasses of water. "You're planning on staying in Kentucky until then?"

"Oh, yeah," he said, as if seventeen days was a lifetime.

"This isn't smart, Demetri," Elizabeth told him, already thinking ahead to day eighteen. That long, endless day when he wouldn't be there, already moving on to the next port in the storm, and she'd be alone. No, it definitely wasn't smart.

"It doesn't bother me one way or another," he said, smoothing the hair off her face. "I look at you, and I don't get smart."

"I should be getting back to the hotel," she said, noticing the magic in the night air was gone, stuffed back into that little bottle that people uncorked when they let themselves forget.

"Sure," he said, pulled open the passenger car door and swore quietly, but she heard it.

"Your arm?"

"It could be my heart," he told her.

She shook her head, wishing he weren't quite so charming, so compelling and so…injured. "I don't think so. Where're you staying?"

His body moved closer, one arm braced against the car. Almost touching, but not quite. She felt it just the same. "The Seelbach," he answered.

At the mention of her own hotel, she raised her brows. *And wasn't that convenient?*

Noticing her suspicions, not that he couldn't help but notice because she wasn't trying to hide them, he looked at her, disappointment apparent in that oh-too-handsome face. "Louisville's not that big, Elizabeth."

She nodded, taking a step back, until she was flat against the car. "All right. We go back. I want to take a look at your arm."

"You're a nurse, too?" he asked hopefully.

And did his mind have to stay entrenched in the sewer all the time? Thinking those sordid, sultry thoughts about the two of them together, rolling around in bed. He wouldn't have a shirt, of course. All that wide, tanned flesh open for exploration. Where she could touch him, trace the long line of his muscles, all the way down...

Elizabeth shook her head. "I'm concerned, that's all," she snapped. "Don't think this is an excuse to get me back into your hotel room."

"You're a cruel woman, Elizabeth."

"Heartless," she said, and then sneaked under his arm to walk around to the driver's side. "But not so heartless that I'm going to make you drive."

He rested his arms on the roof of the car, a moonstruck look on his face, and the air started to sing once again, carrying her right along with its fancy tune. "You like my car, don't you?"

She shot him a sideways look. "It's starting to grow on me, but we're still not going over fifty."

The handsome snake grinned at her, and damn it all if her heart didn't give out one more time.

By the time they got back to the city, Demetri was feeling human again, his needs firmly back under control. He hadn't expected to find that response in her. It had startled him, pleased him, and when he found his mind winding back to the image of her body in the moonlight, he stopped. Froze. And silently counted backward from one hundred. By fifty, he was actually paying attention to her driving again. She handled the car like a champ, her hands shifting like a pro. Someday she could learn she didn't have to take everything slow, but that would come in time.

Everything was good until she was a block from the hotel, and she braked to a sudden stop. The brightly lit awning was crawling with the press.

It was after two in the morning. Didn't these people ever sleep?

News vans were parked outside the front entrance, along the street, down the circle drive. "You think anyone noticed that we left?" she asked.

Demetri saw the pack of reporters still gathered near the hotel's entrance and frowned. "Yeah."

"Can we get to the underground parking some other way?" she asked, making the sweeping assumption that he would know the best way to sneak in, or out, of hotels.

"Go around to the side. There's got to be a place for deliveries," he said, choosing not to confirm or deny her suspicions.

"You know, if you had picked a less showy car, people wouldn't know it was you."

"Don't blame this one on me. Most of the people in the United States don't even know who I am. You're the star here."

"You make it sound like a bad disease. I just don't want people to talk."

"They won't talk," he said, trying to make her feel better.

"Oh, of course they're going to talk. Hell, you go out alone with my great-grandmother and they'd talk."

"Is your great-grandmother anything like you?"

"Does it matter? I'm just trying to figure out a way out of this."

"We could walk through the front door."

She glared.

He lifted his hands. "I'm only trying to help."

"You're not the one with the squeaky-clean reputation, Mr. Casanova."

"I've been trying to be good," he told her, mortally

offended that she hadn't noticed. Dammit all, the woman had no appreciation for the corporal punishment he was enduring on her behalf.

She turned the car with ease, already adjusting to its handling, he thought with admiration. He'd never trusted his car to a woman before. Actually he'd never met a woman he thought could handle it, but he was coming to realize that Elizabeth could handle just about anything he tossed her way. She parked along a side street, sitting there, her thumbs drumming on the steering wheel.

"Now what do you want to do?" he asked, wishing he had an inside source into the way her mind worked. He knew she was thinking, he could almost hear her thinking, but sometimes he didn't have a clue, and he really wanted a clue.

Elizabeth turned to him, the gears still turning in her head. "What do you mean, 'what'?"

"I'm waiting to hear the plan," he explained patiently, because he knew there was a plan.

"I have no plan. Lord, I need to get my head screwed back on straight." She held up a finger. "Wait. I've got it. It's too simple. We go in separately. You go through the front, leaving the car with the valets. I'll duck in the back. They'll never know."

"Never know what? That I popped your clutch?" he asked with a grin, and her eyes shot daggers.

Demetri knew when to quit. "Fine. I'll go in the front. Should we synchronize watches?"

"Are you always like this?"

"I think you're bringing out the worst in me."

"It must be something," she muttered.

"What room are you in?" he asked, ignoring her sarcasm. He was in too good of a mood. For a man with a sprained shoulder and who had been wearing a painful erection for the past three hours, that was saying a hell of a lot.

"The Presidential suite. You?"

"The Governor's suite. I told you that you were the bigger star. You'll still sneak out to my room?"

She looked at him from beneath her lashes. "I probably shouldn't."

"Your decision," he said, then shrugged, rolling his shoulder, wincing once in pain.

"You're faking that."

"You're absolutely right," he said.

Her fingers drummed on the steering wheel, and with her skirt hiked up midthigh, and the hellfire glint in her eyes, she had no idea how appealing she looked at the moment. He'd fake a heart attack if it meant he could have her alone again. This time with a bed.

No, she wasn't like that. He knew it, every man in America knew it, and Demetri had made a promise. To Hugh, and more important, to himself. For once, Demetri—the man—wasn't going to screw up.

Thoughts of enforced abstinence, a bed and her perfectly formed thighs fought it out.

"I think you're faking, but you weren't earlier. I know you got hurt. I want to see if we need to get you to a doctor."

There was no way in hell he was going to see a doctor. He had a race in three weeks and he was going to win it. However, she didn't know that, so Demetri sat there silently with a pitiful wounded-patient look on his face.

"I have to look," she added.

"Of course," he answered bravely, closing his eyes on the image of perfectly formed thighs wrapped about him—

Enforced abstinence.

The pain shot through him again, this time not from his shoulder.

Elizabeth held her head high as she walked through the hotel kitchen, as if women in long dresses did this every day of the week. Apparently at the Seelbach, they did, because no one said a word. She took the penthouse elevator up to her suite and closed the door behind her.

She was alone. In other circumstances, the stately elegance of the room would have made her stay that way, but at the moment, polished oak wood floors, ornate velvet drapes and beautifully carved mahogany furniture didn't inspire her to stay at all.

She wanted to go to him.

Don't be silly, Elizabeth, she told herself, dropping the beaded evening bag on the brocade couch. Inside her chest, her heart was still hammering from the evening's events, and she pushed back her hair, wondering who had turned the universe upside down while she wasn't looking.

Nobody had ever told her about this, the treacherous power of passion. If Demetri were a jerk, or some Don Juan easy-lover type, it would be an easy decision to make. But he wasn't. That was his biggest—and most unforgivable—crime. He was nice.

Well, that, and the sexy part. And the built part, too.

Elizabeth swore to herself. No, she was going to stay here. She was going to lock the door, not answer the phone, climb into her four-poster bed—alone—and not worry about a thing. Which was a great thought until she got back to the bedroom, and started undressing, and suddenly, she was having a steamy flashback to the whole evening's events, and she could feel him touching her, she could feel his voice whispering in her ear, and her body didn't seem to care if he wasn't there or not, because she was purring like a cat stuck in a red-hot heat.

Okay, so maybe she could see him again—but on her terms, and in different clothes. Something sensible, responsible and virtue-conserving. Elizabeth changed into blue jeans, tennis shoes and a shirt with a sweater. Layers. It seemed to Elizabeth that if she couldn't control herself through all these clothes, then she deserved whatever she got.

When he opened the door to his suite, she saw that Demetri had changed, too. Now he was wearing a pair of low-slung blue jeans on lean hips that looked better than any clothing advertisement, a chest-hugging white T-shirt and no shoes. Sadly, while she had increased layers, he had decreased, which she felt gave him an unfair advantage.

"I thought you'd chicken out," he said, shooting her a smile that she was learning to recognize. It was that "I'm a nice guy with no hidden agendas. Won't you come to bed with me?" smile.

Sadly, the smile worked like a charm, and Elizabeth suspected he knew it.

She lifted her brows, giving him her best superior look, and shot into the room before anybody saw her executing what was possibly the stupidest move of her career. "There's nothing that's going to happen here that I would chicken out of. I like your company. I want to look at your arm…and maybe talk," she said, her eyes flickering guiltily away from the heavy muscles in his chest and arms.

"There's not a lot to see," answered Demetri.

"I can be the judge of that," she said, and so he pulled the T-shirt over his head, exposing an angry green-and-black bruise that circled his shoulder and his arm. And even her untrained eye could see that it was swollen, as well.

"Oh, Demetri," she said, because it looked so bad. "You need to see a doctor, honey. That's got to hurt." She lifted her hand, wishing she were a healer or something, because that must be mighty painful, and then, two seconds later, she noticed the rest of the man.

A long, golden torso that was heavily bulked. Heavily, heavily bulked. *Oh.*

Elizabeth's mouth turned desert-dry, and she had to blink a few times before her vision came back. Tanned, smooth muscle tapered down to a lean, defined waist. Good lord, he was a pretty man. Demetri began talking, not noticing her dumb-struck face at all, which was probably a good thing.

"It looks worse than it is," he was saying. "I'll put heat on it for a couple of days, and be good as new. I felt it jerk when I took that last corner. Happens all the time. It's a pulled muscle, maybe a sprained shoulder, nothing really."

Elizabeth considered touching all that warm, hard flesh, but thought better of it. "I can see. You can put your shirt back on there, mister."

Demetri complied, and when he was safely clothed again, he settled on the couch, one arm outstretched along the back. Completely comfortable, while Elizabeth was standing there bouncing on her heels. "You don't play poker, do you?" he asked.

"Nope. Why?"

"Because everything you're thinking is showing up on your face."

"Good, then this will make perfect sense to you. You sit over there, and I'll sit over here," she told him, and she perched on the edge of the vastly uncomfortable straight-backed antique wing chair.

Elizabeth liked looking at him, liked talking to him, listening to the deep buzz of his voice, but she knew this was a fine line she was walking. Tempting fate wasn't something she normally did, because she'd been poor once, twice if you counted the paper version after her father ran off with the money, and she didn't relish being poor again, and if Elizabeth's reputation went down the toilet, well, she wasn't sure she wouldn't end up being poor again.

"Would you like something to drink?" he asked, still wearing that nice-guy smile.

"That's a big no, I think."

His long, capable fingers drew tiny circles on the flowered tapestry of the sofa back. Tiny, hypnotic circles that drew her eyes. His nice-guy smile faded some. "I had to try. How do you turn it off?"

She didn't pretend not to understand. There was something between them, the stillness before a thunderstorm when the atmosphere turns heavy and damp. Elizabeth knew when a storm was coming; usually she could smell it on the air—like now.

Most times she loved all the rain and the fury, but this was one storm that she wasn't sure she could survive. In seventeen days he was going to leave, and she knew she couldn't hold out that long. *Damn.*

"Some of us call it self-control," she told him, sounding as though she was in complete control.

"Some of us have none," he said, as if that was an excuse.

"That's a lie."

He looked at her innocently. "What do you mean?"

"You've got a lot more self-control than you pretend."

The nice-guy smile was now completely gone, and the raw emotion in his face should have scared her. "You make it very difficult."

"That's not my problem," she answered. When she was a kid, her mother had taught her not to poke at mad dogs, or go near a skunk, or go tromping through any vines that had three leaves on one branch. Elizabeth had never been bitten, sprayed or developed poison ivy because of that good sense. Yet here she sat, poking the mad dog, waiting for him to bite, wanting him to bite.

"It is your problem," he said, his gaze skimming over her, and it really didn't matter if she was wearing layers of clothes, because her breasts swelled, and that cursed ache between her thighs was starting to hurt again. Bad.

Quickly she rose. "I think it's time to leave."

The heat disappeared from his eyes. "Don't go. I'll behave."

Sensing the danger had passed, Elizabeth sat back down. "See. You proved my point. You turn it off when you want to. Tell me about Greece."

"Scared, Elizabeth?"

"Terrified. Tell me about Greece."

For a moment she thought he was going to keep after her, pulling at her defenses, but he didn't. He donned his smile once again. "I don't remember much. We left when I was eight. My father worked with computers for a shipping company, and he was gone almost all the time. My mother, she was nice, gentle, but then she died."

"Do you remember her?"

His face grew sad, and she wanted to go sit and comfort him, because he looked to be in a world of hurt. "Vague stuff, mainly. Her singing at night, tucking me in bed, talking soft and gentle."

"Your father never remarried?"

The laugh wasn't pretty. "No, my father wasn't good with relationships. I don't know how my mother could stand it. When he transferred to the States, the three of us moved out to Seattle."

"Three of you?"

"My father, brother and me."

Brother? "Really," she said, dying to ask more, but there was something in his face that didn't invite questions, so she let him go on—for now.

"After we got to Seattle, my father worked until he had enough money to launch his own start-up. It went on from there."

It was very odd, because she couldn't imagine Demetri in a business suit. He had too much energy, he was too restless. "Did you ever work with him?"

"For a few years, not long. I don't like the lumbering pace of business. Too stagnant, but it was a means to an end. I helped my father build it up, but I struck out on my own. I invested in some risky ventures. Some of the bets paid off big. I started racing as a hobby, but by the time I was twenty-five, I knew that I wanted to race professionally. I had the money, so I did."

Elizabeth wanted to know more, but the phone rang, and the little porcelain clock next to the table said it was after 2:00 a.m. She was willing to bet a year's royalties it was a female.

Demetri picked it up. "Lucas.

"Yes, Oliver. I'm fine."

Not a female. Elizabeth smiled, Demetri smiled back.

"No. No, I didn't.

"I don't care what you think. Do you know what time it is? You should be asleep."

She should be asleep, too. Safely in bed rather than sitting here lapping up sweet cream from a man who was probably going to toss her over like last year's leftovers.

"That's nice. I'm glad you're happy.

"I'm alone, Oliver," he said, lying easily.

"Yes. I'm really alone," he said, still lying.

"Really, really alone," he said, still lying, smiling as if it didn't matter.

"No, I'm not interested in having a drink. I'm in bed.

"—alone.

"Really, really alone. Good night, Oliver."

Elizabeth smothered her laughter until Demetri hung up. "Is he always like that?" she asked.

"Almost always. Oliver comes from a large family, and he has a compulsive need to be around people. You might have noticed."

Elizabeth didn't want to talk about Oliver. She wanted to hear about Demetri. She wanted to know every detail of his life, even if it took all night. Especially if it took all night. She kicked off her shoes and buried her toes into the heavy tapestry rug. "Tell me about your brother."

"My brother?"

"You said you had a brother. Younger or older?" Elizabeth had always wanted an older brother, or a younger sister. Somebody to talk to when she could hear her mother crying in the other room. Somebody to play games with her when there was no one around. All Elizabeth ever had was an old guitar that once belonged to her grandfather.

"Seth was younger than I am, by four years."

Was. "What happened?"

"He died in a rock-climbing accident a long time ago. His senior year in high school."

She noticed how still his face was, showing absolutely nothing. No good memories, no bad memories; it was as if there were no memories at all. "I'm sorry. You never talk about him in the articles."

He raised a brow. "You've been reading articles."

"Some. Don't act so surprised. Google is my friend."

"You shouldn't believe everything you read."

As the victim of several false reports herself, namely a secret love child, four supposed trips to rehab and a torrid ghostly affair with Johnny Cash, Elizabeth knew that a lot of things weren't true, so she felt it only charitable to give him the benefit of the doubt. "So I'm assuming you didn't sleep with that princess, then?" she asked, giving a silent prayer that, like the ghost of Johnny Cash, the princess was some figment of the media's overactive imagination.

His mouth twisted, but he remained stubbornly, guiltily silent.

Her fingers ground into her knee. Not Johnny Cash, not even close. When she spoke, her voice was raw and brittle. "Now see, not everything is false, is it? And you're wondering why I'm nervous."

He got up, walked to the crystal decanter and poured himself a healthy two fingers. Once again he downed his drink, and put it aside, never planning on picking it up again. "This isn't the same. Don't judge me by the past. I'm trying. I've never tried before. Give me a chance. Give us a chance, Elizabeth, before you shoot it all to hell."

"Why me? What's different now?"

"You. Me. Everything. The world thinks I'm this hero, but I'm not. You look at me, and I think you see me for what I am, what I want to be."

"And what is that?"

"A man. Just a man."

It sounded so simple. Maybe it was too late at night to think clearly, maybe she was all wound up, maybe she was being stupid, but she was going to believe him—at least for now.

"Do you ever go back to where you were born?" she asked, switching to something harmless.

He shook his head. "No. I don't like revisiting ancient history. I've even forgotten most of the language."

Elizabeth looked at him in surprise. "But it's Greece! I'd love to go explore. I've never traveled much." When she was growing up, Nashville had been pretty much it.

"Even now?" he asked, his face more relaxed, the worry smoothed away.

"I do some concerts overseas, but it's a day there, rehearsal and a day back, most of my time spent at the airport. A concert is no travel vacation, believe me."

"Why don't you come to Canada with me? Take a real vacation?" he asked, looking completely serious.

"Canada?" she repeated stupidly.

"It's not European, but it does qualify as foreign…ish. There's a race in three weeks. The last one of the season. It'd be fun."

"Fun. Drop everything, fly thousands of miles across the country and all for fun," she said, as if she wasn't desperately tempted, as if she wouldn't love to spend more time on the arm of this man who kept turning her head.

He leaned forward, far enough away that she couldn't touch, but close enough that she could smell him, his scent teasing her nose, teasing her mind. She had noticed that he didn't wear some exotic, heavy cologne. No, he smelled so wonderfully clean and crisp and strong and dynamic. Nothing at all but potent, head-turning man.

"Travel is good, Elizabeth. See the country and see how the rest of the continent lives. You stay in the same place too long and you start gathering moss. Think of it as an educational experience."

And didn't he wrap it up in a pretty bow? Elizabeth wasn't fooled. "I don't think cultural education is what you're proposing."

"I'm letting you make the rules, Elizabeth. I'm just blindly following them."

"I still don't trust you."

"But you trust me enough to go to the auction on Thursday?"

"New York is not a week in Canada. I was thinking New York was a day trip. A short day trip."

Seventeen days was bad enough to try to hold on to her virginity, but throwing an overnight trip in the mix? Currently, Elizabeth was deeply steeped in denial, but there was denial and then there was stupid.

"Come with me to Canada. I'll get a plane next weekend, we'll fly. I can show you how good a pilot I am," he said, listening to her objections, and then completely ignoring them.

"Do you fly like you drive?" she asked, not that she didn't trust him in a plane, but he was probably one of those pilots that went upside down and in circles, and then zoomed low to the ground, leaving the passengers' throats somewhere back in Cincinnati.

He grinned at her. "Even better."

Elizabeth held up her hands. "Lord, no."

"All right. We take the Sterling jet."

The word *yes* was sitting on her tongue, waiting to be free, and she searched her mind for something, anything, to keep that word from slipping out. "I have a concert and then I should be getting back to work." It was a poor excuse, not even a logical one, but hopefully he wouldn't notice.

"Where?"

"Here."

"When?" he asked.

"Wednesday."

"This Wednesday? Can I come?"

Elizabeth wasn't sure she wanted him in the audience. Singing for her fans was one thing, easy, natural as breathing. Singing in front of him was like pulling back a piece of her soul and letting him take a hard look. Still, when it came down to it, she was a performer. Maybe the performance would be a little more difficult, but she could handle it. Elizabeth was tough. She shrugged casually, her toes digging into the old rug a little deeper. "It's a public venue. You're a C & W fan?"

"It's growing on me."

"I'll get you tickets."

"I'd like that. Come to dinner with me tomorrow night and I'll tell you about Vancouver. I'll try and change your mind."

"I have rehearsal," she told him, knowing how easily her mind could be changed.

"After rehearsal," he corrected.

"Sometimes it goes late," she told him, hearing the weakness in her voice.

"Even better," he answered.

"I should go," she said. For tonight she'd passed the test. Day one, virginity still intact. Day two, all bets were off.

"I'll see you tomorrow?"

Elizabeth pretended to consider her answer before she nodded. Already she couldn't wait.

"Will you kiss me before you go?" he asked.

"That's all we're talking about—kissing?"

"Whatever you want," he said with an indulgent smile.

"One kiss," she said primly, as much a reminder for her as well as him.

"Come over here," he said, his smile the very picture of temptation.

"At the door, thank you kindly," said Elizabeth, rubbing damp palms on her jeans and walking to the door.

He followed her there, moving with the same natural, masculine grace that he used when he danced, when he drove, when he kissed….

Sweet mercy.

Her heart bumped twice in her chest, and he crooked a long finger under her chin. For a second he stared, simply stared, and she got lost in that deep, dark gaze that kept her from running away. Then his mouth slanted over hers, her eyelids fell, and she found herself drowning once again. She was starting to adjust to this feeling, craving him like a drug.

He kissed her so easily, so gently, so heartbreakingly perfect. Carefully, her hands crept up on his shoulders, around his neck, and when she rose up on tiptoe, he deepened the kiss, forcing them even closer together, so close his heart beat urgently against her breasts and the hard ridge of his body surged insistently between her thighs.

Earlier she'd blamed everything on the bewitching nature of moonlight, but here, there was no moon or stars, merely the bewitching nature of the man himself, and Elizabeth wanted to stay. She wanted to toss her entire belief system in the garbage and sell her soul for one night in his arms. Maybe two.

She could feel his chest empty and expand as he breathed against her, and her hands curled around the security of his broad chest, careful of his shoulder, but she wanted to touch him. She needed him to hold her, to touch her, to love her.

In that one moment he could have taken her, and she suspected he knew it. But he didn't.

Damn him.

He raised his head, searched her eyes, looking so raw, so serious, so resolute.

"You kiss just as pretty as you look," Elizabeth said, putting an extra jolt in her voice, because she needed to keep things light and breezy. She was poised and ready to jump off that bridge, and it scared the fire out of her because now he was the one pulling back.

"You're the most beautiful woman in the world, but I think

you kiss even better." He took her hand, and held it over his heart. "See? That's about one hundred and fifty beats per minute from a man who faces 3.4 Gs on a daily basis."

Oh, dear God, she wanted to believe him. She wanted to think this wasn't a lie or a game, or some devious ploy to get her into his bed. But she knew that anything that looked too good usually was. Still, every time he touched her, she moved one inch closer to the edge. "If you're playing a game with me, I will come after you, and hunt you down like a dog."

"No games, Elizabeth."

This time she searched his face, and when she believed him, her lips curved in a weak smile. She kissed him again. Soft and tender, because she wanted to hope. "Good."

He opened the door, and immediately Elizabeth was blinded by the bright flash of a camera. She blinked, and took a step back into Demetri. He wasn't stupid enough to look as though he was touching her, but she could feel his hand at her back. Warm, strong, comforting. At the moment, she desperately needed that hand.

The reporter was a young man, probably no more than twenty, with wire spectacles that made him seem harmless. Of course, grizzly bears were pretty, too, until you got stuck in their teeth. "Miss Innis? Hunter Lyons, *Starstruck* magazine. Do you want to make a statement for our readers?"

Elizabeth took a long breath and stepped away from Demetri. Far, far away. "Not one you can print, mister."

Demetri put himself between Elizabeth and the reporter. "Leave the lady alone."

"Do you have a statement for our readers, Mr. Lucas?"

"Mine would be worse than Elizabeth's," he answered with a cold smile.

Elizabeth didn't wait to hear more. She ran toward the stairwell, and took the steps two at a time until she reached the safety of her suite.

Once there, she ripped off the layers of clothes, stared at her face in the mirror, knowing that in the morning papers she was going to see her face and Demetri's together. She popped some aspirin to prevent the expected headache and climbed into bed before things could get worse.

Three minutes later the phone rang.

"Are you all right?" he asked, his voice warm with concern.

"A little ticked off, but I'll be fine. I didn't want this to get out."

There was silence for a moment, and she wasn't surprised. How was he supposed to respond to that? Finally he spoke. "I told him that I had gotten you to sing some songs for my aunt in California, and it was late because of the time differences."

"Do you have an aunt in California?"

"No, but I'm not sure the readers of *Starstruck* magazine will know."

"Did he believe you?" she asked, still blindly hopeful. She didn't want the press to intrude. This thing with him, whatever it was, was too new, too fragile.

"Probably not, but it was the best I could do on short notice. Next time, I'll come up with a better cover story. Something about you being a CIA operative. I think that would play well in the media."

Elizabeth smiled, digging deeper into the covers, her toes curling, and she wished she weren't alone. "You were supposed to be a snake in the grass," she whispered, but he heard her.

"I'm just a man, Elizabeth. Nothing more." And then he hung up.

Chapter Eight

On Monday morning, the phone at Demetri's hotel room began ringing early—obscenely early. The first call was from Hugh Preston, who wasn't happy because apparently in the Internet age, pictures and rumors about Demetri and Elizabeth were already starting to fly. It took about fifteen minutes to smooth those ruffled feathers, and when Hugh hung up, not all ruffled feathers were back in place. The next call was from Thomas Preston, Hugh's son, who wasn't happy. Then Melanie Preston, who wasn't happy, either.

Eventually, Demetri got smart, and stopped answering the phone. He was about to drive out to Quest and talk to Hugh, when Oliver knocked on his hotel room door, bursting in before Demetri could stop him.

"You are the sly one, aren't you?"

"What do you mean?" asked Demetri, knowing exactly what he meant, and shutting the door behind Oliver before anyone else heard what he meant, too. Bad actions, bad consequences, bad actions, bad consequences. Yes, Demetri had done it again.

"I didn't realize what the bellman was whispering about until I heard your name, and then I thought, this must be interesting, and then they said something about the magazine reporter, last night, Elizabeth Innis..." Oliver trailed off, waiting for Demetri to fill in the blanks.

"There's nothing," said Demetri flatly, not inviting Oliver to sit down, because that would imply he wanted his teammate to stay. When Oliver didn't pick up on the hint, Demetri checked his watch. Oliver sat down on the couch.

"There was a picture, Demetri."

Yeah, Demetri knew about the picture. He'd seen it in the Louisville paper after Hugh Preston had pointed it out, in frank, graphic terms. "Two people standing in a hotel hallway. Hell, if that was all it took, we'd be an item, too."

Oliver grinned, not quite with the finesse of Demetri, but Demetri knew that Oliver would learn. "Very clever. Exceedingly clever. Why couldn't you have told me?"

"Nothing to tell."

"Was she with you last night?"

"Go to hell," answered Demetri tiredly, feeling more and more like a six-year-old. Tragically, sometimes six-year-old worked best with Oliver.

Oliver beamed. "You play this however you want, I'm only happy that you took my advice. With this, and your win over Marcusi, the timing couldn't be better. Jim said that Anton Valencia rang and left him a message early this morning. Give him a few more days and he'll be begging Sterling to take him back as a sponsor. Maybe you should take Elizabeth out for a night on the town? Something romantic, heart-tugging, that will have the press salivating for more."

With thoughts a long way from heart-tugging, more like violent heart-ripping, Demetri walked toward the door, hoping

Oliver would take the hint. He didn't want to talk about this. With Oliver, with anyone. He'd been trying very hard, working very hard not to screw this up.

When Elizabeth got a whiff of a Valencia endorsement, she wouldn't be happy. He knew that with every fiber of his being. Elizabeth was just beginning to trust him, just beginning to believe that he wasn't exactly who he was, and when Elizabeth believed that, Demetri could believe that, too.

"Leave it alone, Oliver. Please."

Oliver held up his hand. "All right. I won't say another word, but I support this relationship one hundred percent. In fact, let's go out tonight and celebrate. I met a cheeky young blonde yesterday, Sandy, and I'm positive her friends will be equally as friendly. I could tell them about your last photo shoot for the Valencia commercial in Brazil. Women eat that up. Sand, surf, beautiful blondes. This is why I became a Formula Gold driver. What a life..." Oliver ended on a wistful sigh.

"I'm not going anywhere tonight."

"Plans? Hopefully?"

Demetri stood stone-faced and silent.

Oliver, finally taking the hint, stood, but felt the need to tease Demetri anyway, because he was that way. "Taking one for the good of the team, aye? I think I'll ask Sandy if she'll bring a friend anyway. You won't show, and I'll have to console them both."

He would have kept on, but Demetri closed the door behind him. It'd be another two minutes before Oliver noticed he was talking to air.

Not long after, Demetri grabbed a cup of coffee from the lobby and was out of the hotel and driving to Quest.

He had debated about calling Elizabeth, but what was he supposed to say? And she'd find out soon enough, when her PR people called, or her agent called, or her manager called, or Melanie called, and Demetri felt it would be much more beneficial if that news came from someone other than himself.

Deep in his heart, he was a coward, and he freely admitted it, but today he was going to be a little braver. It was a short half hour later when he got to the stables, and found Hugh standing outside the practice track, watching Marcus work out with the gray.

He jammed his hands in his jacket pocket, noticing the wind was picking up.

Hugh saw Demetri, and frowned. Ignoring the frown, Demetri joined him at the fence.

"I didn't expect to see you."

"I know," answered Demetri. "But look, here I am."

"You gave me your word."

"I couldn't stay away from her, Hugh. It's not possible."

"Why not? She's not your type."

"No. She's perfect."

Hugh looked at him once, twice. "What's going on, Demetri?"

It wasn't a conversation that Demetri wanted to have with Hugh. He'd never talked about feelings or emotions. On most days, he didn't have feelings or emotions, because they were invariably bad, but this was different. Elizabeth was different. His feelings for her were different. "I don't know," he answered carefully. "But I respect her, and I'm treating her well, and I wouldn't do anything to hurt her, or her career."

"And when you leave Kentucky and take off for Canada?"

Canada. With Seattle less than an hour away. Seeing his father again. Now that was a mood killer. The only thought that kept him sane was the idea that Elizabeth would be there with him as a safety barrier. She didn't know how much he'd come to need her, and there was no way he would let her say no to this trip. Whatever her rules, whatever she wanted, all he needed was her with him.

"I've got a few days before the race," answered Demetri, as vaguely as possible, because he'd cleared his schedule. Canceled the meetings, canceled the press junket, canceled the photo shoots, all for her.

"I have always liked you, Demetri. I have always loved to watch you race, like the devil was chasing behind you, and we've always been on the same side. But you hurt Elizabeth, or ruin her career, and I will hunt you down like a dog."

"Yeah, I've already gotten that warning."

"From Melanie?"

"From Elizabeth," Demetri answered with a smile on his lips. "I know my private life isn't trustworthy and I know my track record is bad, really, really, bad, but trust me. Please."

Hugh looked him over, found something acceptable and nodded.

They watched as Marcus took the horse through a lap, stretching him to the wider side of the track when the horse wanted to run close to the rail, and holding his head until the last furlong. "The colt's looking good. Every time I see him, he's faster."

"Robbie's done a great job with him."

Robbie was Hugh's grandson, and up until now, there'd been tension between him and the family. "He trained this one?"

Hugh nodded proudly. "Yeah. That's my grandson's work."

Well, well, thought Demetri. The Prestons had overlooked Robbie's talent with horses, but it seemed that had now changed. Good for Robbie. Assuming the stables survived. "Any news on the missing computer tech?" asked Demetri, watching as Marcus finished the practice and led the colt back toward the paddock to cool down.

"Brent's going to talk to his co-workers at the registry one more time to see if they remember anything new."

None of it sounded promising. "What about the owner of Apollo's Ice? What does he say?"

"Nolan Hunter is as shocked as we are. He's insisting that someone is out to tarnish his reputation. I don't know what to think." Hugh shook his head, tongue clicking against his teeth.

The gray pranced around the paddock, starting to show off

for the audience. Hopefully he'd be able to race again soon. "Then I'm glad you took the money. Will this give you some breathing room?"

"That and the money from Elizabeth. We should stay in the black for a couple of months."

Demetri turned his head from the horse and looked at Hugh. "What money from Elizabeth?" he asked curiously, wondering why she hadn't said a word to him.

"She's donating the money from the concert to the stables."

Ahh…that explained it. She'd probably gone and black-mailed Melanie into taking it, knowing Elizabeth. His mouth curved in a rueful smile. "She's trying to help. Your family should take her more seriously."

"We take her seriously," Hugh insisted.

Demetri coughed discreetly. "I don't think she thinks so."

"After the problems a few years ago, Thomas and Jenna felt like she needed to look after her own finances.…" Hugh trailed off, his head shaking slowly from side to side.

"What problems?" asked Demetri, careful to keep his voice casual and flat.

"Her dad showed up like a brass penny, played the adoring father for a couple of years and then took off with several million dollars of her money. Jenna says he's been calling on Diane again."

Demetri thought of Elizabeth's trusting eyes, eyes that saw the world through rose-colored glasses, and his hands gripped the fence a little tighter. His mouth was a little drier, and he worked his jaw, keeping the anger carefully in check. He could cheerfully have broken her father in two. One more thing that she'd forgotten to mention.

"Don't hurt her, Demetri. I've been your friend for a long time, I respect the man you are, but if you hurt my family…"

Demetri met the old man's eyes and nodded. There weren't many people that Demetri would discuss Elizabeth with, but

Hugh was one. He owed the older man that. "She's different, Hugh. How did you feel when you looked at Maggie?"

Hugh smiled, his eyes lighting up with the memory. "Everything made sense. She looked at me, and I knew I was home. The rest of the world didn't matter."

Demetri understood that part. He'd never met a woman like Elizabeth Innis, and he didn't think he would ever meet another one like her again. There was no woman whose company he needed, whose approval he craved. But one thing in his life hadn't disappeared. "And the thrills? The need to take the next corner faster, the next horse harder, the next mountain higher?"

After seeing Elizabeth's gray face at the race, Demetri knew there were going to be problems, but he couldn't change those things about himself. Deep down, he was worried that a foolish thrill seeker was all that he was.

"I'm not like you, Demetri. I take risks, but they're calculated. I always ask myself, what am I willing to lose? I'm not sure losing even enters the equation for you."

Demetri considered the words. "I want my chance. That's all."

The old man nodded, looked at him evenly. "One chance. Don't blow it."

There was a surprise guest at Elizabeth's rehearsal. Her momma. When Elizabeth spied her sitting in the back, her hair fixed nicely, wearing her Sunday dress, she didn't want to jump to conclusions. She didn't want to think that her mother was going to meet Ray, but there were so few things that Diane Innis worked hard for. That no-account bastard Ray was pretty much it. So, deciding that it was better to get the doubts out of the way, Elizabeth propped her guitar at the edge of the small stage, told the band to take a break and put on her best, sweetest smile with an extra kick in her step.

"Momma, look at you!" Elizabeth pulled her up and hugged her, not happy to see that her mom wasn't looking her in the eyes. Still, that didn't mean a thing. Elizabeth was going to think positive thoughts. "You came from Aunt Jenna's to Louisville to go shopping, or just to hear your daughter sing?"

And still, Diane Innis didn't even meet her eyes. No, Elizabeth, don't be thinking those things....

"I thought I'd hear you sing since I was going to miss the concert."

And wasn't that sweet? Dressing up so nicely to come to a rehearsal in some rinky-dink saloon. Her mother looked up—finally—her eyes so pretty with mascara, eyeliner, and wasn't that a touch of gold shadow? Daddy's favorite.

So many evil, vile things roared through Elizabeth's brain, and she hated that her father made her this distrustful of her own mother.

"I saw the paper, Elizabeth. Is there something you'd like to tell me?"

"Lord, why do you believe all those papers?"

"Jenna told me about the two of you at the party."

"I danced with him, once."

"I know, but he's…he's a little fast, don't you think? All that bad business with that married royal woman. Are you sure this is good for your image, sweetheart?"

No, he wasn't good for her image. She'd already heard that once today from Melanie. Melanie was right. Elizabeth had shrugged it off.

"Are you going to lecture me on my foolhardy nature, Mother?" she asked, and saw her mother flinch, which made Elizabeth flinch herself, because being a bitch wasn't something that came easy to her.

She didn't want to argue. She wanted everything to be perfect, she wanted to think that the world would ignore her moments with Demetri Lucas, she wanted to think that this wasn't some wild-hair fling, and she didn't want to think about what would happen after he moved on to faster, more exciting women.

In other words, she was as man-stupid as her momma.

She gave her mother a sorrowful look. "I'm sorry. Can I get you something to drink? A glass of soda or a little touch of wine maybe?" She pounded her hand on the bar with a lot more force than necessary. "Joe! Let's have something to drink? What would you like, Momma?"

"A glass of water is all I need," Diane answered, a tiny bead of sweat forming on her temple. "Isn't it hot in here? I don't know how y'all do it."

Elizabeth kept the smile on her face. "There's a front coming. I think the wind's blowing from the north now. Can't you feel all that cold air?" Joe plunked the water down on the counter, and Elizabeth looked at him, her smile a little more genuine.

"Why don't you have something to drink, too?" her mother suggested. "Bless your heart, you must be parched."

"Joe, pour me a whiskey, would you?" she asked, and he looked at her in surprise. Elizabeth didn't usually drink the hard stuff. It had something to do with all those rehab stories they kept printing about her in the tabloids. She took the glass in firm fingers, then downed it, feeling the burn deep in her gut. Better one-hundred-and-one-proof alcohol than soul-selling guilt. After one long, well-worn sigh, she slammed the glass on the counter and shook it off. "Now, isn't that better?"

Diane Innis looked at her daughter as if she didn't even know her. Elizabeth grinned at her, went back to the stage and picked up her guitar once again. When all other methods of communication failed, there was music.

"This one's for you, Momma," she said, then waved the band back to work. Elizabeth picked out a chord, G major, some gold-dusted love song that wasn't worth the two-ply paper it was written on. Rebecca joined in, Peter's hands moved over the keyboard like flowing water, and soon Elizabeth was singing about tomorrow's dreams and yesterday's promises. In the back of the room, her momma smiled so nice and happy, and up onstage, Elizabeth sang as if her life depended on it.

Sometimes it did.

The music always soothed her, always brought her back to that peaceful place where the world was perfect and love was happily ever after. Eventually, under her daughter's watchful gaze, Diane Innis sneaked out the back way, in her Sunday dress and her fancy gold eye shadow. Elizabeth closed her eyes and sang, because she didn't want to think, she just wanted to feel.

They played for another three hours, until Elizabeth felt a bad tickle in her throat and Rebecca kept casting meaningful glances in Peter's and Calder's direction. Elizabeth wanted to keep going, but then Demetri came in, stood so tall and broad against the back wall. Even amidst the shadows she could pick him out. Every nerve ending on her skin came alive, and all good sense seemed to abandon her.

Is that what her mother felt? Is that why Diane Innis kept panting after that no-account bastard? Elizabeth's smile turned a shade needier.

Rebecca noticed the stranger, and knowing Rebecca, probably recognized him, too. "Elizabeth?" she asked. "You want to call it a day now?"

"I could go for that," put in Peter, lifting his fingers from the keys with a grand flourish.

"Yeah,' answered Elizabeth, dusting her hands on her slacks. It seemed there were some restless urges that her music couldn't soothe.

She puttered around onstage, stalling as long as she could, and in the back of the room he waited for her. He didn't approach, didn't make a move in her direction. Eventually she knew she couldn't stall any longer, especially since Rebecca was using hand gestures to indicate things that Elizabeth didn't want to think about.

His gaze drifted over her, so tantalizingly warm. "Ready for dinner?"

Once again, she pasted a smile on her face, and pushed the hair back from her eyes. "I'm not very hungry."

"If you'd rather go to the hotel alone, I'll understand."

"You saw the paper, too?"

"It was brought to my attention," he said, with half a smile, which was still enough to make her heart speed to syncopated double time. "Are you all right?" he asked.

"No," she said, not a good enough pretender to hide the bitterness in her voice.

He tilted her chin, with long fingers, so strong and gentle. So tempting. "Is it the press?"

"No, family problems."

"Your father?" he asked, his eyes narrowed, and she looked at him carefully. He knew. Darn.

"Somebody talked?" she said, thinking she'd find out and make them hurt.

"Your family cares about you, Elizabeth."

"It's no business of yours," she muttered, because she didn't like the whole ugly mess that made her look like a gullible fool.

"I care, too, Elizabeth."

She wanted to believe that, and so she looked at him once, then twice, and wished she weren't about to replicate the mistakes of her mother. Finally, she sighed, thanking the good Lord that Demetri Lucas didn't care about gold eye shadow, and had enough money that he wouldn't be stealing from her anytime soon. He was after something more valuable.

"Let's find someplace where nobody knows who I am," she said, tired of the mental arguing. Those were battles that she didn't want to win anymore. She wanted to lose. Big, bad, burning up in a ball of fire.

"Are you sure that place exists?" he said.

She grinned up at him, getting a little more reckless. Yep. And I know just where it is."

Demetri waited while she and the rest of her band went to the back. It didn't matter if she suggested going to Mars, he would be fine with it. Something had happened today, and he only wanted the smile back on her face, and the sparkle back in her eyes.

When Elizabeth returned she had removed her makeup, pulled her blond hair back in a stub of a ponytail, and looked as though she was fresh out of high school. But she was right. Nobody was going to recognize her. He offered to let her drive his car, but she declined and he didn't press the issue.

She directed him to a place on the outskirts of town, and she was quiet the whole way there, too quiet. The place was a hole-in-the-wall with a sign that read Junior's and a crooked porch that creaked when you walked on it. Before they walked through the old wooden door, she stuck a Cardinals baseball cap on his head, and for now at least, they could simply be a man and woman out for the night. Once inside, he scanned the room and smiled. It wasn't often he'd been to a place like this. In the corner was a jukebox that played nothing but country and western, and a cooler that kept bottles of beer cold the old-fashioned way, on ice. The place was nearly deserted, a few men watching *Monday Night Football* on the little television in the corner, but that was it. Good.

He folded his arms over his chest, and watched as she bought them two beers, and immediately noticed there was something different here. Elizabeth was walking with an extra uptick in the sway of her hips, and he was absolutely sure she'd never worn jeans that tight before. After she set down the beers on the edge of the table, she flicked open an extra button on her blouse, exposing an edge of something black, lacy and probably twice as deadly as the Eau Rogue turn in Belgium. Demetri swallowed hard, his promise to Hugh ringing in his ears, his promise to himself ringing in his heart.

"You play pool?" she asked, a challenge in her voice.

"Some," he answered, wondering where all this was leading. She took a cue in her hand, curled her fingers around the wood, slowly slid them up and down. Even knowing he was being led by the nose, Demetri locked his gaze onto the sensual fingers, and didn't let go.

"Wanna bet?" she asked.

"What are you betting?" he asked, his entire body eager and dying to know.

Her smile promised him everything. "Whatever you want," she whispered, and her voice promised him a whole lot more.

Ten thousand volts shot to his groin and he groaned, only because he wasn't that strong a man. Demetri smiled tightly. "You should just punch me in the shoulder. I think it'd be easier." He'd been set up. He knew it. Whatever family problems had happened earlier, Demetri was going to be the one to pay, and it was gonna hurt.

"I'm not worried," she told him, leaning low, racking the balls on the table with an expert's hand. Demetri stared straight down her shirt into the creamy white valley of death flanked only by a scrap of black silk. He wasn't sure if she was out to seduce him or kill him, but he thought either way, he'd die a happy man. He'd seen her flirty, and happy, and mad, and worried, but this one, the temptress, was new, and he was enthusiastic.

"Why aren't you worried?" he asked, a stupid question, but there wasn't a lot of blood left in his brain.

She pulled out a tube of lipstick and slicked it on lips that didn't need makeup, but he knew this wasn't cosmetic, this was for show. For him. After she tucked the tube away, she pursed her lips. "Because I'm good. Really, really good."

All remaining drops of blood in his brain disappeared.

There were women that a man could take advantage of in

circumstances like this without feeling remotely guilty. Women who'd been around the block, around the circuit, and weren't virginly intact. Elizabeth "I'm pure as the driven snow" wasn't one of them, even with a shirt gaping over two of the finest-shaped breasts in the history of America.

Damn.

As he watched, she leaned over the table in one long, slow, groin-busting move, and he wondered why they couldn't have just gone to dinner. Someplace that was civilized and stuffy. Instead of this…hell.

Painfully he adjusted his jeans, but nothing seemed to work, so he spent his time watching the blinking neon beer signs instead of that perfect heart-shaped rear. And so the endless night went on. She won game after game, only because he wasn't watching where he was shooting. He was watching her. He watched her down beer like water, outdrinking him two bottles for every one. Each time she got a little looser, a little friendlier. She'd flick open an extra button, and he'd button it back, only to have her flick again when he wasn't looking. Eventually he stopped, because he didn't dare touch her anymore. A bomb was ticking inside him, waiting to go off.

Family problems. She thought she had family problems? He was going to have a coronary and she probably wouldn't even remember in the morning to appreciate his pain. Demetri survived manfully, until she planted a wet kiss on his throat. At that juncture, he knew it was time for a heart-to-heart. He pulled her outside, and she stood in front of him, pouting, head cocked to one side, and dammit all, if he didn't just want to scrap all his high ideals and take her then and there.

But he wasn't going to.

Bad action. Bad consequences. He kept repeating the mantra in his head, ignoring the blood-stirring appeal of those very bad actions he was killing himself to avoid.

"I'm taking you back to the hotel," he said bravely.

"I think I'd like that," she replied cheerfully, curling her arms around him, as if he was a big stuffed teddy bear, safe and comfortable.

"You're going to bed," he continued in that same nononsense voice.

"I'd like that, too," she purred, flicking her tongue in his ear.

"Alone," he said, not nearly so bravely.

She pulled back and frowned, slicked red lips pursed oh-so provocatively. "I thought you'd take advantage of me."

This time, he put her away from him. Ten steps away from him, where he wouldn't stare down her shirt, where her mouth didn't seem quite so…liquid, and where he couldn't smell her scent. "No, sweetheart. It's not going to be that easy. Your decision, not mine."

She swung against one of the wooden posts, grinning like a fool. "All right. I'll decide. You take advantage of me."

They were words he'd longed to hear, but not quite in this context. "Not when you've been drinking or recovering from whatever personal crisis is going on. I want you sober, aware and knowing exactly what you're doing."

"You're no fun," she said, walking off toward the car, and he watched the sway in her hips regretfully.

"You have no idea how much fun I am," he muttered, trudging after her. Married royals thought he was fun. Supermodels thought he was fun. The entire racing world thought he was fun. So why didn't he feel fun?

When he opened her car door, one hand reached out and grabbed him. "I'd like to know."

With gritted teeth, he slowly peeled her hand off his crotch. "In the car," he said, ready to push her in, if necessary. If she grabbed him again, he'd embarrass himself. She was probably too sloshed to know, but that was cold comfort.

She slid in the seat as if she belonged there, arms crossed over her chest, and that peekaboo black edge of lace kept drawing his eyes. "Fun's over."

"No, hell is over," he muttered, slamming his door with extra force.

Her head tilted back against the headrest, her expression all wanton innocence, and the biggest temptation of his life. She caught him looking at her and smiled. Slow, sly and still managing to look like the girl next door. How the hell had she managed that?

He started the engine, pumping the gas. Furiously, Demetri ground through four gears, and they hadn't made it past the drive. If Michael Rossi, Sterling's chief engineer, could have seen him, he would have shot him on sight, but Demetri needed something in his hands, and right now, a gearshift was all he had. The car rocketed into the night, tires squealing. Next to him, Elizabeth's eyes drifted closed.

"You can't take me back to the hotel. The reporters are camped out like vultures. Besides—" her lips curled in a peaceful smile "—I've been drinking. I'm drunk."

Demetri swore quietly and colorfully. "Do you want me to take you to the Prestons'?"

"Heck, no. My mother would never let me hear the end of it, and Uncle Hugh would pull out his rifle and shoot you on sight. There's a motel off the highway up here. Andrew told me all the kids went there after prom."

Demetri didn't want to take her to some no-name motel with dirty sheets and walls like cardboard. And what if the room didn't have heat? He'd have to keep her warm. He'd have to hold her close, all night, wrapped around her…. "There's got to be somewhere else," he said, desperation in his voice.

She lifted her head, and grinned at him with all the confidence of Circe. "Nope. The press has been out for blood. We'll have to hide out if my career is going to stay intact."

"In case you're thinking otherwise, everything is staying intact tonight."

"You don't think I can change your mind?" she whispered, rolling down her window, pulling the ponytail loose. The cold wind blew through her hair, and he wondered where her thoughts were, because they weren't here.

"You can't change my mind," he stated, and it was only the distraction in her face and the misery in her eyes that gave him the strength to resist.

"You going to let me try?" she whispered, her head once again resting against the seat. She was almost asleep.

"No."

"Why not? I thought you wanted me." Her eyes never opened, and he heard the sadness in her voice. Demetri chose not to answer. Sometime soon she'd know how badly he wanted her, and he would probably scare the hell out of her, but tonight wasn't going to be it.

Elizabeth awoke to a splitting headache and scratchy sheets. Good Lord, it was like being poor again. She opened one eye, noticed the world spinning and then saw the man leaning back in a weather-beaten chair propped on two legs. His fitted shirt stretched tight across his chest, his bulky arms were crossed in front of him, and he didn't look happy.

Demetri.

"Where am I?" she asked, blinking at the unfamiliar surroundings.

"Hopefully on the road to three years of complete sobriety. I don't think I can survive if you drink again."

She looked down, noticed that she was still dressed in her shirt and jeans, and he was still wearing the same clothes from yesterday, complete with the baseball cap. So how come she felt like navel lint and he looked good enough to eat? Sometimes there was no justice in the world.

Slowly she sat up, and then promptly groaned.

"There's aspirin and a glass of water next to the bed," he said, his voice full of that smug know-it-all, I-didn't-have-too-much-to-drink tone.

She wasn't sure if he'd stayed up all night or not, but he didn't look tired. Instead he looked so impervious, so unaffected. She wanted to pull him down and kiss him senseless, and he was sitting there, balanced on two spindly chair legs as if he had all the time in the world.

She stole a look at the pillow, saw there was only one imprint of a head. "You didn't sleep here, did you?"

He raised one arrogant brow, still talking in that same smug voice. "In bed with you? No." She didn't like that voice. She wanted his other voice back. The sexy one that tickled up and down her spine like a feather duster.

Elizabeth popped the aspirin in her mouth and watched him, trying to figure out exactly who he was, this man who hadn't slept with her. In case she remembered correctly, and she suspected she did, she had given him more chances than any man deserved.

"Why not?" *Was that her voice that sounded like a sulky kid? Yeah. It was.*

"And fail your little test? No."

This sounded interesting. She didn't know she had a test. "What test?"

"Do you know what you would have done if you woke up in my arms this morning?"

Elizabeth closed her eyes, the visual too tempting to resist. She wouldn't have cared about the headache, or the scratchy sheets or the rattling heater. She knew exactly what she would have done if she'd woken up in his arms this morning. Eventually she opened her eyes with a long, disappointed sigh. "What would I have done?"

"I think we would have made love another time. Or two. Then you would have told me you had to go back to work, and that you'd be in touch. But you wouldn't. You'd always be too busy, and I'd be that snake in the grass that you want me to be. I won't be that guy. Not with you."

Why did he have to be like this? Last night, why couldn't he have slept with her like any other red-blooded man in America would have done? He should have given her the chance to nip at the apple without worrying about the consequences. She'd never been tempted before, not with this soul-stealing need. Last night, she had given it everything she had, and he turned her down.

Darn it, he was going to make this hard. He wanted her to know exactly what she was doing, eyes wide-open. She growled, low in her throat, threw back the covers, and came to stand in front of him. "I'm sober now. Wide-awake. No one will ever know."

"Is that what you want?" he asked, completely casual, not moving even an inch in her direction.

"Yes," she said, but her voice quaked a little more than it should have.

He noticed. Of course. "What are you afraid of?"

She curled her arms over her stomach, saw the trampy edge of the black lace bra peeking out and promptly uncurled her arms, so her brain wouldn't scream "slut." "I'm not afraid of anything. I want a man to respect me, to love me before I make love with him. What's wrong with that?"

He shook his head, his eyes never leaving hers. "Nothing."

"I think you respect me, but you don't love me," she told him, then waited carefully, listening for a protest from him, some words to tell her that she was wrong.

"How do you know?" he asked, which was a far cry from "you're wrong."

"We've known each other a little over a week. I admit, I'm powerfully attracted to you, but love? No. That takes time, and gentleness, and patience."

The chair legs came down on the tile with a resounding thump. Demetri laughed at her, harsh and mocking. "You don't want a man, you want a golden retriever."

That hurt. She knew there were people who didn't think the same way she did, but she let them be. Everybody had to find their own way, and he didn't need to laugh about it. "That shouldn't be funny. What do you want from me? You're not happy that I'm saving myself for someone special. You're not happy that I tell you to take me to bed."

He looked up at the ceiling, he looked down at the floor, he stared at the walls. In fact, his eyes looked everywhere except at her. Finally he seemed to wise up to the fact that she was waiting. "I'm sorry. I know this isn't easy for you. It sure as hell isn't easy for me. I double- and triple-check everything I do around you because I will not screw this up. I will not screw this up. And that's coming from a man who has crashed a multi-million-dollar race car so many times that the insurance companies are waiting for me to die. I'm not good at trying to explain things, and I'm not sure I can even start, but I want you so much that it hurts. I've got a bad shoulder that is nothing in comparison to the ache in my gut. There's a hiss in my lungs when I touch you, and I have the same dreams night after night, when I roll over, and you're there, and I slide inside you, and I think I'm going to die. Elizabeth, I would love to make love to you, but not when you're standing there like Joan of Arc, ready to burn yourself at the stake. If there is one small chance that somewhere in that beautiful head of yours you're going to regret this, then we wait. I wait—and hope to hell that the cold water doesn't run out."

When he spoke, his eyes flashed with something that a more foolish woman would call vulnerability.

Oh, heavens. Elizabeth rubbed suddenly damp palms on her jeans.

She was going to remember this, remember each word, each syllable, the husky shudder in his voice, and most of all, the urgent staccato in her heart.

He rose, towering over her, and she thought about touching him, but he looked at her, his eyes flashing dark and dangerous for a moment. "Don't."

Okay, bad plan.

"Get your purse," he told her. "I'll take you back to your car, and you can drive to the hotel alone."

Elizabeth nodded, and followed him out to the car. When she got back to the hotel, the first thing she was going to do was take a shower. Hopefully the cold water wouldn't run out for her, either.

Chapter Nine

She was going to see him at rehearsal again. Her heart really shouldn't have sung so loudly when he told her, but it did. In return, she promised that she'd stay off the sauce.

"If you want to talk about your father…" he started.

"No," she answered, because today was a new day, and on this new day, Demetri's integrity had hitched up another notch—not because she was being love struck or foolish, but because he'd earned it.

Rehearsal was good, but not good enough. Elizabeth felt rough and raw, and her voice reflected it. They had gone through three sets, and when it came time for her to do her new song, Elizabeth called a halt, her stomach getting nervy again. She didn't want to sing those words. They were too close to what she was feeling.

Behind the small stage, Rebecca was all questions and purposeful looks. "That was him yesterday, wasn't it? I knew it. Calder said he didn't think so, but I told him he needed to get glasses. Lord, Bethy, I think you should do that man for all the women of America. It's your patriotic duty."

Elizabeth blushed, because she'd thought about doing him pretty much 24-7 for the past ten days, but patriotism didn't even enter the picture. "Rebecca, we've been friends for a long time. I have listened to each and every one of your man troubles without saying an unkindly word, but I'm a more private person than you are—"

"You big faker. Is that why you told *Vogue* magazine that you were saving yourself for the right man? Or that the Louisville papers knew about your torrid affair before I did?"

"It is not torrid," snapped Elizabeth.

Rebecca seized on the tiny scraps of information. "So you're not denying there's an affair?"

Right then, Calder ambled up, saving her from Rebecca's relentless, and possibly truth-getting, interrogation. "You got a visitor, Elizabeth. Does that mean we're done for the day?"

Elizabeth's conscience told her that she shouldn't quit rehearsal. They had a concert tomorrow, but on the other hand, she had a hot man cooling his heels for her. It was no contest. "Be at the hall at five tomorrow. Tobey's flying in from L.A. Peter, he said he brought you that Disneyland T-shirt you wanted."

Rebecca shot her a wicked look. "Don't think we won't be looking closely tomorrow."

Elizabeth felt the fire in her cheeks, which hopefully matched the fire in her eyes. "Go home. Go harass some other person."

After they had left her behind, Elizabeth tossed cold water on her cheeks, and then went out to find Demetri. Sure enough, as soon as she saw him, her heart stuttered for a moment. Long enough for her breathing to stop, too. Dressed in black jeans and a white no-collar shirt that was stark against his tan, he looked foreign and exotic against the comfortable, old wood of the bar. Demetri Lucas was a chameleon. She'd seen him in shorts and T-shirt, business suit and tie, and an eye-popping, knee-dipping Italian-tailored tux, and each time it looked right on him, no matter the surroundings.

Quickly Elizabeth shook her head, pulling oxygen back into her lungs, and walked over. Today she even dared to put a hand on his arm. Nothing overt or overly affectionate, but only because she needed to touch him.

"You're here earlier than I thought."

He looked at her hand, his eyes curious. "I'm going to look at a couple of horses at White Creek Stables, about a half-hour drive from here. I thought you might want to go. I could show you a few things to look for when you're buying your horse."

"We still need to buy horses, huh? You talked to Thomas, or Uncle Hugh?"

"Well, since you're donating money from your concert…" he said, with *heavy* emphasis. Heavy, heavy emphasis.

"You're miffed I didn't tell you?"

"You could have told me," he answered, looking well and truly miffed.

"Like you could have told me about the bet with Hugh?" she chided, with a hard look. He had the good sense to look ashamed.

"Lesson learned."

"Thank you. It means a lot." And it did. People didn't want to trust Elizabeth with heavy-duty business things, possibly because she wore sequined vests and heels, which didn't lend themselves to heavy-duty business conversations, but she wanted Demetri to trust her with heavy-duty business things. This was her family. "They haven't learned anything more about Leopold's Legacy's sire?"

"No. Brent's still trying to track down some leads, and in the interim, the cash from my race and your concert will give them a couple of months' worth of breathing room. They need the fees from stabling horses to keep them on life support, and thus, the horse buying." He paused. "So, you're still ready to buy a horse?"

"I sure am. Do you know somebody that I can put the horse's name in? I thought about my manager, Tobey Keller, but nobody would ever believe it. He's very L.A. Not horsey at all. And there's Frank, at Five Star. He'd do it, what with Magnum Records sniffing around after that last album, but I don't trust Frank. He's just out to milk me for what he can get, you know?"

"Oliver's going to do it."

"Oliver?"

Demetri nodded. "He likes you. And he'd do it for you. And me."

"I can do this, right?" she asked, because this reeked of impulsive spontaneity that involved loads of cash, and for all her big talk, when it came down to action, she wasn't so quick on the draw. Yeah, here she was, seriously about to buy some racehorses. *Racehorses*. Quickly she gulped, swallowing some air.

"Yeah, you can do this. You'll be great." He looked so serious, so completely respectful, that it was enough to make a foolish woman cry, but Elizabeth had no inclination for tears. Today she smiled. Life got better if you waited. It always did.

Demetri wasn't usually a pious man, not even close by anybody's standards, but sometimes thoughts of God arbitrarily popped into his head. When he won a race and could walk away in one piece. When he was eight years old and a bright red go-kart with a five-horsepower Briggs & Stratton engine was sitting under the Christmas tree. And then there was today, when he saw that Elizabeth had chosen to adequately cover all those creamy, curvy parts of her that he was trying desperately not to touch—at least not until she was ready. Divine intervention was about the only thing that could help. Today was supposed to be all business, or mostly business, or at least business at the beginning. That was his plan, assuming she didn't mess with his plan, which seemed to happen a lot.

White Creek Stables was west of Lexington, right in the

heart of America's horse country. It was a large operation, not as big as Quest, but with a solid reputation for good stock. Demetri wasn't looking to buy a horse today, unless he saw something nice, but he wanted Elizabeth to know what she was getting into. All during the drive, Demetri explained about the balance, bone, intelligence and athleticism. Elizabeth listened carefully, asking smart questions, really smart questions. There was a lot going on in that beautiful blond head of hers, and she kept most of it from the world.

When she drew him into an argument on whether the length of the hindquarters indicated whether the horse was a good sprinter or a good router, Demetri knew it was no lucky break that she had been so successful at what she did. If Elizabeth Innis had chosen another profession—any profession, he suspected—she'd be just as much a winner.

The owner of White Creek was Morgan Tolliver, a barrel-shaped man with an eye for both beautiful horses and beautiful ladies. After he talked with Elizabeth for a few minutes, he got that look that Demetri was starting to recognize. First came the purely aesthetic appreciation. But then, eight minutes later—Demetri had clocked it—the stars appeared. Elizabeth knew exactly when to flatter, exactly when to listen, exactly when to stare up at a man as if he were the only one alive. Every man with a working heart, a working brain and a working piece between his legs ate it up, and it wasn't an act or pretended with her. It was only who she was. If Morgan had been forty, instead of sixty-eight, Demetri might have worried, but as it was, hey, he could afford to be generous.

After a little while, Morgan took them to the paddock where a prime two-year-old was being prepped for his next race, and waited for Elizabeth to look him over. "So if I see that his hooves aren't aligning in a straight line as he runs, I need to pass on him?" she asked, carefully studying the colt's long-legged gait.

Morgan beamed at his new star pupil. "That's right, Miss Innis, straight and center, that's what you want."

"I'd feel better if you call me Elizabeth."

"Only if you call me Morgan," he said. "So you're getting into horses?"

"I'm exploring my options," answered Elizabeth vaguely.

"You have to be careful where you stable them. I know Demetri's loyal to Quest and all, but there's trouble there," began Morgan, not realizing the minefield he had just walked on.

Before Demetri could argue, Elizabeth stepped in. "I'm only exploring options, Morgan," she said, her words friendly, her eyes not so much.

"Just remember, here at White Creek, all our horses are legitimate."

"I'm sure they are," said Elizabeth, and Demetri hid his smile. He was about to interrupt before blood was drawn, when his cell rang. He looked down, saw it was Jim calling, and he sighed.

"I need to take this. Excuse me," he said to them both. To Elizabeth he whispered, "Don't break his heart."

Jim didn't have much to say. "You haven't been answering your phone."

"Don't feel like talking," answered Demetri easily.

"I saw the papers yesterday," Jim started, but Demetri cut him off, because he knew where this was headed.

"Listen, I'm breaking up here. I'll talk to you next week." Demetri snapped the phone shut.

Elizabeth was looking in his direction and he lifted a hand. She had pondered how his reputation would affect hers, but she didn't appreciate how much her reputation would affect his— all for the positive, and in Valencia's eyes, all for monetary gain. She wouldn't think about that, and he hated that people—some of them his friends—looked at her and saw dollar signs.

No, for the first time in his life, Demetri was going to be careful. Very, very careful, because Elizabeth was worth it.

* * *

He'd been quiet on the drive back, probably too quiet, because she started asking questions.

"Something wrong?"

"No, just business."

"Oh. I know. Sometimes business makes me cranky, too. Especially when Frank gets some wild-hair idea. They wanted me to tour with a rock band. Said I needed a crossover audience. I don't need a crossover audience. Do you think I need a crossover audience?"

He looked at her, breaking into a smile. "No. You're perfect like you are. You know that, don't you? You know I think you're perfect."

"Lord, all those pretty words. You do a woman good. I'm liking this horse thing, getting the urge to shop. We're all ready to go with Oliver?"

"Yeah, the lawyers are drawing up the papers. They should be ready before the weekend's done."

"Well, howdy, partner. I guess we're buying a horse."

"We?"

"Well, me, but you'll be my advisor."

That gave him an idea. An easy way to explain why she'd been seen in his company, a way that might tamp down some of the rumors, and preserve her reputation. "You know, we could say to the press that we have a business relationship." Maybe then Jim, Oliver and Valencia Products would cool their jets a bit, until all the hype died down.

Elizabeth looked at him and shook her head. "And have my family figure out why Quest Stables is suddenly drowning in horses? I think that's a big no, Demetri. It's sweet of you to want to protect my crystal-clean reputation, but I don't need it."

"But if we said something publicly, something that made sense, everybody would back off. I don't like having rumors flying around."

"Don't be worried. I'm a big girl, I can take it. And speaking of that, big girls need to be fed. What's the dinner plan?"

"You want to go out in public?" he asked, not wanting everything he said recorded, his every look photographed, especially now when he knew his face gave way too much away.

"Well, I thought about it," she said, "but we don't have to. Is your shoulder bothering you?"

His shoulder. That sounded like a good answer. Demetri nodded. "I'm sorry about that."

She sat, looked at him and waited.

"What?" he asked.

"You're not even going to invite me up for room service?"

Oh, no. He couldn't do that again. Today had been easy. There'd been people around, and she looked so...virginal. But in a hotel room? For hours? With no one around? What did she think he was made of?

"After our last experience, I don't know that that would be a good idea, either."

Her eyes narrowed. "Demetri Lucas, are you dumping me?"

"God, no!" he managed, wondering where that came from. "I don't want your image to get trashed, that's all."

Sadly, she wasn't buying any of this. "Why the sudden worries for me? I was the paranoid one, but now you're getting all hinky."

Hinky was the polite word for it. He stayed silent until he realized she was waiting for him. "Sorry. Look. I'll get the hotel to keep the floors clear and I'll come to your room for dinner. We don't have to go anywhere, and hopefully that might keep the press at bay, at least for a night."

Hopefully she could keep him at bay, too. One night at a time.

How hard could that be? Demetri looked down at his lap. Sadly, hard didn't even come close.

They ended up having dinner in Demetri's hotel suite, which wasn't as cozy as it sounded, since the formal dining table seated eight. At first, Elizabeth wondered about such a large space, but after dinner, when they moved to the living area, she wondered if Demetri wasn't playing things much smarter than she.

All night he watched her, his eyes resting on her as if she was the dessert menu, but he stayed far out of range, where they weren't even within heavy-breathing distance of each other. She considered joining him on the sofa, but the tension was rolling off him like an August heat wave, and if she lit that fuse tonight, there was no turning back.

Eventually, being the coward that she was, she steered the conversation to business, a safe subject, or so she thought. "Do you think I can go up to New York with you?"

"Are you sure you want to do this?" he asked, his gaze skimming over her, leaving a nearly visible trail of shimmery tingles in its wake. "Do you know what you're getting into?"

Elizabeth had started this conversation with the intention of business talk, but that's not what he was speaking of. Her hands gripped the tiny ornate chair arms, nearly twisting them clean off. "Maybe," she answered, which was about as definitive as she was capable of at the moment, when her tongue felt four sizes too big for her mouth. She wanted to move, she really did, but her legs wouldn't do it. What was she afraid of?

Being stupid, stupid.

"I don't want you to get hurt."

"Are you intending to hurt me?"

"No."

"Then why do you think I'll get hurt?" she asked, which seemed a perfectly logical question to ask.

Unfortunately he didn't seem to agree, because he sat there, silent and mysterious, and here she was, one footfall away from giving it all up, and silent and mysterious didn't bode well.

"Why?" she demanded, a little more urgently this time, wondering what bit of something he was holding back.

"I worry," he told her.

"There you go, worrying again."

"I've done things…" he started, and then closed off, the dark fringe of his lashes hiding his eyes from her.

"Are we talking about the princess here?" she asked, because she was way beyond the princess now. That was past history, and every instinct inside her said to trust him, but sometimes instincts could be wrong.

"No," he answered, leaning forward, pressing his hands together.

"What are we talking about?"

He looked at her, his gaze tracing over her face, and the worry disappeared, as if it'd never been. "Nothing. Forget I said anything."

"I thought you said you were going to trust me with things. I'm asking you to trust me with things now."

The worry returned in full force, and now he wasn't the only one that was worried. Elizabeth was getting concerned, as well. "When we're together, when we're seen together, in public, there are people who will want to cash in on it."

"You're worried about somebody selling some pictures?" she asked, not sure where this was all leading.

Demetri sighed, and then looked her square on. "My people are going to try and capitalize on this relationship."

And then she realized what he was so worried about. *Her.* There was a momentary squeeze in her pulmonary region, because she liked—correction, loved—that he was worried about her reputation. But this did put a new spin on things. He was right to worry. In the whirlwind of the last few days, she hadn't been as clear-sighted as she normally was.

"Are they going to make me out to be some trampy, exotic femme fatale like some of the other women in your past?"

"No, they like your reputation just the way it is."

"Nobody in this world thinks I can be trampy and exotic, do

they?" she asked, peevishly disappointed, because as a woman, she was never satisfied with the status quo, no matter how successful the status quo might be.

Demetri smiled at her. "If they saw you in that black bra, they'd change their mind—real fast."

"Thank you for that," she said, with a sincere nod. "So tell me what to expect."

"Things in the paper. Planted items, a few pictures here and there."

"That sounds like the easy part—all in a day's work. But I'm betting there's a hard part, too. Tell me something, Demetri. What are we doing here?" She could overlook a lot if she knew where his heart was, but hot-handed playboys weren't so quick to expose their heart, or even acknowledge its existence.

He met her eyes, didn't flinch. "I don't know."

Not a yes, not a no, and she wished he could make it easier, but no, he wanted to be honest about things, which on most days, she would applaud, but Lord… "That's not very encouraging."

He managed a smile, a weak one, but it worked its way up to his eyes, and she felt some of her doubts fall away.

"I'm trying to be fair," he told her. "I've never done this, been like this. I don't know what the hell to do."

He pulled his hand through his hair, and looked so out of sorts, so lost that she smiled. This was hard for her, hard for him, trying to figure out the rules and the boundaries when there really weren't any. She didn't date fast men, and he sure as heck didn't cool his heels with slow women. So, this was what they were left with.

"What are you thinking you're going to do?" she asked, wanting to make a joke, but it wasn't a joke. There was nothing funny about the dark thud of her heart, and the deep ache inside her. He did that, made her ache so hard that it was nearly killing her.

"I don't know. I've been trying to seduce you for eleven

days, eight hours and forty-seven minutes, but you're still idling on the grid."

"You had your chance yesterday," she said quietly.

"I'm not interested in a martyr, only a woman."

"Sorry," she said, feeling more and more womanly, and less and less martyr-ly by the minute.

"Do you do this on purpose?"

"What?"

"Put every man through hell. Is this payback for your father?" His words snapped at her, hurting her more than she thought he could. "I'm sorry. I'm tense. So did you see any horses you liked this afternoon?" he asked, neatly letting her off the hook—for now.

The moment passed and she gratefully managed a nervous smile. "A few, and the sooner the better. Melanie said they were tracking down some computer guy, and that maybe he was in New York."

"Dead end," he answered.

"How do you know?"

"I called Hugh this afternoon."

Elizabeth rolled her eyes. "This is my family, but do they tell me the important facts in the case? No. Little Elizabeth. She's a bubblehead."

His mouth quirked up on one side. "If I may make a comment, and you might take this as criticism, but you do foster the stereotype."

"I do not," she protested, because he had no idea what it was like being a woman. A woman had to be smart, and sly, and use whatever she could to make it in this world.

"Don't think I don't know when you're playing stupid."

"I am not playing stupid," she said, although he was probably partly right. Maybe more than partly right.

He raised his brows.

Immediately, rather than admitting her own flaws, she went

on the defensive. "That's such a bear trap. If I admit that I'm an awful person for playing to type, then I'm manipulative, but if I'm not playing to type, then I'm stupid. Which is it, Demetri? Manipulative or stupid? What do you think?"

"I'm not going to answer that question. That's another test."

"Oh, no, I think you should," she answered, starting to have fun once again. She loved teasing with him, when the pressure on her disappeared. That pressure that was always bearing down on her heart, her gut, bearing down right between her thighs.

"Nope, not going to answer that one," he said, crossing his arms across his chest.

"Oh, fine."

"Did your father get in touch with you? Is that why you're…edgy?" This time he was a bit more serious, but she didn't want to talk about her father. She wanted to sit here and flirt and stare at him.

So she grinned her good-girl smile and chatted away. "Now I'm edgy? I'm either stupid and edgy, or manipulative and edgy. And you want to take me to Vancouver because why?" she asked, kicking her bare feet up on the priceless antique coffee table.

"I love your voice, I forget my own name when I watch you walk and against all odds, you own a black lace bra," he said, his voice working that magic all over again. Her feet came off the table, her good-girl smile sliding downhill in a hurry. Every time she started to feel safe, boom, he went and started the fire once more.

"I should get some sleep. I have a concert tomorrow."

"I'm looking forward to it," he answered, and so was she, but she wasn't thinking about the concert anymore.

"I really like you. I really, really, really like you," she told him, standing to go, not wanting to go.

"Good," he said, smiling at her, as if everything was fine, as if he wasn't one step away from going up in flames. She knew otherwise. It was there in the flush in his face and the tense muscles in his arms, and she loved that he didn't think she was silly or stupid for being so nervous about making love with him. It boggled her that a man who was so reckless behind the wheel could be so wonderfully controlled for her.

"Thank you," she told him. It wasn't what he wanted from her, but the words held a lot more meaning than her innocence ever could. No man had ever treated her so well; no man respected her so well.

"What are you thanking me for?"

"For waiting."

He shrugged, as though it was nothing, and she knew what it was costing him. Then he walked her to the door and kissed her, a mere brushing of lips, and Elizabeth found herself brutally disappointed.

"I'll see you tomorrow after the concert. Maybe we can have a late dinner?" he asked.

"That could be arranged," she said, and then peeked out into the hallway, and noticed the strange man loitering in there. Quickly she shut the door. "It's the press. Either *Entertainment Weekly* or the *Enquirer,* not sure which."

"You want me to take them out?" asked Demetri.

"I know just what to do." She picked up the hotel phone and pressed a button. "Security," she said, in a low, desperate whisper, "there's a man hanging around in the hall, looking all beady eyed and suspicious. I think he's trying to break into the room across the way. Can you get somebody up here?" She smiled in triumph as she hung up the phone.

Unfortunately, *temptingly,* when she caught a good glimpse of Demetri's face, she realized that maybe waiting hadn't been a good idea.

He took one step forward, she took a step back.

Not a good idea at all.

One more step and she'd have nothing behind her but a mahogany door.

"How long do we have to wait?" he asked, moving closer. Dear heaven, she loved it when he touched her—everything turning gold and liquid inside her.

"I'm thinking five minutes. Maybe ten or fifteen if it's old Gus who is working security tonight. He's a little creaky."

In the beat of a heart, he was flat against her, those perfectly formed, strong arms holding her tight, keeping her pinned. His eyes were burning, ragged dark, nearly glowing with his need. Oh, she didn't need to see this, didn't need to feel this. She moved once, found a hard ridge pressed against her belly and whimpered. Not in fear—this was the hot flush of desire.

"This way we know when the coast is clear," he told her, and she could feel the sweat burning down her neck, trickling between her legs.

Futilely, she clutched at the solid weight of his biceps, thinking that she might get him to release her, but then her fingers got sidetracked with the bumps and ridges beneath that tight skin. Sweet mercy, that man was strong.

"What about your shoulder?" she asked, the pads of her fingers creeping under the short sleeve of his T-shirt, up and up his arm, fascinated by the corded regions.

He didn't seem to mind. He bent his head, his mouth playing leisurely with her throat. Elizabeth inclined her head, liking this game. She didn't have to worry, or make decisions. He was sweeping all her decision-making abilities away. The late-night stubble was hard and tickled against her skin, but just when she would giggle, he'd take a playful nip.

"It's fine," he told her, his mouth trailing over her throat. His hands reached between them, undoing the buttons on her blouse inch by inch. Not once did she consider telling him to stop, because she wanted to see where this was leading. She couldn't breathe, couldn't move. Eventually he discovered the lacy bra beneath.

"Virginal white tonight?"

"I thought it'd be safer," she said primly, until he bent his head and his mouth closed over her through the gossamer material. Sweet sensations passed through her, the touch of his tongue, the rough abrading of the fabric. At first he toyed with her, as her blood thickened and slowed to a painful crawl. Then the pull of that bad-boy mouth grew hard and serious. Her eyes fluttered closed, and she whispered his name like a prayer of surrender.

This was it. No turning back.

Outside in the hallway, voices grew louder, and he lifted his head.

"It's security," she whispered.

His smile turned wicked. "You're lucky that time's up," he said, then plundered her mouth in a soul-stealing kiss that destroyed the last remnants of her mind. This man could kiss, she thought in a haze. She could feel the hunger in him, the restrained power, all that testosterone charging through him like lightning. It was there in his hard-driving mouth. All that power at her fingertips was intoxicating, and she curled her fingers in his hair, kissing him right back.

The voices grew louder. Now they were just outside the door, and she kept right on kissing him, as if it was the most perfect thing in the world—because it was. His hips ground against her, once, but it was enough. Suddenly in her mind, they weren't fully clothed, pressed against a door. He was with her, lying skin to skin.

She moaned. Dangerously loud.

Elizabeth knew that she didn't want to be a virgin anymore. Not a second more.

Outside the door, the voices grew faint, softer, until they disappeared entirely. When there were no sounds except for her own heavy breathing, he drew back from her, and smiled. With sure and steady fingers, he buttoned up her blouse, as though he wasn't even flustered at all. He opened the door, looked outside. He was expecting her to leave him.

Leave him!

Still feeling the aftershocks in her nerves and her lips, she shook her head. "You like living dangerously" was all she could say, her body itching to feel him again. It was going to be one long, lonely night.

He gave her a quick, hard kiss. "So do you."

That night she made up her mind with no equivocations, no doubts and no worries. It was a decision that'd been bubbling closer and closer to the surface. As she tossed alone in her fancy-schmancy, four-poster bed with six-hundred-thread-count sheets caressing her skin, a crackling blaze popped in the fireplace. Even with all her creature comforts fulfilled, sleep was a long time coming. There was one comfort long denied. Late at night, when the midnight hours crept like molasses, she was lonely.

Her own lyrics came back to haunt her, not just a plaintive refrain, but the puckish irony of life imitating art.

Long, sleepless nights when I'm dreaming of you.
You come and see me there,
Touching me,
Kissing me
Love me.

Love me. She pulled a pillow closer, but it wasn't warm or breathing, and made a poor substitute for a man. And not just any man. Demetri Lucas.

First thing in the morning, she was going to go out and buy something silky and slinky that would slide off the skin in three seconds or less. And wouldn't the press have a field day with that? Not that she cared much about the press at the moment—Tobey's lecture notwithstanding. She didn't want to think that she was caving on her scruples or moral fiber, either, but the feelings inside her were so seductive and so powerful that she wasn't sure what was love, what was lust and what was Elizabeth making poor life choices—which seemed to run in her family.

She didn't have a lot of experience with love. Before, she'd never truly entertained the idea she might be in love because her standards for the definition were sky-high—so high that she'd begun to think she'd never touch it. She'd known him for such a short time, but he always did the right thing by her, and nobody—*nobody*—had ever done that for her before. People always put their interests first with her, always looking for what they could get out of the situation, but Demetri never had. Time after time, chance after chance, he'd put her feelings, her standards, above his own, no matter how painful, no matter how much he disagreed.

Now it was time for her to return the favor. It was time for Elizabeth Innis to put Demetri Lucas first. Silly with the idea of it, she grinned and hugged the pillow closer.

Truthfully, she didn't know how this song was going to end, happy or sad. Their lifestyles weren't conducive to the ideal that Elizabeth kept in her head, but it was better to have loved once, even unwisely, than to miss out on this storm of feelings that was whirling all around her. These past few days, she laughed when nobody was looking, grinned at the mirror because she knew there was something different in her face, and most of all, most tempting of all, she was dreaming about him there, next to her, touching her, kissing her…

…*loving her*….

Chapter Ten

Demetri had managed to avoid Oliver all morning and most of the afternoon, but eventually Oliver kept pounding at his door, and Demetri knew he couldn't ignore the world any longer. "What do you need?"

Oliver walked in, and seated himself on top of the desk, making himself completely at home. Damn. "Great news. Jim will be calling you himself, but I wanted to get ahead of him, so you don't sabotage the mission."

"What mission?" Demetri didn't have a mission. His sole reason for living at the moment was to make love to Elizabeth Innis. That was it. His mind, his body, his heart. Everything was all tied to that one single mission, and he had no intention of sabotaging it.

"Valencia Products. Elena in public relations called me—probably because she likes me, I think—to let me know that rumors of your *alleged* relationship have reached their tender ears, and contrary to having a very public affair with a married royal, having a very public affair with a young, unmarried, very marketable singer seems to make tremendous business sense. I think they have visions of finding the next Posh and Becks, although I told her that you're no Becks."

Demetri closed his eyes, and what started as a bright day had suddenly become very dark. "Why are you telling me this?"

"Valencia wants you to confirm or deny the rumors. Deny them, and they strike the whole thing up to yellow journalism. Confirm them, and we're back, proudly wearing the Valencia logo. Jim is going to call and ask you. This is it, Demetri. You said you'd deliver. I never suspected it'd come this fast."

Demetri poured a shot of bourbon. It was only four in the afternoon, but a man could never numb himself too early. The great thing about traveling over one hundred and fifty miles per hour was that you never had time to stop and think about what you did. You moved and adjusted, moved, adjusted. It was easy and reactive. Now, he was supposed to think about the consequences. Hurt Elizabeth, or hurt his team. Gee, what sweet options those were. Grimly he poured another shot and downed it. In the end, the decision was easy. "I'm not going to comment to anyone—Jim, Valencia, the press, anyone."

Oliver's sigh was long and dramatic. "No one's asking you to lie. They merely want you to tell the truth."

"It's none of anyone's business."

Oliver hopped off the desk and started to walk around the room, his hands flying as he talked. "Oh, come on, Demetri. Do you really think that when a few more media reports hit the news, it's not going to matter one whit if you've denied it? At least this way, you get to control how it comes out. Valencia isn't going to out you and the delectable Miss Innis. Better to let it unfold in the press. I think they think the secrecy is wildly romantic. Bloody stupid if you ask my opinion. So what will you say to Jim?"

Quickly Demetri downed another shot, sweet, feeling the

burn on his throat, and the hole in his gut. "It's not his business. I don't have a comment for anyone."

But Oliver wasn't done. He knew Demetri was in a losing position. Hell, Demetri knew he was in a losing position.

"Deny it then, and be happy, but it's going to come out eventually. Flying to Saratoga together. Flying to Canada together. Do you think you're going to be able to hide that?"

Demetri turned his head, stared at Oliver carefully. The crystal glass popped against the hard wood table. "How did you know?"

Oliver laughed. "People love a secret. The only thing they love more than a secret is telling someone else about the secret they know. Of course, if you're planning to sleep with Elizabeth for a few weeks, and then toss her after the season's over, well, perhaps I could understand why you wouldn't want that one to come out. Dumping Shirley Temple is even more dire than sleeping with the princess."

Demetri swore. "That's not the plan, Oliver. You know that."

"Yes, I do, and all I'm asking is that you tell Jim the same thing. He doesn't have to know the details. All he's interested in—all Anton Valencia is interested in—is knowing that you're serious about her."

"Oliver, I've worked very hard to earn her trust, and trust me, that's not easy to do. What if she thinks that I'm making money off my relationship with her? I don't want that. Valencia doesn't care about her. All they want is someone that will sell more Valencia products. I don't want her—us—to be part of some marketing package. I won't sell her out like that."

"You're not selling her out. You're a product. She's a product. Together, you make a great product. I know that's not why you're with her. Good heavens, even a blind man can see why the two of you are together, but those are the facts, and denying them isn't going to change them. Grow up, Demetri. You're in a business. All I'm asking, all Jim wants, is for you to tell the truth."

"I don't like this, Oliver." He hated it. Elizabeth was different from the other people in this business. She didn't give her name, her image to anyone. And now Valencia would want her on photo ops with him, photographers everywhere.

"For God's sake, Demetri, just tell Jim the truth. You gave me your word. You owe me this. You owe the team this. It's your fault we lost Valencia. Now fix it."

"I didn't engineer this," he protested, not that anyone was listening.

"No one's saying you did."

"It stinks of it."

"You're the only one who thinks that."

She would think that. Elizabeth would think that. "I have to go."

"Do the right thing, Demetri."

Demetri took his coat and busted out of the hotel, ignoring the two reporters that were hanging around outside, angling for comments.

Do the right thing? And what the hell was that?

The hours before a concert weren't an easy time for Elizabeth. After ten years of performing, she had certainly adjusted to the jumps in her stomach, and the extra twenty beats in her pulse, and she stayed away from anything that was rich and had too much caffeine, because that was a recipe for disaster, and with anywhere from two hundred to forty thousand people in an audience, disaster wasn't good for the career. She liked sitting in her dressing room with her old terry-cloth robe and pink fuzzy slippers, sipping on ice water and letting her mind wander.

Today she had company. Namely, her mother, in a sharp green suit and cute black pumps, a new green suede pocketbook and that lovely gold eye shadow that brought out the hazel flecks in her eyes. Elizabeth took a good hard look, felt her pulse ratchet up a couple of beats and tried not to sigh. "I thought you weren't going to come, Momma."

"I felt bad," answered her mother, taking the stuffed leather chair across from Elizabeth.

"You don't like crowds," Elizabeth reminded her, and went back to her own makeup, fluffing up her lashes with mascara.

Diane Innis sat up a little straighter. "It's your father."

"Where is he?" asked Elizabeth, moving from mascara to lipstick, puckering up for the mirror and outlining her lips in a dark maroon that would perfectly match the maroon dress that she was going to wear tonight.

"I thought you had someone to do your makeup for you."

"Only the hair. Nobody touches the face but me. Last time it happened, I went out looking like a hooker. Never again. So, where's Ray?" she repeated, determined not to be diverted, determined to keep her cool. She took the blusher and fluffed up the pink powder.

"He wanted to see your concert."

Blush fell all over her robe and her chin. Not an attractive look. With a long, rejuvenating breath, she went to work cleaning up the mess. Seems as if she spent a lot of time cleaning up a lot of messes. "Daddy's here?"

"Now don't get all upset, Elizabeth. He's changed."

Elizabeth put away the blusher. There was a time for makeup, but this wasn't it. She faced her mother square on. "Leopards don't change their spots, zebras can't lose their stripes, dogs have to bark, and snakes have to slither on the ground. Animals don't change, and neither do people. They're born one way, good or bad. I'm sorry that my daddy isn't one of the good guys, but that's the way it is. Maybe you're happy that your heart keeps getting trampled on, but not me. I can't do this. I won't let him use you, and I won't let him use me."

Her mother's nose pinched in, and Elizabeth recognized her fighting look. She'd seen it often enough growing up, when Elizabeth had failed her first algebra test, when she had spilled vegetable oil all over the kitchen floor and the first time that

Ray Innis had returned home after an eighteen-year absence. "You think this is about you?" her mother said, spoken like a true woman in love.

Elizabeth chose the honest route, standing up and gathering the faded blue terry cloth close around her. "No, it'd be nice if Daddy had feelings for me, but I'm pretty sure that it's all about the money."

"No, honey. It's about the way your father looks at me, about the way I feel when I'm with him. I'm happy. I want to be happy, sweetheart. I want to grin at the world, and spin in circles, so dizzy with it. That's how I feel when I'm with him. That's how I feel when I look into his eyes, and see me reflected there."

Elizabeth swallowed hard, her breathing not so easy. She didn't want to hear those words. She didn't want to know a woman could feel that for a no-account man who could disappear for eighteen years. She wanted to think that happiness and foolhardy grins were reserved for women who had found the exact, most-perfect man in the world. The one man who stuck around, didn't milk you for what you were worth, a man who would spend his years sipping lemonade on a front porch.

Suddenly she looked at her mother, who didn't look quite so foolish anymore. "Oh, Momma, what are we going to do?"

"You have a concert to give. Go out there, smile for the crowds and sing your heart out." Her mother's mouth twisted into half a smile, half a frown. That was her way when she was confused, always riding in the center. "You have so much, Elizabeth. You're so happy. I want some of that happiness, too. You don't need me. If I died tomorrow, it wouldn't matter. At least with Ray, I know that I matter."

Elizabeth hugged her mother close, noticing her mother had lost weight and maybe shrunk an inch or two. "Don't talk like that. Please don't talk like that. I would give up everything if I knew how to make you happy. Get a job, or volunteer, or go travel, or find a hobby."

After Elizabeth took a step back, her mother noticed the pink slippers and laughed. It was about time.

"I'm not worth worrying about."

Elizabeth took one pink-shod foot and brushed it over her mother's. "When I'm done here, maybe we could travel. Go someplace together. We'll go shopping." And not think about men at all.

Diane shook her head. "You got a lot on your plate. A new beau. Don't listen to what I said, Elizabeth. I was being mean. If he makes you happy, you be with him."

Elizabeth thought about that for a second, and then nodded. "He makes me happy, he makes me grin, he makes me spin in dizzying circles."

"Well there you go."

"I wish I could make you happy, Momma."

"Oh, you do, honey. I should tell you that more often. You have a good show. I'll be right up front."

"He won't be there, will he?"

"He said he'd be somewhere in the back. I shouldn't have said anything. I should have just kept my mouth shut."

"Stop fretting, Momma," Elizabeth said gently, because it wasn't so easy to judge from the short side of the fence anymore. After her mother left, Elizabeth went back to the dressing table and stared into the mirror with worried blue eyes.

That evening, Demetri considered bringing flowers with him. Yellow roses, maybe. But there weren't many gifts a man could bring to a woman who had everything in the world. He took his seat in the theater, a hat low over his eyes, not that anyone would notice him tonight. Tonight everyone would only have eyes for her. Demetri included.

When the band took the stage, the crowd whistled and cheered, and when Elizabeth appeared, the applause was deafening. Why was it any surprise that she had an arena full of people that loved her? She found him almost immediately, her eyes meeting his, then dancing away quickly. And it was like that for most of the concert. She was wrong. A CD didn't even come close to the sweet notes that captivated him.

Song after song she sang, singing of her own simple dreams. The song about a hard-drinking man finding himself when all seems lost. The single mother who never thought she could love. There was a theme to each and every song. Every time, someone got rescued, someone was redeemed. And her eyes would flash when she sang, her voice vibrating with the strength of what she believed in.

She made everyone believe.

For two hours he sat, almost motionless, watching her, falling in love again. And when she got to the last song of the night, her gaze reached out once again. Nervously danced away, and the slow strum of the guitar matched the husky call of her voice. Suddenly she wasn't singing about getting rescued anymore. As she sang, her eyes kept drifting back to his, and as his eyes met hers, the crowd disappeared, the noise disappeared and every word seared his brain.

Long, sleepless nights when I'm dreaming of you.
You come and see me there,
Touching me,
Kissing me,
Love me.

The last line was so small, so pleading, and he wanted to be alone with her, to tell her that he did love her, and that he always would. He stayed lost in the song until the arena exploded into noise and light, and he realized that she wasn't singing anymore. The words in his head, the image in his head replayed over and over.

This night Demetri wanted to be everything that she saw in

him, because when she was nearby, he didn't need to drive fast, or get caught up in the rush in order to forget. She made new memories for him. Memories that he wanted to treasure.

Amidst all the cheers, Elizabeth grinned and smiled, and this time she avoided his eyes. Around him, everyone was on their feet, but Demetri couldn't move. He didn't know if he could ever move again.

Tonight. Everything was going to be perfect tonight.

A short time after the show was over, Elizabeth had changed into more comfortable clothes. Now she was visiting with her mother and Tobey in the dressing room, her mother looking so pretty, but so worried.

"He was supposed to meet me back here," she was saying, as if she was surprised that Ray Innis wasn't there. "I don't know where he got to."

"Maybe he's not going to show," said Elizabeth gently, winding her fingers through her mother's the way she had when she was a little girl.

"That's not like Ray," she insisted.

And Elizabeth knew that her mother would imagine the worst, muggings, or car accidents, thinking of everything but the wayward heart of the man she loved. "I tell you what. Let me go ask Bobby if he saw him. Will that make you happy?"

"That's a good idea," answered Diane, her hands stilled in her lap.

Elizabeth walked out to the stage and called the security guard over. "Bobby, my mother was supposed to meet a man here. Ray Innis. You seen him?"

"Nobody here but Mr. Lucas."

"Mr. Lucas is still here?" she asked, her heart beating rabbit-fast.

Demetri stepped from behind the stage curtains. "Yeah. I'm still here. Imagine that."

She wanted to ask him what he thought of her singing, wanted to ask him if he had a good day, wanted to ask him if he would make love with her tonight, but she didn't. "You want to come meet my momma?" she asked instead.

"Should I be nervous?"

"Oh, no, not around Momma. So what did you think of the concert?"

"I fell in love all over again," he said, and her heart stopped. Love? Her mind kept going back on the word, wondering if she'd misheard him, but her ears never misheard anything that Demetri Lucas said. Her ears were smart that way.

Love.

Lord almighty, that a four-letter word could cause her heart to get so fat and swollen, until she felt as if it was going to burst out of her chest. She looked into his eyes, seeing the same dark warmth that had been there all along. All along for her. Elizabeth began to smile, and grin, her world spinning in dizzying circles.

All she could think about was kissing him, and she took a step forward, but right then, her mother's voice broke through the fog. "Elizabeth! Did you find Ray?"

Elizabeth looked at Demetri, blinked twice. He nudged her backstage where her mother was waiting. "Let's go meet your momma."

And wasn't that just like a man. Drop a nuclear bomb in the middle of the room, and then just carry on as though everything was normal. However, sometimes Demetri was the smart one, and as much as Elizabeth loved her mother, that wasn't a conversation she wanted to have around her.

"Bobby hasn't seen him. I'm sorry, Momma."

Diane Innis frowned. "Oh."

Elizabeth looked away, because she didn't want to see the face of a woman who had bet on the wrong man. A woman who gave her heart when it was destined to be broken. Elizabeth didn't need this. Not tonight. She had made her own bet, and she didn't want to know she'd bet wrong, too.

Quickly she introduced Diane to Demetri, who immediately charmed her, asking her how she liked the concert, asking how long she was staying in town, and gradually the worry faded from her mother's face, leaving nothing but moonstruck silliness. It was sad the effect that man had on women. He knew exactly what to say, exactly what to do, exactly what every woman wanted. She wondered if he had a clue about what she wanted.

He met her eyes. *Yeah, he knew.*

A stagehand knocked on the door. "Taxi's waiting, Mrs. Innis."

"You're going?" asked Elizabeth. "I thought you'd want to have dessert, or go somewhere to chat."

Diane was having none of it. "Now, listen, you two kids get on. Mr. Lucas, I think I like you, but you hurt my daughter, I'll have to hunt you down like a dog and shoot you."

Demetri laughed and gave Elizabeth his Hollywood smile. "You are just like your mother, aren't you?"

"We're nothing alike," said Diane, her brows pulling together.

"Don't be too sure about that," answered Demetri, and Elizabeth watched, shocked when her momma smiled, a blush on her cheeks. Elizabeth looked at Demetri and smiled.

Elizabeth went to get her things, and Tobey stood there, with his black silk shirt, sunglasses on his head—in the middle of the night, no less—and he was sporting that stubble on his jaw that was currently in style. That was so Tobey.

"Tobey Keller, this is Demetri Lucas," she said, performing the requisite introductions.

"Good to see you. Liz, you did fantastic. Loved the bit at the end. It was new, sexy, very crossover."

"I don't need crossover," she insisted.

"Do you know the size of the eighteen-to-thirty-four market? They control forty-three percent of the music market. The average age of a C & W music buyer is fifty-seven. Fifty-seven. Now, I'm not trying to tell you how to run your career."

Elizabeth interrupted because she didn't want to talk business tonight. There were better things to do. Shimmery, magical things that made her heart quiver when she thought of them. "Tobey, I pay you to tell me what to do."

"I wasn't sure about this direction. But I can see something. Edgier."

"I like edgy," put in Demetri.

"See, he likes edgy," said Tobey, sensing his ally, or possibly a new business opportunity.

Elizabeth made herself smile. "Can we talk about this tomorrow, Tobey? I'm tired. I'm supposed to be on vacation, but everybody seems to be forgetting that." She didn't give two hoots about vacation. All she needed was to be alone with the man who loved her.

The man who loved her. She repeated it in her head, and if her grin was a little goofy, Demetri had nobody to blame but himself.

Tobey sighed. "I suppose this could wait."

"Good."

Demetri held out a hand to Elizabeth's manager. "Tobey, it's nice to meet you. You've done a great job."

And Tobey jumped right in like the shark he was. "You know, if you're interested in doing something in…I don't know, commercials, maybe men's cologne…"

"We have sponsors, thanks," answered Demetri, the picture of politeness. How did he stay so calm when she was ready to burst out of her skin?

Tobey held up a hand. "I've got to try."

"If I have the urge, you'll be the first I call," Demetri promised.

"Liz. Darling. As always." He kissed the air around her, and made phone-fingers. "We'll talk."

And finally they were alone—for about one second—until the security guard poked his head through the dressing room door. If people didn't get out of the way soon, Elizabeth was going to scream bloody murder.

"Miss Innis, the reporters are waiting outside. I've kept them back as long as I could, but I can only do so much."

"Can you give me five minutes, Bobby?" asked Elizabeth, her eyes never leaving Demetri's face. Five minutes. Sweet heaven, she needed a lifetime to kiss him and all she had was five minutes.

"Sure," Bobby answered, raising a hand in salute, and then, Lord have mercy, they were alone. She ran, nearly toppling him with the force of her feelings, but tonight was Christmas, her birthday and the Fourth of July all wrapped up into one bright, moonlit moment in her life, and she'd never been one of those who waited to unwrap the presents. No, Elizabeth needed to tear into her pretty packages as soon as they were in her hands.

Her heart beat so fast, as though it could fly, and his mouth pressed against hers, desperate and hungry, and her busy mouth kissed him until she wasn't breathing her own breath anymore, only his.

His arms wrapped around her, and they were kissing as if it were the first time. Her fingers tangled in his dark hair, plundering and twisting because finally, *finally,* she could touch him the way she had always wanted to.

When he lifted his mouth, she nearly cried. "I have to get out of here before you talk to the press."

"Why?" she asked mournfully, not nearly ready to release him yet. According to her watch, they had another two minutes and seventeen seconds, and she wanted those two minutes.

"Elizabeth…"

"Will I see you back at the hotel?" she asked, not caring if she was being forward, or slutty, or any of those things.

Now that she'd made up her mind, her decision wasn't going to change. When Demetri looked at her, she could feel the glow starting from inside, working its way from her heart to her smile to her eyes to that damnable ache between her thighs. But tonight, that damnable ache was going to explode into a million little pieces, and she wasn't going to miss it one bit. Her eyes met his, and she quivered once more.

Regretfully, he put her away from him, but he held on to a hand, and she understood the need to touch. She wanted to keep him within touching distance, too. "There'll be a car waiting for you outside," he told her.

"To take me back to the hotel?"

His thumb traced against her palm, rubbing circles there, little strokes of sensation that tantalized and teased her. "Where we go is up to you."

"What are you thinking?" she asked, detecting a surprise here, her mind already itching to know.

"I don't like hiding out in hotel rooms. I don't like the press hanging around. I want to be alone with you, a place where we have more than five minutes. But this is your decision, Elizabeth. It's a suggestion...."

Like a Boy Scout. Always prepared. Always thinking of her. This was her chance. Her last chance to back out. Her fate determined, she nodded.

"I love your suggestion. I'll go back to the hotel and pack some things."

"You don't need much," he said, and he was right. There was only one thing she needed, and he was right here.

"Demetri?"

He looked at her.

"I can't wait."

Chapter Eleven

She packed up what she needed and climbed into the limo, hoping he would be there, but the backseats were empty. It was just her and the driver.

Elizabeth saw the bottle of champagne chilling on ice and began to smile. Close to an hour later, the limo pulled up to an old Victorian farmhouse, right in the middle of Nowhere, Kentucky. There were no house lights, but the full moon was bright, casting the metal shingles in its silvery web, illuminating the weather vane perched proudly on the roof. She expected to see that fancy red car in front, but there was only a single motorcycle parked there. A fancy red motorcycle.

Boys and their toys.

Elizabeth didn't like motorbikes. They were a needle in the eye to everything that was safe and orderly, and as if that weren't enough, there had been that one time when she was tooling down the highway somewhere, and a motorcycle had pulled out of nowhere, speeding up in front of her, scaring forty years off her. She didn't like motorcycles, and as soon as she crawled out of his bed, she was going to tell Demetri just that.

Crawled out of his bed—oh, my—that thought was enough to stop her motorcycle worries, and she took a closer look at the farmhouse.

Through the narrow windows, a golden glow burned, a glow only eclipsed by the one inside her. Anticipation, eagerness and want were all there, and she popped out of the car with more speed than grace. Hurriedly she grabbed her overnight bag, picked up the bottle of wine, sent the driver on his way and took the front steps two at a time.

Good Lord, she loved that man.

The door was cracked open, a beautiful door with a stained-glass window that was full to overflowing with Tiffany flowers and peacocks. When she walked inside, the creaking old floor welcomed her, and instantly she understood why the house was glowing. Candles burned everywhere. On the oak side tables, on the dainty mahogany chairs, their flickering flames of gold danced in the chilled night air. But she wasn't cold. Goodness knows, she was never so warm in her life.

In the back corner of the room, Demetri was sitting on the stairway, in his blue jeans and white shirt, looking more handsome than a man should ever, *ever* be allowed to be.

Elizabeth froze, her heart beating desperately, because this was a line she'd never crossed, and now she found herself toed right up to the edge. When you gave yourself to a man, when you gave him your body, your heart, your soul, you couldn't just ask for it back. Part of her would always stay with him, would always belong to him, never to be undone.

"It's not the Presidential suite, is it?" she said to him, her mouth wanting to smile, but not quite making it.

He stood tall, and walked over to her. She felt a sigh within her, a sigh that bloomed from down deep inside her, from feelings that had never stirred before. "If you don't like it…"

She whacked him on his good arm. "I'm trying not to cry. Don't make me cry."

"It was tough figuring out the perfect place for you. I've spent thirteen days, five hours and thirty-seven minutes thinking about that."

She looked around the house, needing to fix her greedy eyes on something besides him. "It's pretty close."

"Pretty close? This is damned perfect." He looked at her, offended, which was way better—way easier—than that earlier look. The one that was full of so many promises.

"Got you," she murmured.

"Yeah. Yes, you do."

Elizabeth wanted to ignore that, wanted to ignore the purposeful intent in his eyes, because there were a lot of things to get out of the way, but when he looked at her like that, she couldn't think straight.

"Sit over there," she said, pointing to the yellow chintz—chintz!—love seat, and she settled herself on a frilly-looking wooden chair.

He didn't even argue with her, walked over, sat down, as if he was in no hurry at all. Glad to see that somebody wasn't nervous. "I want you to know that there're five bedrooms in the house," he told her casually, crossing one foot over the other. "I wasn't going to make assumptions."

"We aren't going to need any more than one," she said, feeling more confident when he was so far away. Out of touching distance, out of pouncing distance.

One dark brow arched up, pleased and surprised. "We won't?"

She shook her head slowly. "Nope. Does that scare you?"

"Terrified."

"Good. Got life insurance?"

"They won't touch me."

"Figured as much."

For two long moments, she sat and watched him, memorized him. She was still scared, terrified even, but the fears were slowly dying.

"Why are you over there?" he asked.

"So I can talk, and think, preferably at the same time. And I can't think too well when you're sitting close."

"I like that."

"Figured that, too. I keep thinking that I shouldn't trust you, but I was wrong. I misjudged you, and I want to thank you for being so nice."

"I can be even nicer. The night's young."

She gathered her courage and talked in a fast rush, the words tripping over each other. "I love you, Demetri. I don't know any woman that can't not love you, but that's their problem, since I'm the one sitting here now. But before we have sex…"

"Make love," he corrected, and she wished he wouldn't do that, keep making her heart stop.

She sat up a little straighter, because this didn't feel like her tonight. This felt like some other woman. Elizabeth didn't dive in the cold water first, she'd always eaten her Oreo cookies in tiny, even nibbles, and it had taken her three months to learn to ride a bike, four months if you counted proficiency in braking.

However, tonight was a lot more serious than anything she'd ever done before. It wasn't even her virginity that she guarded so well, it was her heart.

"Before we make love, I need to know what you are thinking, because I'm out this door if I'm a fling for you. I don't think I would survive that, and I don't want to be one of those music stars that are in and out of relationships, and rehab, and car accidents, and in general, being unhappy. I want to be happy. I deserve that. I'm looking around here, and I'm thinking you don't do this for everybody, including that royal hussy, although now I'm a little more charitable toward her, because there's not a man alive that could hold a candle—"

"I love you. I fell in love, right from the beginning. Right when you ran into me."

"Lord, you are a foolish man," she said, shaking her head.

"And then when you turned away, I fell in love again. Because of the way you walked."

Her head cocked to one side. "You do like that, don't you?"

"Everywhere you walked, the sun followed like a puppy dog, and I thought how lucky the sun was."

She sat motionless, because she didn't know what to say. Her words had all fled.

"The third time I fell in love with you was that night, when I danced with you for the first time. I didn't want you to ever leave my arms again. You belonged there, and I knew it. And then you sang," he continued. "And I fell in love again. You sang like you believed in the implicit goodness of people, and that the world was some great place, and it didn't seem stupid, or naive. I wanted some of whatever you were drinking."

Elizabeth perched right on the edge of the chair, one more inch and she was gone, and he kept right on pulling. Not with his strength, but with something much more dangerous, much more deadly. "There you go with those pretty words. I want you to know this isn't waterproof mascara."

He crossed his arms over his chest, not even fazed. "But it didn't stop then. Next was the black lace bra."

"I brought it with me."

That stopped him. One booted foot hit the floor. "Don't go there. Not yet."

"Trouble thinking?" she asked, pleased to see him flustered.

"Don't distract me, I'm only up to day four. It continues on and never stops. Every time I saw you, I found new reasons to love you. Even now, every time I see you, I find new reasons to love you. When you told me what you wanted to do for your family, how you put aside pretty much everything and everybody until you could solve their problems…"

"But it's still not solved."

"We'll fix it."

"We?" she asked, smiling to herself.

He nodded.

"You're making a whole lot of promises for a man who wants one romp in the hay."

"Not just one."

"No?"

"Not even close."

However, Elizabeth was close. Her body was covered in sweat and that was wrong, because it was downright chilly in here. Her hands kept twisting in her lap, just like her mother's hands. "Are there flaws, secrets, warts or dead wives or dead princesses, that I need to know about?"

"Trust is a problem for you, isn't it?"

"Double-check, triple-check. Can't be too careful."

"You know there's going to be a lot of publicity. A lot of reporters who are always tagging along."

"Handgun laws are lax in Tennessee and Kentucky…." And then she stopped. *Thirteen days.* Good Lord. She'd known him for all of thirteen days and she was already planning out her life. "How is this going to work?"

"I don't know," he answered confidently, as if the details weren't going to matter at all.

Elizabeth twisted her hands once more, and he noticed. He seemed to notice everything about her.

"You have your chance to walk out, too, Elizabeth. But take it now, because once I've had you, once you're mine, I won't let you go."

She lifted her eyes. "Where do you live?"

"What?"

"Your house? Where do you live? I don't even know where you live."

"I have an apartment in Los Angeles."

"Oh, God, you live in Los Angeles." *He lived in California.* It was a full day of travel going from the East Coast to the West Coast. A full, lost day before she'd get to see him. She could taste the panic in her mouth, coppery and brittle.

"It's only an apartment."

"I hate Los Angeles. I need air, and green grass, and I want a porch." There. She'd told him. She needed to get some of this out in the open, so there wouldn't be misunderstandings.

"I can move," he told her easily.

"How much time do you spend there?"

"Not a lot. Most of the time I'm on the circuit. The season runs from March to November, and I like to ski in the winter, so I'm not home often. My apartment is actually not a lot more than a big storage closet for my stuff."

"I won't see you much, will I?" she asked. She wasn't sure if she could handle that. All those pretty women on the circuit. Tanned, exotic and full of their European ways. She couldn't compete with all that.

"You can see me as much as you want."

"But when you're racing…"

"Dammit, Elizabeth. Don't talk yourself out of this."

"You just want that one romp in the hay," she said, talking herself down from the edge. She moved back until her spine was once again safely aligned with the back of the chair.

"That's not true."

Her eyes narrowed, and her voice was sly. "You really want to be that golden retriever? Cautious, gentle and patient?"

"Get out," he said, low and hurt.

It took a second for it all to sink in. She could leave, walk out the door. This was her chance. Instead she nodded once and looked at him with respect in her eyes.

"Another test?" he asked.

"Don't worry. You passed."

"When do the tests stop?"

"I don't know they ever will. Does that bother you?"

"Yeah."

"Can you live with it?"

"Yeah."

And now there wasn't anywhere else for her to run, there weren't any other questions she could ask. It was time. "Can I come and sit next to you?" she whispered.

This time, he was the one with caution in his face. "What if I change my mind? What if I make you move out to California? Sterling Motor Cars is a California-based company."

"Short visits or long visits?"

"Long visits, possibly years," he said, and she could see the need in his eyes, the fear there, too. It made it easier for her, knowing she wasn't the only person that was jumping off.

"How many years?" she asked.

"Fifty. Hopefully more."

She rose and came to sit next to him on the world's most perfect yellow chintz love seat. "I can handle that," she whispered to him. Through the old diamond-paned windows, the moon shone on candlelight, tracing his face in silver beams, and she felt it again. That moon magic. It always pulled her closer, strong arms that pulled her closer. It felt so right to be there, so comfortable, her cheek against his chest, hearing the constant beat of his heart. He pulled back, and his eyes studied her, unbearably tender, unbearably warm. When he looked at her like that, it burned her, taking all the oxygen out of her lungs, out of the room.

In the end, she had no choice. She kissed him, a brush of lips that was soft, so terribly soft. With his lips, he gently followed the lonely tear that was dripping down her cheek.

It was time.

His mouth was so persuasive, so warm, coaxing her into the magic with him. He brushed back her hair from her face, taking the time to stare, and she could see the moon magic shining there in his face, in his eyes. Everything was so slow, so easy. He slid the blouse from her shoulders, talking to her in deep whispers, his voice gliding over her skin as easy as his hands. He took off his shirt, and her fingers traced and curled, flirting with the hard muscles that were exposed. He was such a pretty, pretty man, so strong, so perfect.

Why did he have to move around the world in a rush? But then he kissed her, his mouth on her lips, seducing her with tenderness, and she couldn't reason anymore. His mouth moved lower, tickling her neck, and she didn't care if she couldn't think. Lower he went, teasing her breasts until she was in a place far, far lovelier than she'd ever known. The gold of the room heated, warming her, and every time he touched her, the candle flames hissed in response. Through the thick silence, she could hear the sounds of her own pleasure. The quick gasps, the desperate urge to breathe. She needed to breathe. Her back arched, and she pressed into him, wanting him closer to her.

He picked her up in strong arms and carried her upstairs, and his mouth never left hers once. The hardness of his arms changed to the softness of the bed, and then he followed on top of her. This time, she was bolder, her fingers undoing the buttons at his fly, wanting to feel him covering her. She wanted to see, she wanted to feel. He covered her, his hard to her soft, so dangerously hard everywhere she touched. She heard the crinkle of foil, heard him whisper in her ear, loving words, loving promises that she would keep forever. With urgent hands, he dipped and stroked, and each time, a new ripple pulsed through her, the sensations widening. The torment continued, on and on, until she was pleading with him, mindless and lost.

When he slid inside her, she felt it through every inch of her body, her mind, down to the dark shadows of her soul. When he thrust, she froze, waiting to feel the tear inside her, the pain of something shattering apart. There wasn't any pain. There was no great bolt of lightning to strike her in two. Like that, her innocence was gone in the quick blink of the eye, in the long beat of the heart, as if it'd never existed at all.

Elizabeth followed him, he held her hands, never hurting her, never scaring her, and she could see what it was costing. He was a strong man, his body so thick and hard, and powerfully built, and all those steely muscles were corded and bunched as he moved. Every time she touched him, she felt those steely muscles quiver with weakness. She whispered to him, whispered words of love that she'd never dared to say before. Somehow, in the velvet shadow of the night, in the soft embrace of the moon, she dared. With the dark pull of desire guiding her, this wasn't a dream anymore. He moved faster inside her, and the lyrics spun in her head, meaningless words that could never compare to this, and she followed—blindly, foolishly—she followed.

Once again her heart stopped, the world poised right on the edge. And then he was

touching her…

kissing her…

…loving her.

Demetri had always believed that falling in love wasn't in the cards. Before Elizabeth, he put love in the same category as politics, philanthropy and sanitation. Somebody had to do it, but it probably wasn't going to be him. For Demetri, it was always about winning, always about speed, always about forgetting, because there wasn't anything he wanted to remember. But tonight, loving her—body and mind—made forgetting impossible.

They made love through the night. *Made love,* like the lyrics from one of her songs. The clock on the wall said it was four in the morning, and he thought she was asleep, curled up next to him, silky blond hair wrapped around his shoulder, dreamy blue eyes that were wrapped around his heart. Demetri couldn't sleep. He was running on adrenaline and his eyes wouldn't close, so he lay there, watching her, his mind filled with the creamy kiss of her skin.

Tonight she'd made love just the way she did everything else—she'd been passionate, giving, a dazzling smile on her face. And tonight, the smile was only for him.

Damn.

He wasn't sure that he deserved it, but he was extraordinarily happy she thought so.

Her mouth brushed his chest, and soft fingers stroked over his shoulder. "How's this?" she asked, almost a whisper. For thirteen days he'd wondered what it would be like to hear that honey voice whisper to him at night, stroking him as softly as her fingers. For the rest of his life he would know.

"Really nice," he answered. He said no more, because she was the poet.

She rose on one elbow, brushed her hair from her eyes. "How's your shoulder?"

"I have good drugs, don't worry about it."

"The bruises have faded some," she said, pressing a kiss there.

"Does that really matter?" he asked, because he had bruises more often than not. But if she kept kissing the weakened flesh, were bruises really a bad thing? He could get used to this really, really fast.

"I worry, that's all." Then she tucked herself next to him. "I want to meet your father."

"Is this another test?" he asked, because he didn't want her to meet Andre Lucas. The world bought into the media creation that was Demetri Lucas, fawning over him and mythicizing him, but not his father. His father saw through the shell, into the man. Right now, Demetri didn't want Elizabeth to know the man he was, the man that could never live up to her standards. She wanted the fairy tale, and he could give her that. But after she met Andre Lucas, the fairy tale would be over. "Maybe you can meet him later," he answered noncommittally.

Elizabeth rose up on his chest again, and her eyes studied him carefully, but Elizabeth, with her rose-colored glasses, would never see the truth.

"You won't like him," he said, because he knew she expected something else from him. A reason. An excuse. Whatever.

"Really? Well, that's interesting. More than two words. Now I definitely have to meet him."

He sighed, pressing her back against him, because he didn't want her looking too closely, even with those rose-colored glasses firmly in place. "Why do you think my father is any more a prince than yours?"

She sat up again. "Is that why you don't see him?"

"No," he said, as he stroked her hair, wondering if anyone would notice if they stayed here forever. Probably.

"So what's the problem? Why can't I meet him? Thanksgiving's coming up."

"I'll be in Canada."

"Oh," she said. "I didn't think about that." And he understood. For Elizabeth, family wasn't thought about or considered, it simply was. Like breathing.

"You don't have to go if you'd rather stay here."

"You're going to laugh at me," she began.

"Why?"

Her mouth worked silently, and he could see dim shadows in her eyes, until finally she spoke. "I worry about you. I feel like if I'm there when you're out on the track, then I know you'll be okay. If I'm not there, then something bad might happen. It was gut-wrenching watching that race in Louisville, but not watching would have been impossible."

His guardian angel, watching over him. He rolled her underneath him, because he didn't have words. In the quiet of the first light of sunrise, he thrust inside her, surrounded by her warmth, her light, her heat. Their eyes locked, because there was no place he wanted to be, but here, joined with her. He loved her well, and when he could feel her gasp, when the golden rays of sunlight gilded her skin, he whispered over and over against her neck.

"I love you."

It wasn't enough, but it was all he had, and he hoped she understood.

Demetri woke to the sound of a cell phone. His. At first he ignored it. You could ignore anything long enough and it would go away, but then two minutes later the buzzing started again.

"You should get that," Elizabeth said, her head emerging from under the covers. "Somebody's bound and determined to talk to you. Besides, I think I want to ogle you naked some more."

Demetri laughed and went downstairs to dig out his phone because today he could handle anything the world threw at him. Elizabeth believed in him. Elizabeth loved him. Amazing how that worked.

Unfortunately, the phone call was from Jim.

Hell.

"Where are you?" Jim asked.

"It doesn't matter. What do you want?"

"We need you for a press conference this afternoon at the hotel."

His one perfect day, and they wanted to ruin it? No way. No way in hell. "I won't go to a press conference. Prior commitment. Sorry."

"It's Valencia. We can tie this up today with a nice neat bow. They're ready to announce the sponsorship, and they want to do it in Louisville."

"No." Demetri hung up, threw the phone across the room, and it promptly started ringing again. Dammit.

Demetri sighed, because he could feel the weight of her stare. He looked up, and saw Elizabeth there, standing next to the balusters, wearing his shirt. Good God, lucky shirt. The white tails skimmed perfect thighs, and she hadn't bothered to button it up, not that he was going to remind her. She walked downstairs and sat in his lap, sunlight trailing behind her. He was dazzled, and she honestly had no idea.

"Honey, it's a press conference. We can go to an auction some other day."

"I made you a promise," he told her, because he didn't want to let her down. Not yet. Not like this.

"And I'm letting you out of it. Do your press conference. These horse-buying opportunities are a dime a dozen. We can go to Keeneland."

"I need to get away from Louisville," he said, because they would use her. Sterling Motor Cars, Valencia Products, the whole Formula Gold organization. They would take Elizabeth Innis and milk every drop of innocence from her, and she'd never realize it.

"Demetri, I love that you want to do this, but if you look at your life, at my life, the fact is that I'm going to have to make some adjustments. I admit, I wasn't thinking clearly about this sort of thing, but, honey, I'm not going to stand in the way of your business."

He was going to tell her. Explain the situation with Valencia. Laugh a little bit about it. Make it sound casual. Just business, nothing more. He could do that. "Elizabeth, there's something you should know…."

"What?"

"Sterling wants to hint about our relationship, make it public in a press conference. With Valencia. I don't think we should do this. I think we should go to New York as planned." There. He'd done it. Of course, he'd glossed over the sordid parts, but if Elizabeth was paying attention, she'd pick up on it. Elizabeth was bright. Another reason he loved her.

"What sort of hints?" she asked, not paying attention to the parts she needed to pay attention to.

"Nothing major," he told her. "It's mainly to announce the

renewed sponsorship with Valencia Products. Anton Valencia will be there."

"Well, that doesn't sound like a big deal, Demetri. I think we should put everything out in the open. Makes our relationship sound more legitimate, less tawdry. Legitimate is good for my career, and yours, too. Even if tawdry has made you some bucks in the past, I think legitimate is the way for you to go now."

And no, there wasn't a cynical bone in her body.

Time for reality to bite. His fingers trailed up and down her arm, and he reminded himself that she believed in him. She had seen the man he was. She loved the man he was. He could do this. Unthinkingly, his fingers tightened.

"You're the reason Valencia came back for the sponsorship. That is, you and me. Our relationship. They see it as a marketing opportunity."

Some of the innocence dimmed from her eyes. "I see."

"I'm sorry. I didn't want this. I don't want this, but it's what it is. It's business."

"I see," she repeated. He'd never glimpsed this side of her before, the closed-faced, hard-eyed businesswoman, and he wasn't sure he wanted to know this side of her. He knew it was smart of her. He knew it was defensive, but it still nudged at his conscience that he was responsible.

His hand fell away. "What do you want to do?" he asked. He had no right to ask her to stand by him in front of the press while his reputation was restored, while her reputation got not-so restored. Up to now, he'd careened along, believing that somehow things would work out. Now who was being naive?

Elizabeth looked at him, her gaze flat. "What choices do I have?"

"Option one. I don't have to do the press conference. I can tell Jim no. Option two. You don't have to be there. Skip it. I'll take the questions and slide through, giving as little information as possible. Or, option three, we take the bull by the horns and deal. Those are your choices." *Or, alternatively, you could ditch me and Sterling Motors and Valencia Products, and tell us all to go to hell.* He left that choice off.

"You go alone," she answered, her voice as flat as her eyes.

"Elizabeth?" he asked, because he needed to know they were okay. He needed to know they could get through this, that he hadn't thrown too much at her too soon. He needed to know that Demetri, the man, was worthy of her. It wasn't true, but he wasn't going to tell her that fact.

"Yeah? What?"

"Are you okay? Are we okay?"

"Yeah, sure. I think I need to take a shower. And get cleaned up." Slowly, she buttoned up his shirt, and he knew they weren't okay.

"I don't have to do this. I can reject the whole deal." Big words. Brave words. Stupid words. He couldn't go back on his team. This was his mess to clean up. No one else's. *Bad actions. Bad consequences.*

She looked up at him, and saw so many things he didn't want her to see in him. "And what happens then?"

Demetri didn't answer. He didn't need to.

"I'll take my shower," she said, and that was the end of the conversation. Decision made. Life goes on. Demetri swore.

Upstairs he pulled on his clothes, and out the window he could see the red bike that called his name, singing in his ear like a siren. So tempting. To race against the demons of the mind and beat them. After a quick look upstairs, he knew he'd have time to burn. Once outside in the early-morning sun, Demetri hopped on, cranked her up, listened to the 1300 cc twin-turbo engine, four cylinders, 150 horses and a zero to one hundred in 3.8 seconds. Sweet. For some people the loud whine of the engine was earsplitting; for Demetri it was a lullaby to calm a restless soul.

He let out the clutch, and was off.

Before he'd had a car, he'd had a motorcycle, an old Honda with a fifty cc engine that was more of a scooter than a beast. But Demetri had loved the bike, loved the way the road flew in front of him. His brother, Seth, had loved that bike, too, and used to take it around the woods behind their house.

Seth...

Damn, someday, he was going to be able to think about his brother and not hurt. But not today. Today, hurting people seemed to be his greatest talent. Demetri took the bike to redline, the soft dirt throwing out to the sides. Second gear turned the trees into brown cotton, in third gear the engine kicked up, the front wheel leaving the ground, and in fourth, the battering wind coaxed tears from his eyes, and the wheel found the purchase of ground once again.

As the tachometer settled to 7000 rpms, the wind was more like a hurricane, ripping through his ears, beating his shirt against his chest, blocking out everything but the speed. The straightaway was perfect for opening it up, and Demetri took it with a dark smile on his face. The world passed in a blur, grass and hills merging together, and he could make out the one incline coming up around the corner.

He punched the throttle, and leaned hard into the curve, but the rear wheel slipped out from beneath him, the engine whining in protest. Demetri put his foot out to brace the bike, but the gravel was an accelerant, not a brake. With a worthless thud, Demetri hit the ground, feeling his shoulder jam once again. But then it didn't hurt so much because three-hundred and fifty pounds of machine was pulling him back toward the trees. Demetri stuck a foot on the ground, and eventually friction did its job, and the bike came to a skidding halt.

Goddamn.

"Demetri!"

And yes, things just got worse. He pasted a hapless smile on his face and pulled up the bike.

He wiped the dirt from his face and his eyes, and watched Elizabeth race over the hill. "Oh, my Lord," she said, her face white. "Are you all right?"

"Damn rocks. Who'd have thunk it?" he said easily, trying to calm her fears. He'd been stupid to push the limits here. The bike was designed for clean pavement, not the uncertainties of Kentucky backcountry. Focus and concentration were a prerequisite in driving, whether a bike or a race car. For the past few years, Demetri had cruised by on aggression and pure speed. Now, watching the concern in Elizabeth's face, he knew he couldn't anymore. There were consequences.

Demetri exhaled slowly. Maybe they weren't perfect, but the look on her face told him what he needed to know. In spite of everything, Elizabeth loved him. Still. He felt the sun shine a little brighter, he felt the shoulder sting a little less.

They were going to be okay.

With gentle fingers she touched his forehead. "You're bleeding."

"I'm fine. Honestly. It was a spill. You should know I'm indestructible."

She shook her head, scolding him like a child. "Have you ever considered another mode of transportation? Walking, for instance? Good Lord, you're going to turn my hair white before I'm thirty."

Teasing. She was teasing, joking. A good sign. Definitely a good sign. Demetri looked at her and smiled. "I think you'd look very sexy with white hair."

She whacked him on his arm, and he knew that loving Elizabeth was not only inevitable, but painful, too. She was wearing trim jeans, and a yellow sweater that clung in all the right places. His body forgot about the pain, forgot about the bike, and thoughts of having her again replaced pretty much everything else.

"Sorry. I don't mean to make you worry," he offered, not that it would stop her.

"What time's your press conference?" she asked.

"Two hours."

"That's not much time to make it back to Louisville."

Demetri looked at her, offended. "In two hours, I could finish Monza and the British Grand Prix. Or, alternatively, we could go upstairs, and I could get reacquainted with the cluster of freckles you have on your left hip."

The warm light in her eyes dimmed. Nope. Not all clear yet.

He took her angel's mouth in a long kiss, because he had no choice. At the moment, he needed her more than he needed to breathe, and as with everything else in his life, Demetri took.

When he lifted his head, she looked a little dazed, and he smiled. "Come on," he said, tugging her hand. "I'll come back for the bike. I need to change, and you'll need to change again. Some of my dirt has rubbed off on you."

After they rounded the hill, the sun shone full in his eyes, but Elizabeth, in spite of her rose-colored vision, seemed to be noticing more and more. Maybe those rose-colored glasses were starting to fade.

"We've got company," she said, nodding her head toward the news van parked in front of the old Victorian.

The press.

Chapter Twelve

Elizabeth heard Demetri swear again, this time in a more descriptive manner. At some time, she would have to talk to him about that, but not now.

That weasel, Hunter Lyons from *Starstruck* magazine, was running toward them, cameras clicking. Whoever invented zoom lenses should have been shot. Demetri pulled her toward the house instead of away.

"What are you doing?"

"Where are you going to go? We don't have a choice."

She looked around, saw the flat lands with no place for miles, and licked suddenly parched lips. "I don't want to talk to him."

"Then we won't," he said, walking right toward the weasel.

"Miss Innis," Hunter called. "You're a hard woman to track down."

"Leave her alone," answered Demetri, still pulling her hard and fast toward the front porch, right past Mr. Lyons.

"Are you still a virgin, Miss Innis?"

Demetri stopped, swore and then popped Hunter Lyons right in the face. Those cute silver spectacles cracked and dangled uselessly to one side. Goodness knows, that sure looked like it hurt.

Demetri didn't wait, but pulled her into the house.

"I don't think you should have done that," said Elizabeth, looking out the window. Hunter got up and dusted himself off, and he and his van disappeared in a red cloud of dust. "But I'm sure glad you did."

"Get your stuff. Let me get cleaned up again, and we'll head out."

She looked beyond the hill, where she knew the motorcycle was still lying, and her stomach quivered in protest. What did he think she was made of? First, the dang press conference, then the weasel Lyons and now this? Elizabeth should have called a halt right then and there, but she couldn't do that to him. She loved him.

A few minutes later she stood in front of the big red beast of a motorcycle, cleaned up, but still looking ominous. "Don't make me do this," she told him one last time, because she knew it wouldn't turn out well, but he smiled gently, and pulled out two helmets from his bag. "All you have to do is hold on tight. You'll do fine."

After riding in a car with Demetri, and now having cruised the roads hugging him as if her life depended on it—which it did—Elizabeth was seriously considering the benefits of hiring a driver. She'd always thought drivers were useless, another toy-monkey luxury for the rich and famous, but now she saw the advantages. Namely, the preservation of life.

Each mile took them closer and closer to the hotel, but she didn't want to go back. In a lot of ways, it was easier cruising on the back of the motorcycle than facing what was up ahead. There were bad feelings inside her, ugly doubts that churned her stomach and worried her mind. By all rights, this should have been a day full of love and nothing to do with business at all. Yet here they were, cruising back to civilization, announcing to the world, the new and extra-strength relationship of Demetri Lucas and Elizabeth Innis—trademarked, Valencia Products, patent pending.

Elizabeth knew how sponsors worked—like vampires, latching onto a vein and sucking you dry. But she knew what she knew about Demetri Lucas, as well. His reputation in business dealings was closer to Dracula than Disney. And it was that key character trait that gave her pause.

Leopards don't change their spots, zebras can't lose their stripes, dogs have to bark and snakes have to slither on the ground. Animals don't change, and neither do people. What wise woman had been dishing out that lecture? Oh, yeah, it was her.

But holding on to him for dear life—now there was an apt metaphor—she knew she trusted him, or wanted to trust him. No. *No.* She trusted him. She did.

Resolutely, she pushed the doubts from her mind, and slowly unfurled her fingernails from Demetri's waist. Her breath returned—barely. In truth, there were worse things than being forced to sit so close to Demetri, his back pressed tight against her. But man, he gave her a fright more than once—pulling right and left between the cars stuck in traffic, running more than one yellow light, and cutting through the alleyways when the light was against them.

What should have been an hour's drive took thirty-five minutes, and soon they were jetting along the main roads of Louisville, driving along the wide banks of the Ohio River, past the Waterfront Park dotted with red-leaf trees, and past the gleaming building facades of iron and glass until they reached downtown.

If it was anyone else but Demetri, she probably would have keeled over in a faint, and why she wasn't flat on the ground now was a tribute to how far they'd come. When they pulled onto Jefferson Street, Demetri stopped a few blocks from the hotel and pulled off her helmet to give her a long, lingering kiss.

"Okay, I guess that means I'm still alive," she mumbled, slightly woozy from the ride, the kiss and the general headiness of being next to so much man.

Demetri shot a dark look down the street, toward the front of the hotel, where the news vans were already gathering. "I'm really beginning to hate this town."

"Where's your spirit of adventure?" she asked, not so happy about the town, either.

"Screw adventure," he muttered.

"You still need to clean up the scratches on your head. After all, you'll need to look pretty for your press conference. God knows, they'll need bouncers to catch all them women swooning." Elizabeth frowned. "Don't let them women start tugging at your clothes. I should come with you," she said, and then felt the stomach churning start up again. "I don't want to come with you."

He looked at her, concerned. "You don't need to go. I can handle this."

She met his eyes, saw her own worries reflected there and then got off the bike.

"Wait a minute," he said, pulling her toward him.

"What?" she asked, losing herself in the dark stare, wondering how this had happened so fast, so furious…so right. Please God, let it be right.

"I love you, Elizabeth," he said, nearly drowned out by the beeping car horns, the noise of the engine and the road crew that was filling potholes down the street. However, she heard, feeling that glorious skitter inside her, that bubbling of joy that seemed to spill out and drench everything with a golden haze. She smiled, her eyes giving her away, and the doubts faded to nothing. When they were alone, it didn't matter what the world thought. The important thing was that they were together.

* * *

Demetri went upstairs and changed into the dark blazer that bore the Sterling Motor Cars crest. Today, the blazer put a sour taste in his mouth.

When he was a boy, it'd been the go-kart, then the motorcycle, and then the Mustang at sixteen. Demetri had known from early on that he wanted to go fast. When he had donned the business suit—a futile attempt to please his father—the suit had felt too tight, so he had changed careers. Time passed, the dream started to take hold and become real and eventually he was wearing the signature blazers that belonged to the men who drove the fastest, drove the hardest, won the most.

He'd achieved his dreams, he'd touched the top. Everything he touched turned to gold. And yet, where did a man go after that? What did he do? Demetri was thirty-five, not sixty-five, yet as he looked back on his life, it felt like a lifetime. A lifetime passed. Now his dreams were changing. He was changing.

Before, he probably would have zoomed past the dark side of the business, but today, after being with Elizabeth, he couldn't zoom past it anymore. A knock sounded and he hoped it was her, but it was only Oliver, dressed and grinning ear to ear. "How was last night?"

"What last night?" asked Demetri.

"I have my sources," answered Oliver. "Actually, you're all over the telly."

Television? Already? Demetri closed his eyes, took some pills from the table and popped them in his mouth, but he knew the painkillers weren't going to be enough, not nearly enough. "What do you mean?"

"That magazine reporter dashed into the news station. Must have been right after you smashed in his nose, because the plaster looked fresh. Nice job, by the way. If you're lucky, he'll need surgery."

Demetri didn't want to think about this now. "You're kidding."

"No, although I think Anton Valencia is probably grinning ear to ear. Cuffing a reporter? It doesn't get better than that. Is Elizabeth coming, as well?"

"No. She's opting out."

Oliver rubbed his hands together. "Strategic thinking. Playing coy. I like it. Let's go downstairs," he said, more like a kid at Christmas than a man facing the bloodthirsty sharks of the press.

While they were waiting for the elevator, Demetri took a long look down the hall, wondering what she was thinking, wishing they were back at the old house, far away from the rest of this hell. However, the sooner he got it over with, the better.

When they got to the hotel reception room, the media was spilling out into the hallways. The backdrop behind the podium sported three emblems: Formula Gold. Sterling Motor Cars. Valencia Products. When Demetri stared at the harmless, sterile images, it seemed easier. It didn't feel so much as if he was selling her out. And Oliver had been right. Demetri didn't have a choice. It was a lose-lose situation. Better to take a deep breath, beard the lions and then hope like hell that everything worked out in the end. He ran his races much the same way.

The room was buzzing, and he saw Anton Valencia, the marketing director, Elena, a pretty blonde who never seemed quite genuine, and Jim Sterling all making their way to the front.

He could do this.

Jim came up to him, grabbed his hand and pumped it up and down.

"Where's Elizabeth?" he asked, searching behind Demetri.

"Go to hell, Jim," said Demetri, smiling pleasantly.

"She'd be a nice touch."

The smile faded. "Leave her out of this. Far, far out of it. I'm doing this for you, for Oliver, for the team because I owe all of you. That's it."

"All right," he said, and they went up on the stage where Oliver was already flirting heavily with Elena. Anton Valencia gave Demetri a long look, but said nothing, only a nod, and then the press conference began.

Everyone had their speeches, everyone but Demetri, but when they opened up the floor for questions, it was Demetri who was getting bombarded.

"Are the rumors true about you and Elizabeth Innis?"

Demetri shook his head, managed an easy laugh. "No comment. I think we're here to talk about cars. Not women."

"This morning did you hit Hunter Lyons, Mr. Lucas?"

Elena stepped forward, a cloud of heavy perfume following behind. "I'll take this one. I'm sure each and every one of you realizes the extraordinary circumstances that have arisen recently, and we at Valencia Products ask that you respect Mr. Lucas's privacy, and Miss Innis's as well. Come on, guys, lay off. Give them a break."

It was the perfect setup. So cozy, so friendly, so completely admitting that the relationship was going on. Demetri could do nothing but sit there and smile.

After another fifteen minutes of weak denials, Jim called a halt and they managed to escape to the adjoining room behind the stage, free of press, free of gawkers. Free of everyone but Elizabeth, standing against the back wall in her jeans and yellow sweater.

Anton Valencia was the first to say something to her. "We're really happy to be back on board with Sterling. I didn't know you're a fan of racing."

"I'm not, Mr. Valencia. Honestly, it turns me a bad shade of green," she said, and Demetri came to stand behind her. Anton was discreet and perfectly polite, but Demetri wanted her out of there as soon as possible. In a lot of ways, the press conference hadn't been awful, and she'd escaped untouched. He wanted to leave her that way.

"Call me Anton," Valencia said, oozing charm. Normally Demetri liked the man, but normally Demetri didn't feel as though he were walking on hot coals, either.

Elizabeth smiled, dazzling Valencia and Demetri both. "Anton, then."

Elena and Oliver walked up, Elena's head bent toward Oliver's. "I'm sure we'll be seeing more of you in the future," she said, holding out her hand to Elizabeth. Demetri intervened, because he'd done his part. Hell was over.

"We have to go," he said, and ushered Elizabeth out of the room.

"I like him, Demetri. Friendly, charming. I'm glad the two of y'all got back together," she said, as he led her through the hallways to the service elevator.

No matter the circumstances, she always believed in the absolute goodness of the world. It was the main reason that he loved her and wanted to protect her from the big bad that was waiting out there for her. Right at that moment, he thought he could.

Elizabeth was relieved the obligations were out of the way. When they got back to her suite, she flipped on the television, curious what the press was saying about one sniveling Hunter Lyons. It didn't take long to find it.

"This morning, reporter Hunter Lyons from *Starstruck* magazine was assaulted by Formula Gold driver Demetri Lucas. Apparently there will be no charges filed. Mike, let's show that clip from Hunter."

"You shouldn't watch that, Elizabeth," Demetri said, putting strong hands on her shoulders. Without thinking, she leaned into him, feeling that same maddened shock to her senses she always felt when he touched her. The drugging need that made a mockery of the tender love songs that she sang.

"Oh, it's not too bad, and you sure look pretty on television.

Movie-star handsome," she said, her voice starting to shake. His hands curved around her, fanning out over her abdomen, sending fire licking inside her, starting to melt her insides once again.

The screen flashed to Hunter, a bandage on his nose, and some bruising around his eyes, which Elizabeth supposed was what happened when you stuck your nose in where it didn't belong. However, Mike and Sandy weren't finished with the discussion.

"And even more Formula Gold news. In a stunning about-face decision, Valencia Products is once again on board with Formula Gold team Sterling, headed by lead driver the darkly handsome heartthrob Demetri Lucas, and that charming golden boy Oliver Wentworth. Why the turnaround, Mike?"

And apparently Mike knew the skinny. He chattered right in, and Elizabeth was acutely aware of the stillness in Demetri's hands. "Sandy, it's marketing, marketing, marketing. With the swirl of rumors surrounding a romance between country-and-western good girl Elizabeth Innis and perpetual playboy Demetri Lucas it's a win-win for Valencia."

Looking at it from the business perspective, Elizabeth could see that yes, if she and Demetri were together, it was a huge pot of gold poured right back into his pocket. A huge pot of gold. It had sounded so businesslike when Demetri was talking about it earlier, so meaningless, but it really wasn't so meaningless after all. The desire stopped licking at her insides. Instead, something dark and shabby and foul took its place.

Perpetual playboy Demetri Lucas.

Elizabeth knew her words. Perpetual meant forever. Forever meant forever. A leopard didn't change its spots, a zebra couldn't lose its stripes and perpetual playboys didn't change in fourteen days. If she'd known how often she'd be singing that same damned refrain, she would have never said the words in the first place.

"That's why they wanted Sterling back?" asked the stupid

girl broadcaster, giving all women reporters everywhere a bad name, and at that, Elizabeth pulled herself out of those comforting hands that seemed to madden her senses and numb her foolish brain, both at the same time.

"We don't have to watch this," said Demetri. However, Elizabeth wasn't about to turn off Mike and Sandy. For all that mindless chattering, this was some downright fascinating stuff.

"I think I should," she said, still managing to smile. It was a little hard, but she did it.

Mike jabbered on, smiling with perfectly capped teeth. "Sandy, I think the endorsements will start flooding in for Demetri, and Valencia is looking for a new spokeswoman for their line of cosmetics, marketed under the Softsilk name. Elizabeth would be perfect. It's a fairy tale come to life, and he'll be riding the tide."

"Sounds like perfect timing for Demetri, Mike."

The pretty-boy broadcaster smirked, definitely smirked. "Oh, yeah. It took a lot to temper the bad publicity from the royal scandal, but taking a sharp 180—that's, well, I have to say, this move is a lot like he drives."

This move is a lot like he drives.

Demetri clicked off the television, and the silence was deafening. He looked at her, but she was sad to see that words of indignation weren't springing to his lips, and eventually she didn't want to stare at him anymore. She looked down, saw her hands twisting together and balled up a fist and socked it right into the back of that pretty antique sofa. She hoped the damned thing broke. "Sterling's primary sponsor is Softsilk? I didn't know that. They've been wanting me to do commercials for them for forever. Small world."

She saw him wince. "I don't know what all their brands are."

"What sort of man falls in love in fourteen days?" she asked, meaning it as a rhetorical question, but it was actually a pretty good one. One of those thought-provoking questions that she hadn't considered twenty-four hours ago, or forty-eight hours ago, or seventy-two hours ago, when she had given up her heart—her *heart!*—to this…this… Sadly, she looked at Demetri. Even now, she couldn't think bad thoughts. Instead, when she looked at him, she got lost, not wanting to look away.

Finally he spoke. "I know what you're doing. Don't think this, Elizabeth. I love you." He said it so softly, so sincerely, so heart-weepingly false.

"What sort of deal did you cook up with Valencia?" she asked, not that she wanted to know, but there was a small, sane part of her, one that wasn't love-struck crazy, that could still think with rational logic.

It took a second for him to meet her eyes. One second too long. He looked at her, cagey and guilty, a man who wasn't happy with himself. "I didn't do anything, Elizabeth. I haven't talked to Valencia. I have kept our relationship far, far away from business."

Elizabeth smoothed her hair with shaking hands. "Sandy had a good point, don't you think? Why, if I looked at this with my businesswoman's eyes, I'd say that you've got a pretty good thing here. Cleaning up your mess, they get a sponsor, and wow, everybody's happy."

Demetri turned, looked at her again, the dark eyes that she loved so serious, so somber. "It's business, nothing more. They saw a good PR opportunity, and they took advantage of it. After the rumors started," he stressed. "Not before."

"They've been after me for months."

"I didn't know that, Elizabeth. Hell, I didn't even know they made shampoo. I race cars."

"So what about leaks to the press?" she said, thinking back over the past few days, how the press always seemed to be lurking around. Demetri was a smart one. Good at finagling what he wanted. He could tip off a reporter without thinking twice.

"Stop. It's the press we're talking about. It's not like I needed to leak anything." He took her shoulders in his hands, kneading, caressing, and she stepped away.

Okay, maybe she would trust him on some of it. The press was like a flock of vultures, picking on the bones. But there was one stinkin' problem, one big question that nagged at her. "How did they know where we were last night?"

That seemed to hit a raw nerve. Demetri rounded on her, eyes shooting fire, that big chest heaving, and when he spoke, his voice rumbled louder than thunder. "They're the media. It's their damned job to know."

Sweet mercy, she wanted to believe, she truly did, but she wouldn't go through this again. With her father, it had hurt, but she had never loved him like a real daughter would. With Demetri, it had been perfect. The sweet, succulent passion that had overcome almost everything. Almost.

"What am I supposed to do? Am I not supposed to doubt you? Am I not supposed to think?" she asked, the words desperately quivering, right along with her nerves.

Demetri stared, the gentle eyes going cold and black. The room chilled until she needed a sweater, anything to warm her. A strong set of arms. *No.*

"You're supposed to trust me," he answered, hands jammed in the pockets of his fine blue blazer.

"I want to. I want it more than anything, but I'm not sure I can."

He cocked his head, assessing her. "Nothing's changed," he told her, but everything had changed. Suddenly she was second-guessing all the steps, all the words, all the touches she'd known. It wasn't fair.

"Before I didn't have reporters talking like I was wearing a price tag on my head." Realizing there were no strong arms that she could lean on anymore, she curled her arms around her stomach. It didn't help, so they fell weakly back to her sides.

"I don't need the money. I could buy you over three or four times, Elizabeth." She noticed that all the pretty words of love were now gone.

"All those business deals you had, all those cutthroat racing moves, that's who you are. Stepping all over whoever you needed to step over to get what you wanted." She had known it was part of him, that need to win, whatever the cost, whatever the price. Racing, business…*love.*

Stubbornly he shook his head. "When I'm with you, when you look at me, I want to be that man that I see in your eyes. I didn't know he even existed, but he does. *He's here,*" he insisted, jamming at his chest with his hand. "That's who I am, Elizabeth, and you have to know that, you have to believe that, or he won't exist anymore."

The vulnerability in those eyes was killing her, making her weak, and she didn't want to be weak. "Don't put this on me. You control your own destiny and your own decision making, not me."

"And I had nothing to do with this," he insisted.

"I can't do this," she answered, her voice as weak as her heart. "I can't do this."

When she said that, all the fight disappeared from him.

"I don't get it. I said the exact right things, I did the exact right things, but it wouldn't have been good enough for you, would it? Maybe not the Valencia deal, but there would be something. Some piece of gossip, some ill-timed statement from a friend, and we'd be doing this all over again, wouldn't we? We'll be doing this every time, won't we? Your test will never end, because I won't ever meet your standards."

And there he was, putting all the blame on her. Her conscience flared up, angry because she didn't deserve it. Angry because she did.

When she looked at him again, her eyes were cold, frozen, because something warm in her had died. Elizabeth had grown up. "I think it's time that you leave now."

He didn't look back. Not even once.

The next morning, Elizabeth went back to Quest. She should have run to Nashville, or gone home to her mother in Memphis, but even now, a part of her didn't want to go too far away from him. She hated that she was that weak.

It was late afternoon before she dared to spend time with Melanie, whose eyes were sharper than most. Melanie took her riding to the ridge, a place for sharing secrets and giggles, not heartbreak and tears. Elizabeth wouldn't be the first one to break the tradition.

"How're you doing?" Melanie asked, as if Elizabeth were the one with all the problems.

"I'm fine, cuz," she said, curling up on the grass, watching the clouds. The weather was colder today, dark clouds rolling in from the west. There'd be a storm, and this time, she would welcome it. It suited her frame of mind. The darkness, the cold.

"What happened?"

"I only wanted to spend some time with my favorite cousin. What's wrong with that?"

"Normally, not a lot. But in light of the television reports…" Melanie trailed off suggestively.

"Can we not talk about that, Melanie? I will eventually, because you know me, can't shut me up. But not yet. Today, I want to look at the sky and not worry about a thing."

"I know you're mad, Elizabeth.…"

"You were right, Melanie. I should have listened to you, but I didn't. So, bravo, cuz. You were right.…" She pulled at the grass, jerking it out by the roots.

Melanie's gaze was a lot more disapproving than comforting, which was Elizabeth's first clue that this wasn't going to be the Pity-Fest that she craved. "You shouldn't quit on him."

"*Now* you're switching sides?" This was totally unfair. Elizabeth needed support, not Benedict Arnold.

"He's been working with Marcus and the horses. Marcus said in the beginning Demetri was wasn't paying attention, but he started to care. He's a good man, Elizabeth, and he's different since you. He cares."

A tiny part of Elizabeth wanted to believe, a tiny part of Elizabeth did believe, but the cautious part of her knew better. "He cares about his business deals, but not everybody wants to sell themselves out for soft and shiny hair with bounce."

Melanie laughed. "I don't think that was his intention. He's not a part of this and you know it. It's business. He's not like that."

"No. He's exactly like that, and that's part of the problem."

"I've known him for longer than you have."

Elizabeth wanted to laugh. Yeah, the whole world had known him for longer than she had. "Is Brent back?"

"He was supposed to fly in this morning."

Finally, an excuse to talk about something else. Elizabeth took it and grabbed it, because she was weakening, softening. Before you knew it, she'd be decked out in gold eye shadow and calling the sky green. She jumped to her feet and dusted off her hands. There were problems here. Problems to be solved.

"Well, why are you wasting time with me? Melanie, you should be down at the house."

It was Melanie's turn to go deep into denial. "I don't want to know, Elizabeth."

Elizabeth leaned over and gave her cousin a weak hug. "Come on. I'll race you back. This time, I'll take that twenty-dollar bet and raise you a couple of hundred."

Melanie shook her head, and climbed on the gray. "You hear that, sweetheart? Elizabeth wants to be parted from her money." She leaned low, whispered in the horse's ear and then they were off, and Elizabeth didn't catch up to her cousin until she was back at the stables, whistling, grooming the gray as if she'd been there all day.

"You ready to see if your brother's back?"

Melanie shook her head. "Not really."

Elizabeth held out her hand. "Come on. We'll go see together."

Brent was the second-oldest son of Thomas Preston. Not having the genius of his older brother, Andrew, not having the horse sense of Melanie, he was still the first one to jump into a scrape when someone needed help. The last few years had been hard on him and it shone in his blue eyes. He was talking with Hugh and Thomas, the three heads huddled together, when Elizabeth and Melanie found him in the library.

Melanie ran to her brother and hugged him tight, the way brothers and sisters were supposed to behave, supporting each other, always there to stick up for each other. Elizabeth watched, until Brent saw her, gave her a casual wave.

"I'll catch up with you later, Elizabeth—and think about what I said," Melanie told her, before the Prestons shut the door on Elizabeth once again.

Nearly forty-seven minutes later, the doors opened up, and Brent stormed out, the door slamming behind him. Thomas Preston followed, and whatever had transpired, it sure wasn't pretty.

Elizabeth looked at Melanie silently, her eyes questioning, but Melanie only shook her head. Elizabeth peeked in the doorway, saw Uncle Hugh sitting, his shoulders slumped, his eyes droopy.

"You mind if I come in?" she asked.

He gestured to a chair. "Make yourself at home, Elizabeth. You're always welcome here."

"And thank you for that," she said. "I don't mean to intrude, but what did Brent find out? Did he find the computer tech? Is anybody closer to clearing this thing up?"

"No. He thinks he's found a connection in Ireland—"

"Well that's great news!" she nearly yelled, because somebody, somewhere needed to hear great news, and Elizabeth was going to hold tight to whatever good she could.

"But it's only Brent heading off on a wild-goose chase." Hugh ran a hand through the remaining wisps of gray on his head. "Thomas is ready to quit. I look at what my family is going through, and I don't think it's worth it."

Thomas Preston? Quit? Elizabeth looked at Hugh, mightily alarmed. "Quit? What do you mean exactly by the word *quit?*"

"We're talking about selling the stables."

"No!"

Hugh looked at her, surprised. "Sometimes things are more trouble than they're worth."

"This is your life. This is Uncle Thomas's life. This is the entire Preston heritage. Y'all can't sell that off."

"But no one's happy. Brent's mad at me. Melanie's walking around on eggshells, Thomas closets himself in the study, talking on the phone, trying to convince the owners to leave their horses at Quest."

"I can give you enough money to get through this."

"Elizabeth, you have no idea how much it costs to run an operation this big. We have a staff of over fifty employees that I need to take care of. The money from the concert, Demetri's race. That'll buy us two months, tops."

"There's more where that came from, Uncle Hugh."

He shook his head, his face turning stubborn. "No, Elizabeth. The ban may never be lifted. You don't send good money after bad."

"I can't believe you. You're just going to walk away from all this, walk away from everything you love—just give up without a fight?"

"You gotta know when to throw in your cards, isn't that right, Elizabeth?" Then he looked at her, blue eyes still sharp, still seeing so much, and suddenly they weren't talking about the stables anymore. "So what's it going be, Elizabeth? Fight or walk away?"

Elizabeth slammed her palm on the wooden chair arm, and it stung, but she needed that pain. "I don't understand. You were against this. You and Melanie both. What's changed?"

"Demetri. I got him on the phone yesterday. Yelled and bellowed at the man. And you know what he told me?"

"What?" asked Elizabeth, not wanting to be curious, but everything about Demetri made her curious. Even when she should be careful about that man, she wanted to know everything he said, every detail about his life.

"He said he loved you. He talked in a lot of ways I've never heard Demetri Lucas talk before. I think he's changed. I think it's good for a man to change. Maggie changed me, Elizabeth. When that happens, you can't walk away."

Elizabeth looked at her uncle, and felt the single tug at her heart. "I don't know, Uncle Hugh. I just don't know."

There must be a time in every woman's life when she has to see that perhaps perfection has its flaws. It wasn't an easy turnaround for Elizabeth, who had always assumed a prince wore a shiny gold crown that never rusted, consistently brought the princess to orgasm with only a deep look and could slay dragons with no loss of blood or injury. But these past long, dark hours had given her time to question her own ideals.

In her heart—the one organ that she relied on more often than her gut—she knew that Demetri hadn't parlayed their relationship into an advertising sponsorship. She didn't know how she knew, she just did. And it wasn't her foolish mind that brought her to that conclusion, but her far more sensible heart.

He had laid everything out in front of her, and she still hadn't trusted him, but not anymore. Today was a new day.

Her decision to call him was easier than she thought, and she dialed Demetri with fingers that didn't want to stop shaking.

"We need to talk."

"Really?" he asked coolly. *Dammit.* She'd been so proud of herself for being bighearted and all-forgiving, and here he was going to make her work for it.

"Can I see you this afternoon?" she asked nicely.

"I'm going to the track. I have a race to get ready for."

"It's important," she said, wishing he were just a hair less stubborn than her. Their life together wasn't going to be easy. "Please."

Apparently begging worked wonders. "Where?"

"I'm at Quest, but I don't want anyone to see us right at the moment. There's a field just east of the house."

"I'll be there in half an hour."

He was there in twenty minutes, and she didn't ask how. Damned fool. He was going to get killed and make her cry, and she would kill him all over again for that.

"What's the problem?" he asked, stuffing his hands into the pockets of the black leather jacket. Her eyes traced over him, relearning the lines and angles. She didn't think she'd ever get tired of looking at that face with all those dips and furrows. So handsome, so strong.

Focus, Elizabeth. Keep on track, here. "Hugh and Thomas are thinking of selling out, Demetri. I won't let that happen. Are you in this, or not?"

"I thought you didn't trust me."

She waited a beat, because she had hoped to breeze right past things, back to where they were before, but there was a coolness in his eyes today, and she knew this discussion was going to cost her things. Namely, a little bit of her pride. "Do we have to talk about this now?" she asked, stalling for time, because her pride was a precious commodity and not to be wasted lightly.

"Yeah, I think we do." He looked down at the ground, gathered his thoughts and then looked up again. Some of the coolness had left his face, and she noticed the glimmer in his eyes. The glimmer of hope. "I'm sorry about what happened. I didn't like it, but I was put in a bad position. I didn't have a choice without hurting people that I don't want to hurt. I love you, I will always love you, but we live in a world where people say things, where people will continue to say things. You're going to have to accept it, Elizabeth, because there are a lot of things I can change for you, but that's not one."

She wanted to kiss him then and there, but they needed to talk first. She'd called him for a reason.

"Oliver's going to be buying some horses. Probably one hundred, or maybe two," she stated, not even phrasing it as a polite request.

"Oliver's very excited about the prospect," he said, a smile pulling at the corners of that perfect mouth. God, she'd missed that smile. She didn't realize exactly how much until right this moment, when her knees felt a little jittery.

"I think he needs a whole fleet of horses," she said, locking her knees firmly in place.

"We'll go to Keeneland tonight. It's the opening reception and the auction. But there's something you should realize, Elizabeth. If the ban doesn't get lifted soon, Hugh won't have a choice, whether Oliver stables new horses there or not."

"Then we'll think of something else," she said, not allowing him to doubt.

"We?" he asked, looking at her curiously.

"We," she said firmly. "I've got money, and there's all that money of yours that you keep bringing up. I think it's time you spent it on something worthwhile."

Again with the smile. Again her heart stopped, exactly like before. Oh, Good Lord, this man was going to be the death of her.

"You trust me?" he asked, his eyes still wary.

She nodded once.

"I missed you last night," he told her.

"Are you going to kiss me?" she asked, because eating crow hadn't been as hard as she thought it was going to be, and he had the world's most kissable mouth, and it belonged to her. *Only her*.

Demetri shook his head. "I have to go to the track. And I work better when I don't think about you. If I kiss you, if I touch you, I'm not going to be thinking about the track."

"Really?" she said, inordinately pleased by the idea of it.

"I'll pick you up here tonight. Wear something nice."

She smiled, her mind already racing.

He turned and opened the car door and was ready to climb in when he stopped. "And, Elizabeth?"

"Yes?"

"Pack your stuff. You won't be coming home."

He got in the car and drove off, leaving her with nothing more than an open mouth, tingling breasts and that damnable ache back between her thighs.

Oh, sweet mercy.

Chapter Thirteen

After spending three hours sweating at the track, Demetri was no closer to the driver's cup. Today Oliver had outdriven him, fair and square. No, when it was all said and done, Demetri's shoulder ached, he was going to see his father in a week, and all he wanted to do was grab Elizabeth and lose himself inside her again.

At the moment he felt like the dinosaur he was.

However, even dinosaurs need to drink, so after cleaning up, he met Oliver in the bar. "Where's Elizabeth?" asked Oliver, probably not the smartest question he could have asked.

"You're lucky she's speaking to me," Demetri said, a little more bitter than he intended.

"Why is this my fault?"

"Oh, let me think. The leaks to the press?"

Oliver didn't even pretend to be innocent. "I might have mentioned a few things to Valencia's PR people. Elena's really quite charming when you get to know her well. She might have mentioned a few things to the press. However, I didn't wallop Hunter Lyons, but I would have liked to. He's a dirty bastard. You're much better off without him."

"You don't even deny it, do you?"

"It all ended well. We got our sponsor back. My spot is safe, and you have Elizabeth," Oliver answered with a blameless grin, before ordering a couple of bourbons, Kentucky's finest. Demetri took the shot in one gulp. It was smooth, sweet and didn't do a thing to take the edge off.

"You owe me, Oliver. And I know exactly how you can repay the favor."

"Oh, fine. But someday, I'm going to be in the driver's seat. You know that, don't you?"

Demetri laughed. "Keep dreaming, Oliver. Keep dreaming."

At Keeneland, Elizabeth had never seen so many horses in such close quarters. Temporary stalls were set up around the grounds, grooms parading horses in a circle, people dressed up like Sunday church, women in hats and gowns, men in dark suits and ties. The horses didn't seem to mind, either.

It felt strange wandering through the grass in heels and Oscar de la Renta, but sometimes Demetri looked sideways at her, taking in the royal-blue dress, which accented her eyes nicely, and her other parts—which she wasn't shy about using when the occasion demanded it. At these moments, the hardship of her heels sinking into the soft ground was well worth the price. Besides, he looked mouthwateringly nice, too. He'd worn a tux—again—and she really liked him in formal wear. All crisp and sharp, and elegant.

They walked around the grounds, trailing behind Oliver— Oliver and his entourage, which was probably the more polite word. He'd brought a "secretary" who probably wouldn't know dictation if it came up and bit her in the most likely artificially shaped butt. After the secretary came another two women.

Twins. After one too many sultry giggles, Elizabeth turned to Demetri and rolled her eyes.

"It's like this everywhere for you drivers, isn't it?" She could see the come-hither looks that Demetri was getting, and all from women glittering with jewels and their faux tans.

"Jealous?" he asked.

Elizabeth snorted. "'Course not. If you choose to spend your leisure time with some peroxide blonde with hooters the size of Everest, then I'm not concerned at all. Although I will say it doesn't speak highly of your character."

"Hooters the size of Everest?" he asked, his mouth curving in a darned irrepressible grin.

"It's an exaggeration, Demetri. Nothing more," she answered pertly.

However, he wasn't done. He bent low, whispering in her ear. "I've never been attracted to women with large breasts. I like something more perky, firm, hand-size."

"Hand-size," she repeated, wondering if she was ever going to get used to this volley of heat inside her, the one he created with a look, a touch, a word.

Demetri nodded, the devil dancing in his eyes "Want me to show you?"

Quickly Elizabeth whacked him on his good arm, before she got any more lurid ideas than the ones that were zipping in her brain. "We're here to buy horses," she said, but he saw the blush in her cheeks and laughed.

Fortunately, she spied a pretty filly with a golden blond coat and the softest brown eyes. Heartsongs's Folly. Elizabeth stroked the horse, while Demetri looked her over. "This one?" he asked, and she nodded.

He asked the owner about her pedigree and racing history, and then made a mark next to her name. "Next?" he asked, and they walked on. In less than an hour, Elizabeth had picked out twenty horses, Demetri had found forty-seven, and even Oliver had found some horses he liked, as well. It wasn't a stableful, but it was a start.

The moon was high in the night sky when the auction started, and Oliver knew his part well. He bid and kept winning, and at the end of two hours, he was the proud owner of some sixty horses, at which time, Elizabeth decided she could forgive him his womanizing ways. "Thank you," she said, managing a smile for his three women, as well.

"Shameless," she whispered to Demetri later, as he led her out on the dance floor. "It's just embarrassing how those girls are hanging all over him."

The music began slow and sultry, and soon enough, Elizabeth was curled into Demetri, showing the other girls exactly how shameless was properly done.

In the car that night, she asked him about Canada. She'd been to Toronto, and played a concert once on the Canadian side of Niagara Falls, but she'd never been to Vancouver.

"It rains a lot," he told her, in a tone that didn't invite more conversation.

"You race there every year?" she asked, because when Elizabeth wanted to know something, it took more than a tone to stop her.

"Not all the time," he answered, his jaw locked tight, and she could see the way his hands nearly strangled the steering wheel.

"It's sure close to Seattle," she said, wondering what had happened to the easygoing man she'd been dancing with, because he was fairly burning up with tension, and not the good sort, either. "Close to your home. Will your father be there?"

"I don't know," he answered, shifting hard and fast, sending her back against the seat with a lurch. The car shot forward, and Elizabeth grabbed the door handle. "That's mighty fast," she told him as he took a turn and left her insides scattered back on the road behind them.

He didn't respond, and after that, she kept quiet, wishing he trusted her as much as she'd gone and trusted him. Maybe in time.

He took her back to the old Victorian, and the grounds were quiet tonight. Too quiet. "No Hunter Lyons?" Elizabeth asked as he led her up the creaking steps. "How'd you know it'd be okay to come back here?"

Demetri's hand tightened on her arm. "Suspicious?"

"Nope," she said, keeping it light. "Just asking."

"This is what you get when you hire a security force the size of a small third-world country."

She looked around, noted absolutely nothing and no one. "Wow. They're like ghosts."

"We're safe," he said, and they went inside.

It was black tonight, no candles burning this time, only a sliver of moonlight that shot like brilliant prisms through the old glass panes. Elizabeth shivered in the cold.

Demetri didn't wait, but grabbed her as soon as the door slammed shut. She was in his arms, his ravenous mouth tearing into hers, and there was no magic this time, no time for thinking at all. She was dizzy with the urgency as he took her in the dark. He'd always made things so pretty for her, but not now. This was desperately new, and she wanted to know where the darkness took her.

The tear of her gown ripped through the quiet, and then his hands were on her, rough and reckless, driving her with that same hard aggression with which he drove his cars.

Faster and faster, jolting whimpers from her mouth. Pleasure, so much dark pleasure pumping through her blood, her heart beating so fast, too fast. He took and took until her body was drained and limp, and then he braced her against the wall, big hands clutching underneath her hips, holding her as though she weighed nothing. Greedy lips fastened on her breast until she was going to die all over again. She cried out, nonsense words, wanting more. She wasn't sure she was going to survive this storm that he was whipping up inside her, but she was eager for more. Elizabeth had sensed this wildness from the moment she met him, but…heavens, her heart thundered in her ears, the drenching pressure spinning and swirling all around her.

Then he plunged deeply, thrusting hard and fast, and pulling her further over the precipice. Her legs locked around his waist, her back arched, and she gloried in his strength, mindless with it. In the darkness, she could hear his rough whispers, see the shadows in his eyes and feel the strained iron in the muscles of his chest.

Again and again they went over the edge, and each time she thought there was no more, he brought her to climax again. At long last, Demetri buried his face against her neck, his body stilled, and then he emptied himself into her. The moon had disappeared, the prisms of the windows gone, leaving only the shadows spinning in the dark.

"Are you all right?" he asked, their bodies still joined together.

"No," she managed.

"I'm so sorry," he said, his lips warm against her face, grazing her cheek, her swollen mouth. Then he cradled her up in his arms and took her upstairs, took her to bed. He didn't say anything else, and neither did she. Elizabeth should've been frightened by what he'd let her see, but down deep, she had sensed all along there was more of him hidden underneath. Demetri had been so patient and charming with her, a remarkable—and somewhat contradictory—accomplishment for a man who spent his days testing the limits of gravity and physics.

His shoulder might be healed, but there were wounds still to be tended. All through the night she stroked him, soothed him, until finally, as the sun started to rise, he slept.

The next three days were some of the best in his life, and after they were over, they had another one hundred horses to add to their stable. At night, she was in his bed. That first night, he hadn't meant to be so rough with her. He knew that Elizabeth deserved better than that, but sometimes he felt the void inside him, and he wanted to fill it, wanted to fill it with her.

After that one incident, he'd made it up to her, always gentle, always careful. Sometimes she'd do something, nip at his skin, take him in hand, and the darkness would begin again, but he always tamped it down, and Elizabeth, who could never keep quiet about anything, didn't say a word.

Vancouver was coming. He could feel it. His skin was getting tight, and he was always shifting, always moving, trying to relax. Only with Elizabeth did he truly relax. She could make him comfortable, but even Elizabeth couldn't make him forget.

He had so many memories of his brother. The way Seth had always tagged along, the way he had tried to imitate Demetri. Demetri had encouraged it, had fed on it. The day they'd gone rock climbing, the day Seth had died, Demetri had taken on a steep cliff, and of course, *of course,* Seth had wanted to follow.

Those memories were never far away, and that afternoon on the track, maybe he took more risks than normal, but he didn't care. Demetri was indestructible. It didn't matter how fast he went, it didn't matter how hard he cut the wheel, it didn't matter how many times he crashed, every single damned time, Demetri walked away. For Seth, it'd only taken one fall, one life snapped out in an instant. Life wasn't fair, and no matter how many times Demetri tried to even the odds, no matter how many times Demetri laughed at the Fates, his life never snapped. Not even close.

Demetri shook off the old memories; right now there were new worries to handle, namely Hugh.

On Wednesday, he and Oliver went to Quest, while Elizabeth drove into Lexington to talk with her manager. They found Hugh and Thomas sitting in the observation area, watching the gray colt race, and comparing notes.

Demetri performed the introductions, and then Oliver, being

well coached, got straight to business. "I'm hoping you have some space at Quest," explained Oliver, taking a seat at the conference table.

Thomas turned to Demetri, his eyes curious. "How much space?"

"I have almost two hundred horses that I need to put somewhere," said Oliver proudly.

"Oliver's a little green," Demetri explained, and Hugh looked at Oliver suspiciously, but Oliver only shrugged innocently.

"You have space here?" he asked.

Hugh looked as if he was going to object, but Thomas stepped in before he could. "You know about the ban?" he asked, but Oliver had been prepped well about that, as well.

"It won't affect their reputations. None of the horses are ready to race yet. Mainly they're yearlings. A couple have racing histories, but most are green—just like me."

Hugh peered at Demetri, the faded blue eyes not missing a thing. "I thought you said he didn't know horses."

"He's a fast learner."

"I do swing a mean golf club," added Oliver.

"We're not in a position to say no." Thomas nodded curtly, his steady gaze focused on Demetri, and Demetri felt the itch return. There were men in the world who would never understand him. Thomas Preston. Andre Lucas. Most people bought into the lightning-fast veneer, and when they looked deeper... Demetri looked away. "Is Marcus still here?" he asked.

Hugh nodded.

"Good. Thomas, could you show Oliver around and introduce him to Marcus? I've told Oliver great things about his work, and Oliver has tons of questions."

"Sure," answered Thomas, and Oliver bade his goodbyes with the proper amount of pomp and circumstance, and then left Demetri alone with Hugh. Again, just as planned.

"How are things?" asked Demetri.

Hugh sighed, running a hand through what was left of the gray hair. "Brent left for Ireland today. He tracked down a vet who worked at Angelina Stud Farm when Apollo's Ice was there. Brent's also going to head over to London to talk to Nolan Hunter—the viscount who owns Apollo's Ice."

"What are the odds that any of this will pan out?"

"Long, but it's all we've got to go on at the moment."

It might not have stopped Hugh, but the light was missing from his eyes, and there were deep lines in his face that hadn't been there before. Demetri hated to see his friend so beaten.

"You're not going to lose this place," he promised.

"I don't know."

"I think Elizabeth would shoot you if she heard you say that."

"I'm glad to see at least one set of problems got solved."

Demetri nodded.

"She won't like your racing, Demetri," Hugh said, a warning in his tone.

Demetri wasn't worried. Not about Elizabeth. "She's fine with it."

Hugh laughed. "You are a blind fool, aren't you?"

Once again Hugh had missed the steel in Elizabeth, but not Demetri. He loved her for many things. He needed her for her strength. "You seem to underestimate her, Hugh."

"I don't." Then added after a beat, "Not all the time, anyway."

"We'll see you after we're back from Canada. I'm going to marry her."

Hugh rose, and saw him to the front of the offices. "Melanie owes me two hundred for that one. I told her I knew things, but she thought Elizabeth couldn't stand you." He looked toward the main house, smiling once again. "I'll go see her now. God, it's good to be right."

Vancouver in November was never a good place to race. The streets were gray and rain-slick, reflecting like deadly mirrors.

The wind from the bay blew in cold, wet blasts, and then there was the problem of Demetri's nerves. He never liked this race, never liked being this close to home, never liked being this close to the place where Seth had died.

With Elizabeth by his side, he'd thought he'd be able to shake some of it off, but this time, Elizabeth with her all-too-knowing eyes only added to the burn inside him.

That first night in the hotel, he tried to distract her, but Elizabeth was never easily distracted. It was late, after the chaos of the press conferences, after the trials of dinner and after the requisite photo-ops with the sponsors, and all he wanted was to go upstairs and take her to bed. It was the one place that he found peace.

"What's wrong?" she asked as soon as they walked through the door, astute blue eyes watching him too closely.

He slung his dinner jacket over the couch, and loosened his shirt and tie. "Nothing that can't be fixed with this," he answered, holding her, and getting lost in the wonder of her kiss. Every time he felt it, the calming effect of her heart beating so close to his. Such a simple thing that he craved like a drug.

"Now will you tell me what's wrong?" she asked when he lifted his head, not nearly as lost as he was.

"Nerves."

She made a rude noise. "That dog don't hunt, Demetri."

Instead of answering, he unzipped her dress, watching it slide over her shoulders, fascinated by the smooth silk of her skin. He didn't want to talk, he needed her, needed this.

She watched him, eyes still all-knowing, but this time when he took her in his arms, she was smart enough to not look any deeper. He knew she might not like what she found.

On Friday night, Elizabeth and Demetri met his father for dinner in a tiny seafood restaurant out on the water. Oh, Demetri had made all sorts of excuses, saying they were too busy, that he wanted to kick back and relax. However, Elizabeth was too curious to meet the only family that Demetri had.

Ever since they'd gotten to the city, she knew that something was eating away at Demetri. His eyes weren't watching her like before. Whenever she got too close, his gaze would dart away, looking beyond to the next horizon. When they arrived at the restaurant, Andre Lucas was sitting quietly at the bar waiting for them. The resemblance between father and son was remarkable. Demetri's father was nearly as tall, the same dark, searching eyes, but his hair was steely gray, and where Demetri spoke with an all-American accent, the Greek influence was there in his father's curt words.

Demetri performed the introductions, his voice tight, his smile strained, and Elizabeth could feel his tense arm muscles underneath her fingertips. She wondered if this had been a bad idea, pushing for this meeting as she had, but it was too late for regrets. Best to push away and get through the night. Not that it was easy. Whatever had happened between the two men, there was bad blood here. Andre Lucas was charming with her, using the same pretty words that Demetri did, but whenever he looked at his son, his eyes chilled.

After they finished with dinner, her cell rang. She was dying to ignore it, but Demetri looked at her.

"Aren't you going to take that?"

"I can wait," she said, not wanting to leave the two of them alone.

"It could be important."

And Andre Lucas was just as insistent. "You go. Leave us alone to talk."

With a reluctant sigh, Elizabeth took her phone and made her way to the bar.

"She's very nice." Demetri's father swirled the brandy in his glass, and Demetri knew it was easier for his father to stare into his glass than to look at his surviving son.

"She is," he agreed. "How are you?"

"As well as can be expected," answered Andre, his tone sharp, never forgetting, never letting Demetri forget.

"Whatever."

His father pushed an envelope across the table. "Your check."

"I don't want it."

"I don't, either," replied Andre, and Demetri grabbed the envelope and ripped the whole thing to tiny pieces.

His father was angry, eyes narrowed, jaw locked, but Demetri had known he would be. That was why he did it. It was a game they had played for years. Before Seth died, it had been about Demetri testing the reins. Now, the game had teeth. Sharp teeth that stung.

"You enjoy this?"

Demetri laughed, because "this" was hell. The strained relationship, the monosyllabic conversations. Their relationship had never been easy. Demetri had been the wild child in the Lucas family, and his father blamed him for corrupting Seth. "I hate this."

"You shouldn't be racing anymore. It's a miracle you've survived this long."

"Do you care?"

"I'm still your father."

Demetri stared impassively. "I'm not going to retire. What would I do?"

"Live like the rest of the mortals. You have more than enough money."

"You're still working," Demetri reminded him.

"Work is all I have left."

"That's a choice you made, Father."

Andre Lucas pulled some bills from his pocket and laid them on the table. "This was a mistake."

"It was what you wanted," Demetri reminded him.

"I thought you had changed."

"No, still the same reckless, irresponsible son that I've always been. Isn't that what you said?"

His father stood, his face cold and stubborn. "Will it always be this way?"

"Will you ever forgive me?" Demetri shot back, and as soon as the words were out of his mouth, Demetri swore viciously. He didn't want to need his father, and he didn't want his forgiveness.

But in spite of it all, he found himself watching his father anxiously, waiting for an answer to the question he had no business asking.

His father didn't answer. Andre Lucas simply regarded his son one last time, and then he turned around and left.

One o'clock in the morning was what the bedside clock said, and Elizabeth knew that Demetri hadn't slept. He lay there, staring up at the ceiling. Eventually he stopped pretending and got up to get dressed.

Elizabeth sat up, peered at him in the darkness. "Where are you going?"

"To the track," he answered, and then he stalked out the door, the devil nipping behind him.

Elizabeth got dressed and followed, watching him from the edge of the track, the high-pitched whine of the engine like the sounds of a bad dream. The red car dodged around the track, veering drunkenly, but he hadn't had more than a glass of wine at dinner. That was nothing but Demetri being stupid.

After he had burned up a tank of gas, Demetri stopped, and drove the car back into the garage. It was then that he noticed Elizabeth, and he walked over, hands jammed in the pockets of his jeans.

"Why are you here?"

"It seemed like a nice night to sit and watch cars running around in circles. Why are you here?"

"I have a race in two days. The trials are tomorrow."

"Such dedication," she snapped. "What happened tonight?"

He took her hand, his eyes changing in a flash from hard to hot. "Let's go back to the hotel. You're right. I shouldn't have come."

"Why don't you tell me what's eating at you?" she asked.

For answer, he kissed her—long, hard, practiced seduction, nothing more. "Let's go back," he whispered, after he lifted his head. Elizabeth studied him, hiding behind his Hollywood smile, moonlight glancing off his face.

They went back to the hotel and made love in cool, silken sheets, and eventually Demetri fell asleep, his breathing even and calm. For the remainder of the night, it was Elizabeth who lay there, staring up at the ceiling.

Demetri came in third in the trials. Two slots behind Giovanni Marcusi and one slot behind Oliver. Afterward, he stalked over to the garage, because the wing had moved in his third lap, causing him to lose precious time on the corners, and he knew that Rossi hadn't tightened it as he'd asked.

Rossi approached, his face creased in a smile. Yeah, Rossi could smile. He hadn't come in third.

"Why didn't you double-check the wing?"

The smile disappeared. "I did."

"Yeah, right."

Rossi stood an inch closer. "I did. You don't believe me, look at it yourself."

Fine. Demetri went to yank on the red fiberglass, and his injured shoulder got shot to hell, but the wing didn't give an inch.

Demetri swore as the pain exploded up and down his arm once again.

Goddamn. Twenty-four hours. He only had to get through the next twenty-four hours, and then he could get out of this godforsaken place, and leave his past firmly behind him.

* * *

That night, Elizabeth barely saw Demetri. There was a dinner for the drivers. The press hounded them with questions, but Demetri was all Hollywood. All smiles and charm.

The big faker.

She had thought she'd be able to talk to him once they were done, but he had an excuse for everything. He needed to go down to the garage to check on the car, but Elizabeth knew they weren't allowed to mess with the cars before the race. Oliver wanted some advice on the track, but Oliver was busy with the two brunettes he'd met in the hotel bar. Eventually Demetri stopped making excuses to her and simply left.

Back in the room, alone, Elizabeth paced and muttered, and paced and muttered, but it didn't do any good. After seeing the haunted look in Demetri's eyes, she wasn't sure she could do anything at all.

Early on race day, the rain started in earnest first thing. It wasn't those heavy, earthshaking thunderstorms like the ones back home, with crashing lightning and booming thunder. This was gray, dismal and the constant drip-drip of rain that made you forget what sunshine looked like. Elizabeth stood at the hotel window, the dark clouds low over the water, cursing the gray world, cursing the gray color of her heart.

Since they'd arrived in Canada, it seemed as though nothing was going right. She wasn't sure what was eating at Demetri, and he didn't feel the need to talk. This morning, he'd been gone before she woke up, leaving a note to say that he'd be at the track and would be back by lunch.

Elizabeth was alone at a time when she really didn't want to be alone. She picked up her phone, started to call Tobey, but she didn't want to hear any of his business talk today. Today, she just needed a friend, somebody who was in worse straits than she. Somebody who would take her mind off her problems.

Melanie answered on the first ring.

"What are you doing?" asked Elizabeth, sounding happy and cheerful and everything that she wasn't.

"Sleeping," she said in a groggy voice.

Elizabeth's eyes flew to the clock—9:00 a.m. That meant it was 6:00 a.m. back home.

"Oh my gosh. I'm sorry. Go back to sleep, we'll talk later."

Melanie sighed. "No. I should be up anyway. It was a long night last night."

"Why'd you stay up late? Something I should know about, cuz?"

"Brent came home."

Normally the return of Melanie's brother would be a good thing, but Melanie sure didn't sound perky about it. "So I guess he found something?"

"The vet was dead. Shot in a botched robbery."

"Dead? Could he have been targeted?"

"Maybe, but there's no way to know if it's connected to Apollo's Ice."

"Well, Brent will have to find something new."

"There is nothing new to find, Elizabeth."

"There's always gotta be something new."

"Not always. Sometimes it is what it is. Listen, I need to get dressed. I still have horses to train. Marcus put in his notice. I'll be helping Robbie with some of his work."

Elizabeth collapsed on the couch. This couldn't be happening. Not to the Prestons. "I'm sorry, Melanie."

"Don't be, Elizabeth. You tried. You having fun in Canada? Everything going okay out there?"

"It's great," answered Elizabeth, lying to her favorite cousin. "The weather's so calm and peaceful. All this rain makes you want to curl up in front of the fire, and just read a book all day."

"You'll have to tell me all about it when you get back."

"Sure. Don't worry, cuz. We'll figure something out," she said, and then hung up quickly before Melanie could disagree.

For three hours she waited, pacing, thinking, twiddling her thumbs while all around her the world was falling apart. By the time Demetri finally appeared, Elizabeth was pretty much a basket case.

She launched herself at him, and felt a moment's peace when his arms came around her, but it sputtered to nothing when she noticed the way he was holding his left arm.

"What is this? Why are you favoring your arm?" *Not now. Please Good Lord, don't let this be happening now.*

"It's nothing," Demetri answered.

"You can't race like this. Hell, you can barely lift it."

"That's not true. Some heat, pills. I'll be fine," he said carelessly, tossing away her concerns as if they were nothing.

"You can't race," she said, saying her words slow and careful, as if it would help him to understand.

"Yes, I can. I'm headed for the track. Are you coming with me, or not?"

He was looking at her as though today was any other day, as though this whole trip hadn't been full of potholes and problems.

"You can't go."

"I can," he said, stubborn, and she realized that he wasn't going to live. He was going to stand there, and be stupid, and reckless—and dead.

She rounded on him, thinking hard about whacking him on his injured arm with the sole purpose of hurting him so badly that he couldn't race, hurting him as badly as he was hurting her. "Listen to you! You are too stupid to live and don't care about dying."

Demetri laughed, and it wasn't a pretty sound. "I'm indestructible. Haven't you figured that out yet? It doesn't matter what I do, I always come out fine."

She rolled her eyes, wondering if he really believed everything that was coming out of his mouth. "What do you need to prove? Since we've gotten here, you're different."

That made him stop pretending. He glared at her, his jaw set as stubbornly as his heart. "How do you know, Elizabeth? What if this is me? What if this is all that I am?"

It was her turn to laugh. All this time she'd thought she was the stupid one. Couldn't he see who he was? Couldn't he see what was inside him? Good Lord, she did. Each and every day. "You know that's not true," she snapped.

"Come on, you're smart. You didn't want to believe I could be anything but what I was. An irresponsible driver who ran over whoever got in his way. A man so reckless he didn't deserve to live." His smile was so cold, she shivered.

Elizabeth shook her head, abandoning this argument because he wasn't going to see sense. He had made up his mind. "I'm not going to watch you kill yourself, Demetri. I can't."

"Then don't," he told her easily, as if he didn't care.

As if he didn't care.

"That's what you want?"

"No, but I can't change who I am, and you can't change who you are, so I think we're stuck."

"You don't mean that," she said, but she knew he did. She could tell by the hard stone in his eyes. There was nothing soft or gentle there, none of the tenderness she'd seen before. This man was a virtual stranger to her. "I won't be at the track this afternoon, Demetri. You're on your own now." It was a warning shot, designed to snap him out of it. It didn't work.

"I'll manage," he said, and she knew he would. He'd zoom right on without her, while she would die. No. Quickly she went to the closet and started throwing her clothes in a bag, not caring if she was breaking hangers left and right, not caring if her things wouldn't fit. It wasn't as though she was the world's best packer. Hell. She wiped her eyes, because water was bad on silk.

"What are you doing?" he asked, as if he didn't know.

She looked up at him, because she couldn't do this. She wouldn't do this. "Letting you manage, since you seem to be so good at it. I'm not nearly that talented."

"You're leaving?"

"Yeah."

He stayed silent, his eyes steadily regarding her, not even upset.

"You're not surprised," she said, noticing the quiet resignation on his face. A man who drove himself to win at all costs, but when it came to them, he was going to quit before he'd even started.

"We're too different. I wanted to change for you. You do that to people. Make them want to be better. But I'm not any different. People expect things from a race-car driver. I'm reckless and irresponsible, and that's not what you want. That's not what you need. Sometimes two people meet, and there's a chemical imbalance in the brain brought on by an overabundance of dopamine. Once those effects wear off…" He shrugged, as if what they'd had was nothing more than a mental defect. What was hardest for her was that she knew—*knew*—that he had changed for her. He just didn't believe it himself. He didn't believe in himself.

She'd thought trust was his problem, but that wasn't it. He didn't have faith. In her, in himself, in anything that didn't travel over two hundred miles per hour.

"Do you love me?" she asked.

"No," he answered, and she knew it was a lie. There was something dead in his eyes, something scary, and Elizabeth had no stomach left for thrills and chills and hot-rod drivers cruising on Dead Man's Curve. She wasn't going to watch him. She couldn't. She loved him too much.

"Dammit, Demetri. I can't do this."

"So you keep saying."

She stopped trying to pack, because the tears were getting in the way. "I'll send someone for my things. I have to leave. I have to get out of here."

"Do whatever you need to do, Elizabeth."

"You're wrong about so many things, I can't even begin to count." Frantically, she brushed at her cheeks, took one final look at him and slammed the door shut behind her.

She wasn't going to watch the race. She wasn't. So she took off in his favorite candy-red car and drove up Highway 1, listening to the race on the radio instead. Everything was fine until she was a good two hours out of the city. So far away that she couldn't make it back to watch no matter how badly she needed to.

Marcusi was ahead, Oliver in second and Demetri was third, and she didn't want anybody to be ahead of Demetri, only because that meant he would do something stupid. It was who he was. It was the reason she wasn't there, watching the race in person as she should've been. But no, he had to be stubborn, and stupid, and sure enough, he tried to pass Oliver. She'd prepped herself for this, talked herself into not panicking, but when he started to pull ahead, she pulled her car over, because she couldn't drive anymore. She needed to sit there, and pray. But she couldn't even do that, because she heard the squeal and the skid, and…

…ohGod ohGod ohGod…

…the crash.

Chapter Fourteen

They wouldn't let her in to see him, and wouldn't release any information. She wasn't family, and Demetri didn't know she was there, because the last time she saw him she had told him she couldn't do this. Elizabeth the coward. Elizabeth the quitter. Elizabeth the smug one, so sure she was right about everything.

She sat huddled in her corner of that antiseptic room, making all sorts of deals with God, because Demetri had to live. She'd watch every car race known to man. She'd make commercials, gazillions of commercials; she'd hawk every shampoo a woman could ever need. She'd be more patient, more caring, less judgmental. Elizabeth loved him and it really didn't matter how he drove or how he lived or how pigheaded he was.

In the big scheme of things, all she needed was for him to live.

When Jim Sterling came around the corner, she nearly kissed him. "How is he?"

He blinked at her. "Demetri's going to be fine."

She collapsed on the orange-cushioned seats, her head between her knees, and took long, deep breaths. *Thank you.*

"And Oliver?"

"He's in there with him now. Do you want to go see him?"

"Please."

Demetri had never liked hospitals. They were for people who had weaknesses, people who were lacking in some way, and he didn't like to acknowledge his weakness. Shortly after the doctor had taken an X-ray, Demetri had a sling for his shoulder, and another dose of pills. He didn't need the pills and he didn't need the sling.

For Demetri, the pain was nothing compared to the guilt inside him. After the doctors released him, some of the Sterling crew were there, but Demetri shrugged them off, wanting to be first in line when Oliver could see visitors.

"How are you?" he asked, entering Oliver's room, noticing the pale face and the huge cast on his leg.

"I've been better," answered Oliver, stiff upper lip firmly in place.

"The doctor said you broke your leg in four places." *And I'm responsible.*

"Good thing you picked the last race of the season to go all out on your teammate."

"I'm sorry," said Demetri, and he was. Bad actions have bad consequences, and he didn't want that anymore.

"I'll race you next year, and this time, I'll take the podium."

"Aren't you mad?" asked Demetri. It'd been a stupid mistake to try and pass Oliver. It had cost them both the race.

"Mad at you?" asked Oliver.

"At me."

Oliver looked at him for a minute, thinking silently before he finally began to talk. "You're the best driver I've ever seen.

You take chances and you don't care. Everyone else pulls up at the last minute, but not you."

"That's not necessarily a good thing, Oliver." Looking at Oliver, he saw his brother, and he didn't want Oliver to end up like Seth.

"For now, for me, it is. When I grow up, I want to be just like you."

The compliment embarrassed him. He didn't deserve it, so Demetri laughed.

Oliver managed a smile. "Don't think you're going to take the cup next year. There's a new sheriff in this town."

Demetri nodded once. "Yeah, I think there is. Take care of yourself, Oliver."

"You, too. I'll see you in a couple of months."

Maybe, thought Demetri to himself. Maybe not.

As he headed down the hospital corridors, Demetri didn't feel the familiar urge to run anymore. He was tired of running, and he was too old for it, anyway. No, it was time to face some things about himself. Not good things. Elizabeth had been right.

He looked up, blinked twice, not sure if he was dreaming, because she'd always been there in his dreams.

She ran toward him, her eyes red, and he hated himself for making her hurt. And then he was kissing her, and he didn't care about his arm, didn't care about the hospital, didn't care about anything but this. The rest of the world didn't matter. Not now.

He lifted his head, and moved away, but Elizabeth needed to touch him, needed to keep him close, so she reached out with shaking hands. She couldn't stop shaking. She needed to stop shaking, or those rehab rumors were going to start right up.

Oh, God.

Her fingers traced along his arm like a blind person feeling her way, and his eyes weren't cold, or hard, or anything like before. He looked perfect to her. "Do you hurt?"

"Not my arm," he said, and took her hand. They made their way down the hall into a waiting room where they could talk and be alone. There were so many words that were still in the air between them. There was an orange couch that matched the one in the hall, and she settled herself on it, waiting patiently. However long it took, she would wait for him.

Demetri sat, then stood, then paced, and finally faced her. He'd only said the words aloud once, the day he tried to explain to his father. That hadn't gone well. The events of that day ran in his head like a newsreel. He'd never tried again, but he needed to now. He needed for Elizabeth to believe in him. She needed to know the whole truth about who he was, and then she could decide. "I need to talk to you. There are things you should know about me."

"You don't need to tell me anything. You don't owe me anything," she said, looking up at him, unblinking, faith unflagging. She had been right about that, too. He didn't have her faith.

"Yes, I do," he said. "You need to know." Carefully he studied the world map on the wall, his eyes fixed firmly on the Atlantic Ocean, never deviating. "We'd gone hiking. I was twenty-two, Seth was seventeen. It was Saturday, right before Labor Day, and we headed out to a granite monolith that was sixty miles west of Seattle. It's one of the most popular and difficult climbing destinations on the West Coast. A place for real men to go. Yeah, right. On top of that dome, it was easy to think you were king of the world, and on that day, we did. Seth had spent the entire trip up talking about Ashley Hollenbeck—that was his girlfriend at the time. I don't even know what she's doing anymore. She never spoke to me again. He kept begging me to let him drive. I told him no because he didn't have a license and he drove like a pansy, anyway. He laughed about it. He'd only made it four meters down before he came off-rope and fell."

For long, stupid minutes he had stared like a mindless idiot at his brother's body down below, wondering what had happened. Finally, Demetri stopped staring at the map and turned to see Elizabeth's face.

"It was an accident," she said, her faith still unflagging.

"Yeah, but it was one of those accidents that never should have happened," he answered, because he didn't deserve her faith. He was reckless, and careless, and stupid. Those had been his father's words.

"Your brother must've been something," murmured Elizabeth.

"He wanted to be me. If I drove fast, he wanted to go faster. If I aced a test, he wanted to do better."

"It's probably hard living in your shadow, Demetri."

She had it so wrong. "He shouldn't have lived in my shadow. I should have lived in his. Sometimes you remind me of him."

"Me?"

"He loved everything. Found the silver lining in everything and everybody."

Elizabeth smiled at him, and he loved her smile, loved the way it pierced right through him. She picked up his hand, curled it over her own. "Well, it's not that hard when you know what you're looking for."

"It was my fault," he reminded her, because he wasn't about to let her gloss over this.

"He made a choice," she answered, still glossing it over.

"If I had been more careful, he'd be alive."

Elizabeth rolled her eyes. "If I'd been born with red hair, I could've been a rock-and-roll star." Then she turned serious, her fingers tightening on his hand. "You can't blame yourself for this."

"My father does."

"Don't be as stupid as your daddy, Demetri. Be smart. Like me."

"Like you?"

"Heck, yeah. You're the gentlest, most patient, albeit stubborn, man that I know. You're the only man I love. Dark secrets and all."

"I like when you look at me like that," he said, because he could see himself in her eyes, see his potential there. At thirty-five, he'd thought his life was over. He was wrong. It was just starting. "Don't leave me, Elizabeth."

"No, I don't think I will."

For long minutes they sat together. The hospital air chilled, and Elizabeth waited for him to say more. So many things made sense to her now, and she hated that he carried so much of the burden alone. Not anymore. This was her new deal with God. She was going to stop being so high-minded and judgmental. Sometimes things went fast, and sometimes things went slow, and she had to be prepared for both. That was part of her new deal with God, too.

"I'm going to retire," he said, which wasn't anything like what she was expecting.

She took a good look at him, wondering if this was some passing change-of-life phase, or if that serious look in his eyes came from something else. "Because of today?"

"Some. But, I've been thinking."

"Uh-oh."

"I told you I hadn't changed."

"That is what you said."

"But I have. It's been a long time coming, and I've tried to ignore it, because I didn't know who I was, or what I could do with my life. But now I know. I think we should take that stableful of horses you keep talking about, and buy a place to put them in. We'll buy some of Hugh's and open up a stable of our own. We can hire Marcus to train. If we buy a majority interest in Something to Talk About, he can race until the Prestons get their problems worked out. Whichever of the Quest horses need to race, they can at our stables. And then, when the scandal is over, they go back to Quest where they belong. Courting Disaster can race, and those two hundred other horses as well. You know, we own two hundred horses. We'll have to put them somewhere."

"Courting Disaster?" she asked, skirting right past the other part. That "stable of our own" part that reeked of permanence, roots and drinking iced tea from the porch swing.

"You'll have to meet her. You'll like her. She's got long eye-lashes, too."

"You're serious about this?" she asked, because she needed to double-check and triple-check this to make sure she understood correctly. She wasn't going to make assumptions that would swell up her heart like a balloon, only to have it popped twelve months later.

"Yeah. I wasn't sure what I was going to do after this season anyway. It's not the same. Besides I need to give Oliver a fair shot. If I'm still racing, he can't win." He said it as a joke, but that didn't hide the undertones. Serious undertones.

"But what about the need for speed, the thrills, the chills?" she asked.

He looked at her and managed a smile. Not Hollywood, all Demetri, making her heart stop all over again. "I think having you in my bed is about all the thrill I need at the moment."

She wanted to believe him, wanted to believe in this, but still she wasn't convinced. "That's mighty pretty, but I'm not sure I buy it."

"Yeah, I deserve that, but I realized something today. I don't want to die. I used to think that if I died, it would be the ultimate screw-you to my father. But I don't want to die. I want to grow old. I want to grow old with you. I didn't have much to worry about before, but now I have you." His hand tightened on hers, his fingers lacing and unlacing with her own.

Elizabeth frowned at him. "You worry about me?"

"Somebody's got to."

"You really thought this through?"

"Yeah. You make me think."

She shook her head. "I don't know. I still can't see you sitting in the recliner reading the evening news…."

"A recliner? Uh, no. I'll keep the car if it's okay with you."

"Only if you're going to let me drive it."

"We could get two and then race," he said, serious enough that she knew it was going to be all right. Her heart swelled up a few inches more.

"I think you need to let me drive," she said, not stupid enough to race him, unless he gave her a four-hour head start.

"You look very sexy when you drive. I don't mind. But you can't drive all the time."

And there they were, talking about the future. Their future together.

"Have you thought about kids before?" she asked, deciding to go for broke.

"Not once."

"I have."

"I thought you might."

"I want kids, Demetri. A whole houseful. Does that scare you?"

"Nope," he said, with absolute certainty in his eyes. There was faith there. Faith in her, in him, in *them*. Finally.

"Confidence," she said with a bright smile. "I like that in a man."

This time he tucked her under his arm and stood, walking with her out to the parking lot. Suddenly he stopped. "I don't know how to get home. We'll have to call a cab."

Home.

Elizabeth repeated that inside her head, because she really liked the sound of it. Her mother had a cross-stitch picture that hung on the wall, an old English cottage with smoke puffing from the chimney. There was a pretty pink border with flowers and vines and elaborate yellow letters that said home was where the heart is. All her life Elizabeth had thought that was true. But now she knew that sometimes, one heart wasn't enough.

Sometimes it took two.

Elizabeth smiled up at him, smiled up at the sun that was poking its way through the clouds. "You keep smashing up your cars. However, today is your lucky day. We'll take your car home. I stole it. But this time, I think I should drive."

"Only if you can push it over seventy. A good engine is like a horse. You have to exercise it in order to keep it running smoothly."

"Eighty, and not a hair more," she insisted, which was about as big a compromise as she could go.

Demetri looked at her and laughed, and she felt that tug at her heart again.

Yeah, everything was going to be just fine.

* * * * *

Romantic
SUSPENSE

Sparked by *Danger*,
Fueled by *Passion*.

USA TODAY bestselling author

Merline Lovelace

Undercover Wife

Secret agent Mike Callahan, code name Hawkeye,
objects when he's paired with sophisticated
Gillian Ridgeway on a dangerous spy mission
to Hong Kong. Gillian has secretly been in love
with him for years, but Hawk is an overprotective
man with a wounded past that threatens to
resurface. Now the two must put their lives—
and hearts—at risk for each other.

Available October wherever books are sold.

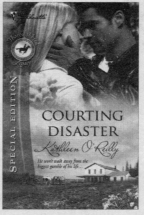